A Girl in Winter

A Girl in Winter

a novel by
PHILIP LARKIN

The Overlook Press
Woodstock, New York

First published by Tusk/Overlook in 1985 by
The Overlook Press
Lewis Hollow Road
Woodstock, New York, 12498

Library of Congress Cataloging in Publication Data

Larkin, Philip.
A girl in winter.

(Tusk Books)
1. Title
PZ4.L328 Gi   1976   823'.9'14   75-27291
ISBN 0-87951-217-2 (paperback)
ISBN 0-87951-039-0 (cloth)

If you would like a hardcover edition of this work for
your permanent library please write to THE OVERLOOK PRESS,
Lewis Hollow Road, Woodstock, New York, 12498.

To
BRUCE MONTGOMERY

PART ONE

I

There had been no more snow during the night, but because the frost continued so that the drifts lay where they had fallen, people told each other there was more to come. And when it grew lighter, it seemed that they were right, for there was no sun, only one vast shell of cloud over the fields and woods. In contrast to the snow the sky looked brown. Indeed, without the snow the morning would have resembled a January nightfall, for what light there was seemed to rise up from it.

It lay in ditches and in hollows in the fields, where only birds walked. In some lanes the wind had swept it up faultlessly to the very tops of the hedges. Villages were cut off until gangs of men could clear a passage on the roads; the labourers could not go out to work, and on the aerodromes near these villages all flying remained cancelled. People who lay ill in bed could see the shine off the ceilings of their rooms, and a puppy confronted with it for the first time howled and crept under the water-butt. The outhouses were roughly powdered down the windward side, the fences were half-submerged like breakwaters; the whole landscape was so white and still it might have been a formal painting. People were unwilling to get up. To look at the snow too long had a hypnotic effect, drawing away all power of concentration, and the cold seemed to cramp the bones, making work harder and unpleasant. Nevertheless, the candles had to be lit, and the ice in the jugs smashed, and the milk unfrozen; the men had to be given their breakfasts and got off to work in the yards. Life had to be carried on, in no matter what circumscribed way; even though one went no further than the window-seat, there was plenty to be done indoors, saved for such time as this.

But through cuttings and along embankments ran the railway lines, and although they were empty they led on northwards and southwards till they began to join, passing factories that had worked all night, and the backs of houses where light showed round the curtains, reaching the cities where the snow was disregarded, and which the frost could only besiege for a few days, bitterly.

2

"What are you singing about?" said Miss Brooks, sniffing. "I'm perished."

"Well, the pipes aren't hot," said Katherine. "They never are."

"It's a plague. I could say a few choice words to that caretaker."

"The whole system is too old to be any use, I suppose."

"They should do something about it. And look at the room we have to use. Two basins! And only one mirror."

"And that has spots on it."

"My married sister works in an office," said Miss Brooks, with melancholy envy. "They've got a gas fire."

"I wish we had any sort of fire."

"Yes, and that isn't all. On a cold morning like this you can have a cup of tea there if you want. *And* another in the middle of the morning. Well, that puts a bit of heart in you, doesn't it? Look at us."

"Anstey has a gas fire. I suppose that's all that matters."

"Talk of the devil," said Miss Brooks gloomily.

They stood for a moment by the loaded book-trolley, looking up the long avenue that opened between the oblique shelves up to the counter. Both of them wore red overalls. The high windows were frosted over, and the double row of hanging electric lights were all switched on, although it was only twenty to ten. Individual lights over shelves were left until the doors were opened to the public.

Mr. Anstey had come banging through the entrance wicket, and was leaning over the counter, holding a sheet of paper and talking at Miss Feather, hitting the sheet with his pipe-stem. Miss Feather's untidy grey head was bent in respectful attention. He had not lowered his voice, but the rebounding echoes prevented them from hearing what he said.

"I'll tell you something," Miss Brooks went on. "Once I got Feather to ask him about tea—before your time."

"What did he say?"

"Oh, you know what *he* is." Miss Brooks dragged a handkerchief from her sleeve and wiped her nose. "Where was it going to be made, who was going to make it, where was it going to be drunk, were assistants to have time off to drink it—making as much of everything as he possibly could. He said 'he couldn't see his way to granting our request'."

"I can just hear him saying it," said Katherine. "Why does he have to talk in that silly way? I think that annoys me as much as anything about him."

"Oh, he probably swallowed a dictionary at an early age," said Miss Brooks with vague facetiousness. "Or he was made like it."

Katherine finished sorting a row of books on top of the trolley and glanced at Miss Brooks. "I really don't believe you mind him at all."

"Well, minding people doesn't do any good. I don't let him worry me."

"I wonder what he's bothering about now."

Mr. Anstey's ratchet-like voice was arguing away, Miss Feather's dancing before it like a leaf in a storm. They mingled with the echoes awoken by the least sound—the shuffle of feet, the clack of a ruler, the thuds as the assistants smartly pushed back books onto the shelves. Katherine

13

and Miss Brooks separated, each moving along the particular section of shelving that it was their business to keep in order. Soon everything was ready for the day's work—the books in smooth, unbroken lines, the date-stamps adjusted, the files of tickets at the counter pushed into tight columns. They met again by a special display shelf on Japan.

"What about your mittens? Aren't you going to wear them?"

"I would for two pins. D'you think anyone'd laugh?"

"Of course they wouldn't."

"Another ten minutes and we'll have those doors opening and shutting."

"Well, it's Saturday," said Katherine. "Be thankful. The end of the week."

"I wondered what you were singing about," said Miss Brooks, departing.

On the way back to the counter, Miss Feather, released from Mr. Anstey, came up to Katherine as if uncertain who she was.

"Oh, Miss Lind——"

"Yes?"

"Oh, Miss Lind— You remember you were doing the Bureau work, when Miss Holloway was ill? When was it, now?"

"About a week ago, I think."

"Yes. . . . Well, the university say they haven't had that book on Uganda back yet, by Fielding. Mr. Anstey was just asking about it."

Miss Feather was over forty. She had a withered, sly face, and a conspiratorial way of glancing on all sides as she spoke and rarely looking anyone in the face.

Katherine frowned.

"Uganda by Fielding? I don't remember. Is it marked as returned in the book?"

"Yes, it's marked as returned, but they say they haven't

14

had it," Miss Feather repeated, as one who has found it necessary for years to repeat everything. She slipped a pencil into the pocket of her overall.

"If it's marked as returned, it must have gone, surely," said Katherine, without conviction.

"Well, they say they haven't had it, so would you look round, dear, and see if you can find it? It may have been put on the shelves by mistake. And tell Mr. Anstey if you find it. These little things take up so much time."

"Yes, I will if I find it."

Katherine turned back and went to the Africa section, her right hand raised, her right elbow in her left palm. Although her eye was casual it was nearly the first book she saw, slipped neatly into place in the row of drab leather spines. A glance inside the cover showed her the label of the university library. She turned it moodily in her hands, then tucked it under her arm and returned to Miss Feather, who looked at her with a degraded wisdom.

"Here it is, Miss Feather."

"Ah, I'm so glad. Would you put it on Miss Holloway's table, then? And you might just tell Mr. Anstey it's been found, and that we'll send it off straightway."

"Yes, all right."

Miss Holloway was not in her room—which was really a combined store for new books, and a book-service room as well as where Miss Holloway did her cataloguing—so Katherine left the book on the table and went along to Mr. Anstey's office. This was in a dark passage ending in a twisting iron staircase that led up to the back of the reference department. She knocked on the door, and after a pause the familiar voice told her to enter.

There was little expression on her face as she closed the door behind her. Indeed, there rarely was: her pale, shield-shaped face, dark eyes and eyebrows, and high cheekbones, were not mobile or eloquent. Nor, more curiously, was her mouth, which was too wide and too full-lipped for beauty.

Yet because it was alert and sensitive it should have been most expressive. Almost she looked as if her lips were bruised and she had to keep them unfamiliarly closed. Yet at other times a faint look of amusement stole into her face, as if with pleasure at the completeness with which she could cover her thoughts. And when she spoke it was with a foreign accent.

The room was prodigiously warm, with a vehement gas fire turned up to the fullest extent so that the tips of flame licked the air. A china bowl of water stood in front of this, where a disintegrating cigarette-end floated. Everything was very untidy: around the walls between bookcases and filing cabinets were stacked books and box-files that had not been referred to for months. Then there was an inner ring of similar papers that had been unattended for weeks: at the centre of this was a large roll-top desk, covered with letters and typed sheets and catalogues, where Mr. Anstey sat. A telephone stood by a large tin of cigarette-lighter fluid.

He was giving his usual performance of being too engrossed in matters of importance to notice her entry, and held a flimsy typewritten list which he checked with a pencil, his pipe gripped by his teeth with a snarling grimace. Every now and then he gave a liquid, energetic sniff. He was a thin, wizened man of about forty, with a narrow, lined face and delicate spectacles. His suit was grimy, she disliked his tie, and he wore a pullover whose sleeves came down below his cuffs. His hair was carefully oiled, and occasionally his face twitched: he resembled a clerk at a railway station who had suffered from shell-shock.

Within his reach there was a shelf where a used cup and saucer stood.

She waited in front of him, looking with distaste at his bent head. As though she were not there, he got up and rummaged in a file, looking cross. The smoke from his pipe smelt sweetish. Not till he was settled back at his desk did he say in an affectedly-preoccupied voice:

"Well, Miss Lind?"

"The book on Uganda has been found, and will be sent off at once."

He gave no sign of having heard. In a minute or two he said in the same voice:

"Where was it?"

"It had been put on the shelves."

Mr. Anstey made a final note on the list, folded it and placed it in an envelope, scribbled something on a memorandum pad and duplicated it on a dog-eared calendar, saying at length:

"What was it doing there?"

He removed his pipe, took up a pencil, and began prodding the ash down, looking at her in a wooden, distant way.

"It was a mistake, I'm afraid."

"There are two mistakes there, Miss Lind, pardon me," Mr. Anstey said in a suddenly loud and quarrelsome voice. "The volume should not have been marked as returned. That's the first one. Then, it should not have been placed on the open shelves. There are two mistakes there, Miss Lind, do you follow me?"

"Yes." She said this neutrally, to avoid calling attention to her own refusal to give him any sort of title. Inwardly she summoned patience to meet what he was going to say, for he always said much the same things.

"And neither of them, if I may say so, should have been made by anyone with an ounce of what we English call savvy or gumption or . . . *nous*." He sidled in front of the gas fire, holding a paper spill to the glowing bars. "Certainly not by anyone possessed of the superior education you have received. . . . Perhaps the youngest junior, whoever she is, with her head full of jazz-tunes or boy-friends or the latest 'movie', or whatever they call them, she might do it, but I don't look for it from you, because I have been

17

led to believe that you have been taught to think and this sort of thing is, to put it crudely, just downright damn-foolishness." The flame grew near his fingers, and he gave a few frantic sucks at his pipe before dropping the charred butt into the bowl of water. Then he resumed speaking in the voice that was natural to him, drained of all humour or friendliness, a voice that might be used on the stage as typically insulting. "I've every *sympathy* with the mistakes a man or woman makes due to inexperience or insufficient whatyoumaycall. There are certain things in this profession that can only be mastered after long—just by doing them until you can foresee any eventuality that may arise in the course of the . . . business." He thrust forward his jaw nastily, as if she had provoked him in some way. "I'm not one of your university fellows, Cambridge or Oxford, who comes along and says, 'Oh yes, I can learn all about this how-d'you-do in five minutes'. I've seen these johnnies, and you can take it from me they're precious little use when it comes to a little serious work. No, I came into this profession from the bottom"—he gazed at her once more with the wooden, distant expression that seemed to pinch his nostrils together—"and what small degree of eminence I have attained has been gained simply by *knowing my job* inside out, backwards and forwards, and however you please." He put his pipe back into his narrow jaws, but it had gone out: this time he felt for matches, sniffing.

"Now, of course," he recommenced, sucking greedily at the bitten stem, "I don't know what you are intending to do with your life, whether you are intending to follow this profession or not. I don't know and, frankly, I don't want to know, for that is a question that every person has a right to settle and to decide for him- or herself, *but I am telling you this*: that if you decide, yes, I will follow this profession, I will study and devote my energy to the attainment of this . . . career, *you will find*"—he stressed the three words with his pipe—"that an ounce of *good business sense*, such as you need to run any factory or . . . business, that'll be worth all your Shakespeare and Doctor Samuel Johnson and whateveryoucall. Of course"—he changed his tone to one of indulgent explanation—"I'm not saying anything so foolish as that such knowledge is not of inestimable value, but what I am trying to explain is that once a year a fellow may come in and say, 'Oh, Mr. Anstey, look here, I want to know all about Elizabethan Drama', or some obscure branch of phonology or morphology or whatever it is that you happen to be familiar with—well, there you are then, out trots your education. But *nine-tenths* of the time, *ninety-nine-HUNDREDTHS* of the time, you are simply having to fill the position of an ordinary office boss who happens to be dealing with books instead of houses or perambulators and so on and so forth." Mr. Anstey prodded his pencil into his again-extinct pipe, and produced this time an inexpensive lighter with a large flame. "Now you've started on this job with a very good, valuable education, better by a very long chalk than I ever had, and none the less valuable for being obtained in another country, as human knowledge is the same in England, France, Germany or anywhere on God's earth." Here he gave a short laugh. "But if, as I am saying or rather suggesting to you, you should in the fullness of time achieve a position comparable to mine, you will find that three-quarters of your time is taken up by looking out for and clearing up after some crackheaded girl who thinks she's wrapped up a book and sent it to Wigan or Timbuctoo, when all she's actually done is to put it on the shelves where it oughtn't to be." He laughed again, and pulled at his pipe, surrounding his head with blue, sweetish smoke.

Katherine looked at him as if he were an insect she would relish treading on. "I apologize for the mistake," she said furiously, "but I don't think that——"

"Well, well, Miss Lind, that's how we have to spend our

time," Mr. Anstey interrupted halfway through what she had said. He sat in an ugly position and slapped his thigh ruefully, grinning at her with his face distorted sideways. "Worrying about fiddling little details that won't matter in six weeks to you or me or anyone else, while the really important things go hang." He made a theatrical gesture of resignation. This was another of his performances, that of the man forced to spend his time on things that were beneath his intelligence. "I've had work in this drawer now four years, original and it may even be valuable work on classification, waiting till I can spare a week or so. . . . Well, it doesn't do to stop and think. That way madness lies, as whatyoucall says. All I can do, and all you can do, is to get on with the job in hand. That——"

There was a tap on the door, and Miss Feather entered, glancing round as if she suspected there were more than two people in the room. Mr. Anstey at once put on his distant expression, saying in a preoccupied voice:

"Yes, what is it, Miss Feather?"

"I'm afraid one of the juniors is feeling badly, Mr. Anstey. She isn't fit for work."

"And who is it, Miss Feather?" This was a third manner, that of the judiciary alert to learn all the facts of the case.

"Miss Green. She really looks very ill."

"What's the matter with her?" he demanded harshly. "Is she sickening for something, influenza or measles or——"

"She has very bad toothache, and she wants to go home. I think it would be as well to let her. She won't be much use here, really."

"Go home! It's a dentist she ought to go to," said Mr. Anstey contemptuously, as if detecting a subterfuge.

"I think she will, if we let her go home first." Miss Feather, perhaps alone on the staff, had the knack of keeping Mr. Anstey fairly close to the point: she inserted submissive, insinuating remarks that urged him gently back to the path she wished him to follow.

"Where does she live? Is her mother on the telephone?"
He picked up the directory, disregarding Miss Feather's
denial, and discovered she was not.

"It's quite a long way," said Miss Feather. "I wonder
if it wouldn't be better to send someone with her. She
seems almost likely to faint."

"Why not give a holiday all round?" agreed Mr. Anstey,
with a crowing, hysterical laugh. "I'll go with her myself
if it means getting the morning off!"

He laughed alone.

"I think the best thing would be to send someone with
her," repeated Miss Feather, glancing furtively at the
clock on the mantelpiece. Mr. Anstey, chuckling good-
humouredly, stuck his pipe back into his mouth and
turned again to his papers.

"Yes, all right, all right," he said with indulgent im-
patience, as if they had both been wasting his time. "Send
someone with her. I don't mind who. Send someone—ha,
ha!—you'd be glad to get rid of for an hour or two."

They left him enclosed in his unbreakable belief that all
things depended on him, and that he managed, despite
an overwhelming weight of work, to administer every
detail efficiently.

When they were outside, Miss Feather said:

"Perhaps *you* wouldn't mind going, Miss Lind."

3

What would the Fennels think of this, Katherine wondered.

She stood waiting in the entrance-hall of the library,
three minutes later, as she had been bidden. This was a
dim, unheated place, with double swing-doors leading out

into the street: two sets of glass doors lay on either side, to the Lending Library and to the Reading Room. The only piece of furniture was a large double-sided stand, painted duck-egg green, for Official War Photographs. This was now covered with pictures of destroyers, aeroplanes, and tanks in the desert: sometimes urchins crept in and stared at them, or prised out the drawing-pins to steal. High up on the walls, in the shadow from the blacked-over windows, hung worthless paintings by local artists.

What would they imagine from her letter? To them, the phrase 'working in a library' would call up a picture of calf-bound aisles, with her holding hushed conversations with professors, or drowsing at a mahogany desk: they would be under the impression that the work involved some form of studying, unaware that library assistants are forced to do everything to books except read them. They certainly would not visualize the daily round of string bags, trembling old men, tramps reading newspapers through magnifying glasses, soldiers asking to consult a medical dictionary. Not that they were stupid, but these things did not come into their ken. Or was it simply that she could not imagine them having any thought of such surroundings as these?

Perhaps she should not have written to them. On her arrival in England over a year ago, she had thrashed that question out with herself, and decided that she should not. They would not want any such unexpected liability from the past. And it might even be that they would dislike dealing with her because of her nationality, for the English, she found—and the Fennels were nothing if not English— were characterized in time of war by antagonism to every foreign country, friendly or unfriendly, as a simple matter of instinct. It might even be socially awkward for them to meet her again. And although as the months passed she came to think these things less and less likely, she had kept to her original decision mainly from shyness, though there were minor questions, such as whether they still lived at the same address, that also deterred her.

When she had written, therefore, she had written on an impulse—a reflex action from seeing their name in the papers, or rather, a name she connected with them. She had written to Jane, because Jane had been mentioned, and Katherine was troubled by misgivings that either or both the parents might by now be dead, and there was even the chance that Robin had been called up and already killed or wounded. It was not very likely, but she thought it best to go softly until she knew how matters stood. So a week ago she had been waiting anxiously for a reply. And it had come—not from Jane, which was understandable in the circumstances, but from Mrs. Fennel, written on the same notepaper that Robin had used, with the house and the village and the telephone number stamped boldly in blue at the head of each page. The mere sight of this brought such emotion that she could hardly read it, and had to go through it several times before she could gather its meaning. They were glad, Mrs. Fennel said, to hear of her again: they had often wondered what had happened to her, but they had never dreamed she was in England again. She should have written to tell them. Jane thanked her for her sympathy, and would write herself later. In the meantime, she would send Katherine's address and the news of her to Robin, who was in the army (though still in England) and would no doubt write to her himself. In closing, the three of them sent their very best wishes.

She had written off at once a letter of thanks—stupidly, for there was nothing to thank them for. But thankfulness was what she felt. That night she had been too excited to sleep, and had smoked many cigarettes, finally, after midnight, starting to dust her room and set it to order, half for something to do and half because she felt the need to make some kind of preparation. Really she would have liked to have gone out and walked the empty streets.   It that was against the police regulations. Finally she fell o reading the letter again, staring at the blue embossed heading, and went to bed so restless and exhausted that something really important might have happened—the war might have ended, or an invasion begun.

All the week she had been waiting for Robin's letter. So far it had not come, but the interval lulled her excitement to a powerful, delicious expectation, strong enough to carry her through the daily work that she normally found dis-agreeable. Wondering what the Fennels would think of it all, and in particular what they would think of Anstey, cheered her as if she had found allies, where before she had been alone. If it weren't for Anstey, she knew, she might find the work at least tolerable. But she loathed him so much that at times she wondered if he really was so bad, and whether there weren't some blind spot in her that prevented her seeing him naturally. The other assistants seemed to find him a standing joke—even to like him while agreeing he was quite impossible, as if cursing the weather. But she had disliked him on sight, and as she got to know him better her dislike increased. She could never dispel a feeling of incredulous rage when they met, for he always seemed to be deliberately insulting her. She found him so objectionable that she was almost forced to think that there might be some tone in his voice or turn in his phrases that all English people would instantly take to mean that his sawn-off brutality was only a jocular way of speaking, not for a moment to be taken seriously. It was possible. But she flattered herself that she knew English well enough to detect any such thing, and besides, she had disliked his face before she had heard his voice, and what he said seemed typical. He was theatrical, scraggy, and rude.

Still, she had got through another scene with him. In time, perhaps, he would lose his power of infuriating her so regularly. And this morning, as all the week, none of

24

this seemed very important: it was only when there had been nothing else in her life at all that it made her desperate. Now, when she could not help feeling that in a matter of weeks, perhaps, all might be altered, she could take it lightly.

Certainly it had ended better than they usually did. Usually she felt that the one thing she wanted to do was get out of the library and as far away as she could, and that was almost what she had been told to do. True, it had been rather an insult in itself. But it was quite of a piece with the way they treated her. She had been appointed temporary assistant, which marked her off from the permanent staff: she was neither a junior a year or so out of school who was learning the profession, nor a senior preparing to take the intermediate or final examination. It meant that she could safely be called upon to do anything, from sorting old dust-laden stock in a storeroom to standing on a table in the Reading Room to fit a new bulb in one of the lights, while old men stared aqueously at her legs. Behind all this she sensed the influence of Mr. Anstey. There was a curious professional furtiveness about him, as if he were a guardian of traditional secrets; he seemed unwilling to let her pick up any more about the work than was unavoidable. Therefore any odd job that was really nobody's duty fell to her, for Miss Feather, who was a pale ghost of his wishes, had caught the habit from him. It annoyed her, not because she gave two pins for library practice, but because it stressed what was already sufficiently marked: that she was foreign and had no proper status there.

Still, this errand was better than most. It would be easy enough, and almost anything would be worth getting away from work, even though it meant going out into the cold. She could slip into a café for a hot drink on the way back, and if possible might even call at her room to see if any letters had come. It was strange to be expecting letters again. That depended largely on where Miss Green lived. She was not certain who this Miss Green was. There were several juniors, and she only knew the pretty one by name, Miss Firestone. The others were not remarkable and she had nothing to do with them.

She waited impatiently. After a time a girl came out and moved slowly up to her, dressed in her outdoor clothes. She would be about sixteen, and Katherine recognized her face.

"Are you Miss Green? I'm coming along with you."

Miss Green nodded stiffly. She was thin and dressed in a beige coat that did not suit her: her face was poorly-complexioned and she wore spectacles. Her mouth was held as if her teeth were stuck with toffee.

Katherine looked at her uncertainly, wondering how ill she was. It happened that Miss Green was the first member of the staff she had ever spoken to, for when she had come to work on her first morning she had met Miss Green in the entrance hall, and had asked her where Miss Feather was. Miss Green had stared and answered in offhand nasal tones that she would be in the cataloguing room, without saying where that was, and had disappeared. That had been nine months ago and they had not spoken since. She worked mainly in the Junior Department.

"Is your toothache very bad? Do you feel well enough to start?"

Another nod, as if crossly asserting she had no need of dependence. Katherine, feeling some sympathy was called for, said:

"I'm sorry it's so bad."

"Oh, that makes it feel better already," replied Miss Green sarcastically, with a huddled movement of the lips as if eating a sweet. She pushed out of the double doors without holding them open afterwards.

Exasperating brat, thought Katherine, following her, but it was a relief not to have to pretend sympathy. They

26

stood for a second on the top of the steps, the cold rising up their skirts, and began to walk down as a clock struck ten-fifteen. It was a Branch Library and stood on one corner of a crossroads, a residential avenue and the fag-end of a long street lined with small shops that ran, gathering importance and size as it went, nearly to the centre of the city. The Library was an ugly old building built up on a bank, where laurel bushes grew: the bank was now covered with snow and littered with bus-tickets. A newspaper had been carefully folded and thrust into a drift, where it was frosted stiff. A cart creaked past, from which an old man was flinging shovelfuls of gravel, swinging the spade in an arc that spun the gravel thinly. As they went down the steps Katherine looked disproportionately strong and dark beside Miss Green.

At the bottom they were met by an urchin with very red face and hands, who eyed them suspiciously, saying in a hoarse voice:

"Is this where the books are?"

Miss Green walked on without replying, so Katherine had to stop and give directions. The boy shrank from her foreign voice: in his left hand he held a sixpence. Glancing round while she hurried after Miss Green, she saw him go up to the main entrance though she had specially told him to go round to the Junior Department.

"I say, where do you live?"

"Lansbury Park."

"You're catching a bus here?"

A nod.

"Then we shall change at Bank Street?"

"There's no need for you to," said Miss Green shortly, as they reached the bus-stop. "I can go home alone quite well."

"I shall go with you as far as I can," said Katherine. "I'm not coming back before I have to."

"Well, that's your business."

27

"Are you sure you're feeling all right?"

"Perfectly."

Lansbury Park was excellent: it would take them right across the centre of the city, and her room was quite near Bank Street. She could easily call there on her way back. In fact, as Miss Green seemed so independent she might leave her at Bank Street as she suggested, and spend the rest of the time in her room, in a café, or looking round the shops. Would there be a letter? Robin surely must have had time to write by now, if he wanted to. Perhaps he was not greatly interested to hear that she was in England again. Of course, he wouldn't be as excited at the prospect of meeting as she was: in any case, no-one had said anything about meeting yet. But she would have expected him to write quickly out of politeness. It might be that he was stationed in some inaccessible spot—Ireland, perhaps—which letters took days to reach, or possibly he was busy on a scheme or battle-course that left him no time for writing. Or Mrs. Fennel might not have written as quickly as she implied she would. It was all very tantalizing. But surely every day that passed made the arrival of a letter more likely.

She stirred impatiently as they stood by the bus-stop with a few other people. Miss Green stood a little away from her, as if disclaiming any relationship, and Katherine glanced at her every now and then to make sure she was all right, which was after all what she was supposed to be doing. She looked pale and badly-fed: her thick-lensed spectacles stretched over her ears, meaning she had worn them for a long time. If her eyes had grown weaker, that would explain the petulant backward lilt of her head, which made her look scornful and stuck-up. Her hair was arranged limply on the top of her head, and her wrists were very thin. And she was in pain. Katherine was sorry for her: she looked so pathetic and spiteful; and if it had not been for her she would now be working resentfully till one o'clock.

28

There seemed so many things to be happy about. She could not have named them, but as the large Corporation bus came up she felt that even the cold was delightful. Miss Brooks would see it in terms of the deadening snow that was littered everywhere, but to Katherine the frost made everything stand alone and sparkle. Even getting on the bus gave a momentary flicker of pleasure, as if she were entering on a fresh stage of some more important journey. She rubbed a space clear on the window as they moved off, watching the shops of City Road go past. City Road was several miles long. In the middle of it were twin scars where tramlines had been taken up. In some of the little shop-windows candle-ends were burning to melt the frost from the glass. They were all very much alike, selling tobacco and newspapers, or bread and canned food, or greengroceries. But they made a living from people dwelling in the many poor streets around them, who went no further for their shopping. As it was Saturday, there were plenty of them about: women of the district carrying baskets from one shop to another, leaning on the counters for five minutes' dark, allusive conversation, waiting patiently outside butchers' and fish-shops. Here and there old men, muffled up to their scrawny necks, leaned against walls filling their pipes with stenching tobacco cut and sold in sticky segments. Files of papers hung outside the news-agents. Yes, she thought, imagining the wedding rings and the scale-pans gritty from weighing vegetables, they'd certainly wonder how she got here. This kind of scene—though it reminded her of them—would mean nothing to the Fennels at all. They only noticed things that artists had been bringing under their noses for centuries, such as sunsets and landscapes. Or was that unjust? It was all very well saying the Fennels would notice this or that, but her memories of them were not at all clear. When she stayed with them, she had not been half observant enough, thinking no doubt that she would never see them again, so that all that remained was a mingled flavour of where they had lived and how they had treated her, and the kind of things they had said. Could she remember what they had looked like? She remembered Robin's face clearly, and Mr. Fennel's to a lesser extent: Mrs. Fennel had grown confused with one of the mistresses at school. And Jane she could not remember at all. That was odd. Katherine reckoned on having a good memory for faces.

The truth of the matter was, she could not now keep them out of her mind, and they were constantly linking up with whatever she thought or did. She looked from the unevenly-travelling bus, and saw a cheap dress shop, where a bare-ankled girl was arranging a copy of a stylish model; then a linen-draper's, with an old ceremonial frontage; a milk-bar, permanently blacked-out, with the door ajar and no-one on the tall stools; a pawn-shop window crowded with old coins, shirts, a theodolite, bed-pans and a harp; a public-house door with a bright brass rail, just opening; a sudden gap of high, papered walls and a heap of bricks, furred with frost, where a house had been destroyed. There was nothing in all this to remind her of them, yet it did.

The bus stopped, restarted, took on more passengers. The buildings outside grew taller and impressive. The streets were wider; they at last came to the end of City Road and circled slowly along one-way streets in the centre of the city. Many people hurried by, with a flickering of white collars and newspapers. They passed the cathedral yard, glimpsed the long, soot-encrusted glass roof of a railway station, halted at a set of lights by a doorway bearing a dozen professional brass plates. Here and there girls dressed in overcoats sat huddled in cigarette-kiosks, reading, and down a side-street a man was selling baked potatoes from an ancient roaster.

She had left Miss Green to herself: they were sharing a double-seat downstairs. Miss Green was nearest the gangway, and the bus had become so crowded that a shopping basket swayed above her head, from which hung the end of a leek. At every movement of the owner it tapped Miss Green's hair. But she had looked mutely in front of her and said nothing.

Now she leaned against Katherine.

Katherine accordingly gave her more room. But Miss Green said:

"I don't feel well. I'm sorry. I must get out."

Katherine glanced at her. She looked ghastly.

"All right."

She signalled to the conductress, and got Miss Green to the platform at the back of the bus. At the next stop it swerved alongside the pavement and put them down. Miss Green went and sat on a low wall from which the railings had been removed, her head low. Katherine stood by her.

"Do you feel faint or sick?" she asked helplessly.

"Sick," said Miss Green after a while. She tilted back her head as if the cold air were wet muslin laid across her forehead.

They had not reached Bank Street, but it would have been the next stop. This was a large square, the formal centre of the city, two sides of which were taken up by the Town Hall and Municipal Departments, under which the bus had dropped them. In the middle of the square was a small green, with flowerbeds and seats; over the branches of the leafless trees on the third side was the high-pillared façade of the Central City Library, and on the last side were low reticent shop windows, tailors and jewellers. The green was covered with snow.

Katherine was uncertain what to do. She had had no experience of English invalids: if she went quickly to a chemist's she would not know what to buy. If Miss Green asked for anything, she would do all she could to get it, but in the meantime she did nothing, looking at the thin neck bowed within the chiffon scarf. Pain was so remote from what she herself was feeling that she felt helpless. Possibly Miss Green would not have thanked her for any offer of comfort.

So she waited. At last Miss Green raised her head.

"Buses seem to upset me sometimes," she said, in little more than a whisper.

"How are you feeling? What would you like to do?"

"I don't want anything. Just rest for a bit."

Katherine looked round her.

"There's a shelter place in the middle of this green. There'd be a proper seat there. You shouldn't sit on the cold stone."

Miss Green gave no sign that she had heard. But after a minute she looked up.

"Where?"

"Over there. Do you think you could walk it?"

"I can try."

Katherine stooped and took her thin arm. Together they crossed to the green and went up the path to the shelter, crushing a light layer of frozen snow. The benches were dusty with frost and the laurel-bushes rustled. She got Miss Green up the steps into the dingy interior, and sat her on a wooden seat. The place was bitterly cold, but built substantially: it had a drinking-fountain let into the wall, and a plaque saying it was to commemorate a coronation. There seemed nothing for the moment Katherine could do, so she leant in the doorway with her back to Miss Green, to give her time to recover herself, and stared out at the grey tracing of branches and the dark buildings beyond, their upper storeys sprinkled with lighted windows. It looked as if after all she would have to take Miss Green home. Then there would be no time to go to her room before returning to work: indeed, if they went on at this present pace it was doubtful whether it would be worth going back to work before lunch at all. She was working eight hours a day this week, from nine till one and three till seven, when the Library closed. In any case she could call at her rooms at lunchtime: it wouldn't make more than an hour's difference. The longer she put off making sure there was a letter or not, the longer she had something to look forward to. In the meantime she lolled in the doorway as if on guard, surprised at finding herself in this strange place, while behind her Miss Green pressed her hands to her eyes, letting her spectacles lie on the smooth wooden bench. There was one-way traffic round the square, and she watched the taxis and saloon cars go by at a distance, the noise of them sharpened on the cold air like a knife on a whetstone.

After a while she glanced round.

"How are you feeling now?"

Miss Green rubbed her forehead. She had taken off her gloves.

"A bit better, I think."

She blinked at Katherine: without her spectacles she did not look nearly so disagreeable. Her lips were childish and pouting.

"Is there anything you'd like to do? Would you like to have something hot to drink somewhere?"

"Oh, no, that would make me feel worse."

"Brandy would do you good."

"No."

"Well, rest a bit longer, then. There's plenty of time."

"A drink of water, perhaps," said Miss Green, timidly, after a pause.

"Water!" Katherine looked round. "Well, there is a drinking-fountain here."

"Oh, but they're filthy," said Miss Green, wrinkling her nose.

"Well, it may be frozen." She pressed the button experimentally, and an uneven trickle of water came out of the lion's mouth. She passed her hand through it, and was amazed at its coldness. It might have been a stream drained from plateau after plateau of ice, running down tracks of stones still above cloud level. She withdrew her hand quickly.

"It works, but it's terribly cold."

"Oh, but it's not healthy. All sorts of people use them —old tramps and——"

Katherine looked at the chained iron cup. "Well, if there are any germs the frost will have killed them." She ran the water again momentarily, to test it once more. It numbed her hand, like a distillation of the winter. "But you needn't use the cup—you could drink from your hands."

Miss Green got up very gingerly and came over to stand by her as if walking barefoot on ice.

"I don't like to," she said, with a deliberate expression.

"Why not? Make a cup of your hands. I'll keep the water running."

Miss Green ducked her narrow shoulders, cupping her palms together. She gave a gasp as the water touched them but sipped at it. Then she dabbed her forehead with wet fingers.

"It's so cold it almost stops my tooth hurting."

She bent to drink again, and Katherine saw as she raised her head afterwards that she was gasping at the chill of the water and half-smiling, the tiny hairs around her mouth wet. Katherine, who ever since she had got up that morning had been thinking of the Fennels and herself with increasing excitement, was suddenly startled to sympathy for her. Till then she had seen only her ugliness, her petulance, her young pretensions. Now this faded to unimportance and she grasped for the first time that she really needed care, that she was frail and in a remote way beautiful. It was so long since she had felt this about anyone that it came with unexpected force: its urgency made her own affairs, concerned with what might or might not happen, bloodless and fanciful. This was what she had not had for ages, a person dependent on her: there were streets around that she must help her to cross, buses she must help her on and afterwards buy the tickets, for the pain the girl was suffering had half-obliterated her notice of the world. In the dull suburb was her home, and she must help her to reach it safely, and hand her over to whoever would take care of her next. It was so unusual that she knew it to be linked with the thankfulness she had been feeling for the last few days: it was the unconsidered generosity that follows a rare gambling-win; for the first time in months she had happiness to spare, and now that her passive, pregnant expectation had suddenly found its outlet, it was all the more eager for having come so casually and unexpectedly, leading her to this shelter she never knew existed in the very centre of the city.

She gently took her arm.

"Would you like to rest a little longer? But we shall be cold if we stay long."

They sat together on the seat under the scrolled plaque, Miss Green huddled into herself, and Katherine glancing first at her then out through the doorway; there was a path outside where chance heelmarks seemed eternally printed in the frost. Through the light mist she could see the ornamental front of the Town Hall under the flat shield of the sky, dark and ledged with snow. But all the white-grey patches were not snow, for as she watched they revealed themselves as pigeons, a score of them launching off into the air and hanging with a great clapping of wings. Then the whole flight dropped, rose over the intervening trees across the traffic, and landed on a stretch of snow not fifteen yards from where the two of them sat, coming up as if they expected to be fed.

4

They remained silent for a few minutes, while Miss Green
finally composed herself, putting on her spectacles and
looking at her face in a handmirror. After this she powdered her nose and chin, making herself no less unattrac-
tive. The bones of her wrists were prominent and her hair,
done to resemble the fashion, seemed lifeless. Katherine
looked at her anxiously.

"Do you feel better now?"

"Yes, a bit." Miss Green swallowed. "This tooth has
always been a trouble." Her voice had no volume, and
sometimes rose to a whine to make itself heard.

"What's the matter with it?"

"Well, there was a time when I didn't go to a dentist for
nearly two years. Then it got very bad, and I had to go,
and he filled it so that it was nearly all filling. Then some
time ago all the filling came out and it started to hurt. He
filled it again, but it went on hurting, so he gave me some
stuff to put on it, and that stopped it hurting. But now it's
started again." She looked at Katherine with weak, self-
pitying eyes. "Last night was terrible. I didn't get to sleep
till four, and then I woke up before seven. It was awful. All
my face—the whole of my head seemed to be aching."

"A headache? The one starts the other."

"Yes, I suppose so, but I do get terrible headaches in
any case. And when I've got one, I just can't do *anything*.
Mother knows there's nothing for it but to keep me in
bed with aspirins in hot milk. And very often I'm sick too."

"But do you have them at work?"

"They don't come on during the day as a rule. At night
sometimes. Most often I wake up with them. Then I don't
go to work, I just stay in bed."

36

"Perhaps you should have stayed in bed this morning."

Miss Green replaced her gloves with a genteel gesture. "Mother did suggest it. But it wasn't hurting so much when I got up, and it doesn't do to stay at home too often, does it? Mr. Anstey can be very rude."

"He gets worse every day. He's got the manners of a dustman."

"How funny you should say that," said Miss Green with a faint giggle, "because his father was only a Corporation workman. They used to live in Gas Street."

"Is he married? I wouldn't be his wife."

"His wife died over five years ago."

"I'm sorry for her," said Katherine. "She must have had a dog's life. He's so *stupid*. We don't get on at all."

Again Miss Green gave the ghost of a giggle, as if she were watching another person break a rule.

"Of course," she said, a trifle more animated, "he's only temporarily in the job at all. Mr. Rylands was the real head, you remember. Or did you never see him?"

"No, I never did."

"He was a very different kind of person altogether. Young and very well-educated. He had a university degree. But when the war started he had to go into the army, unfortunately."

"Then they appointed Anstey, did they?"

"Yes, he'd started as a junior assistant as soon as he left school and had been there ever since. He was senior assistant when Mr. Rylands left. I suppose they felt they had to appoint him."

"I can't think why."

"He knows the work, I suppose."

"Well, perhaps he does. But he doesn't know how to behave. He shouldn't have any sort of authority."

Miss Green looked at her stealthily.

"Have you been having a row with him?" she asked.

"Not so far. Just one of his little lectures, this morning. One day, though, oh, one day——!"

She gazed out of the shelter at the motionless branches: Miss Green studied her for a moment or two. Near at hand a sparrow was pecking for crumbs at a paper bag, and beyond it in the middle distance a tramp was looking into a salvage bin. The traffic circulated under the porticoes of the high buildings, the cars sounding their horns like ships lost at sea. She was glad to see that Miss Green had a little more colour.

"Do you feel well enough to go on now?" she asked, turning back to her.

Miss Green nodded and rose, but as she did so a sombre look came over her face. She put her hand up to her cheek. Katherine hesitated.

"Is it hurting?"

"Yes, it——" Miss Green looked at her fearfully. "I think it's coming on again."

"Oh, surely not."

"Yes, it is. Oh, dear. It must have been the water, drinking."

Katherine's heart sank. "Is it bad?"

"Yes, I think so."

There was a silence. Miss Green pressed harder against her cheek.

Katherine shivered slightly in the cold. "Wouldn't it be better to go to a dentist straightaway?"

"Oh no. I'd sooner go home."

"But it would be just as bad at home."

"Yes, I know, but——"

"I should go to a dentist now," said Katherine. Miss Green did not answer, but looked so miserable that Katherine made up her mind to put an end to it for her. "Really I should. Then it would all be over."

"I daren't," Miss Green said brokenly.

"But you wouldn't have any more pain. Then you could

38

go home. You'd have the whole week-end to get over it."

"I'm afraid," said Miss Green, dryly tearful. "It would hurt so."

"You could have gas."

"It's so expensive."

"But you wouldn't feel a thing. It would be over before you knew it."

"This is much worse than it was before," gasped Miss Green in a kind of sob. "I'm——"

She turned away, hiding her face. Katherine realized that she was in no state of mind to make decisions, and determined to act.

"I'll tell you what. There's a dentist near where I live, only three minutes away. In Merion Street. We'll go there."

"Oh, no!—who is he? I want my own dentist."

"Where does he live?"

"In the next street from us. I'd better go home——"

"It would be much better to get it over first. You can't stand any more of this. Come along now—you won't feel anything."

"But what's he like? Have you tried him?" cried Miss Green, shrinking as if asked to jump from a window into a sheet sixty feet below.

"It'll be all right. Really it will." Katherine pulled Miss Green's arm: the girl resisted a little, then finally gave way. "It'll be much the best thing. Don't be afraid."

So Miss Green, looking dazed at the pain rooted in her head, allowed herself to be led across the snow and across the street, avoiding the traffic, and a brewer's wagon drawn by two dray-horses that tossed plumes of breath into the cold air amid a jingling of medallions. Merion Street was a narrow connection between one of the streets leading from this square and Bank Street, where they had been going. On one side of it were dark offices, the premises of an oculist, a chemist's shop. On the other were the back

39

entrances to some large stores, and the warehouse of a wine and spirit merchant. The two of them passed unremarked along the wide pavements, for everyone out that day seemed contracted by the cold, having no attention to spare for others. A warm breath came from the swing doors of a club just before they turned into the narrow entrance of Merion Street, which bore its name high up on the wall in elaborate and out-moded letters.

"It's just along here," said Katherine. They reached an entrance with a plate bearing the name of A. G. Talmadge. Miss Green looked apprehensively up the dark steps, like a dog knowing it has been brought to be destroyed.

"I think——" she began, in a whisper. "Is this it?"

"Don't be afraid," said Katherine, wishing that in some way she could put more strength into Miss Green's thin body. Her wristwatch said five to eleven. They mounted the steps, and climbed the stairs to the first landing.

There was a sour smell here, as if the floors swabbed by the cleaner were never properly dry, and the woodwork was varnished a dark brown. The landing should have been lit by an inaccessible window, but this had been painted over with streaky black paint, and they had difficulty in seeing more than the outlines of things: the banisters, a bucket of sand on the linoleum. Then they noticed a small board directing them into a poky corridor. They could hardly see. There were four doors in this corridor, with glass upper panels: two of them were blank. The others said "waiting room" and "surgery".

Katherine tried the first one. It was locked.

"Perhaps," said Miss Green, whispering, "there's nobody here."

"Surely there must be," said Katherine. She was somewhat puzzled.

Then a shadow rose slowly up against the glass panels of the surgery door, and hung there for a moment, making the passage even more obscure. It was broad and humped, as if bent in thought. They watched it silently. At last the door began to open, and a man stood on the threshold, his hand groping in his jacket pocket. He looked at them, fingers still busy.

In the darkness of the corridor they could see that he was a youngish man, but he had about him no youthful qualities. He wore spectacles and had pale blue eyes. His arms and shoulders were powerful, and he was dressed in a pale green sports coat buttoned closely and looking too small, and tubular flannel trousers. He half-resembled an idiot boy whose body had developed at the expense of his mind.

"Good morning," she said. "We——"

"If you're looking for me," he said, disregarding her, in a slow, flat voice that sounded as if his tongue was too large for his mouth, "I don't work on Saturday mornings."

"Oh—but my friend here——"

The man did not answer. Lowering his head, he took a Yale key from his pocket and opened one of the nameless doors. When he was in, he pushed it nearly shut, so that they could not see what was inside. They heard something close, and water running.

So they waited in the half-darkness, Miss Green changing her hold on her handbag every thirty seconds. She cast a glance towards the stairs, but there was nobody about. The whole building seemed deserted.

When he came out again, he looked dispassionately at them.

"What's the matter?"

"My friend has a——"

"Pardon?"

It was harsh, a protracted bark. She realized he was slightly deaf.

"My friend has a bad tooth that ought to come out."

The dentist ran his hands through his pockets, took out

a bunch of keys, worked the separate Yale key onto the ring, and slid them back into his trouser-pocket.

"I don't work on a Saturday," he said gratingly. "My assistant isn't here. She doesn't come on Saturdays."

There was a short silence. There was no noise of traffic: only a very faraway sound of typewriters.

He moved suddenly. "Which of you is it?"

"My friend." Katherine pointed.

He inspected her with lowered head.

"Are you in pain?"

Miss Green nodded dumbly.

"It's very bad," said Katherine desperately.

The dentist searched through all his pockets, this time without finding anything. After a pause he turned his back on them.

"Come in."

They followed him into the surgery. He indicated that Katherine should sit on a little straight-backed chair against the wall, next to an unlit gas fire. Miss Green drifted uncertainly towards the professional chair that was bolted to the floor in the middle of the room. Though Katherine wanted to support her, something kept them from speaking to each other: the very atmosphere separated them, surrounding Miss Green and placing her beyond any assistance. She was committed now. Katherine told herself it was all for the best.

The surgery was as dingy as the passage outside, with the same sticky-looking, brown wainscoting. The carpet was red, blue, and green, the wallpaper dusty yellow. The chair faced the windows, the lower halves of which were boarded over, and the crooked shape of the drill hung high up by a cluster of frosted-glass lights.

These the dentist switched on.

"Will you sit in the chair?"

Miss Green sat with her back to Katherine, nervously smoothing back a strand of hair: she shifted her shoulders once or twice. Still holding her handbag, she carefully aligned her feet on the iron foot-rest. Then cautiously, almost suspiciously, she let her head lean back against the leather pads.

The dentist went over to her and took her handbag away. "We don't want that," he said, as if in a remote corner of his brain he thought he was being funny. Then he came towards Katherine and lit the small gas fire at her feet with a bang. He had put on his white coat.

"Now which tooth is giving pain?"

"At the back—here——" Miss Green made inarticulate noises, a finger to her mouth. It seemed she had to tense her whole body to make her voice audible at all. The dentist bent over her, thrusting a mirror into her mouth, polishing it and looking again. Then he swung a little circular tray nearer his reach: on it, long, pointed instruments were laid out on a rack. Taking one, he bent over her, his own mouth slightly open. The elbows of his white coat were dirty.

At length he announced: "There's a lot of filling in it," going across the room to a small cabinet of flat drawers. He returned with two tiny bits of metal rolling in his palm, and pulled down the drill, which had been folded high and remote, till it elongated like an insect's leg. He began fitting a head into the drill.

Miss Green spoke up in her taut, trembling voice:

"Are you going to——"

"Pardon?"

He flicked on the drill with his foot and bent over her, knowing she had spoken.

"You aren't going to fill it, are you?"

"Fill it? No."

The noise of the drill was insidious, a slack noise. There was a knot in the belt where it had broken and been mended again, and the knot ran round the short, endless course, silhouetted against the window.

Miss Green whimpered as he began drilling. It seemed her nerve had broken at the first touch of the revolving drill-head, that she now had no restraint and was crying whether she was hurt or not. Her little, half-smothered noises hardly sounded human at all: Katherine leaned forward, aware that though she could hear them the dentist could not.

There was a faint cracking, and the dentist stopped the drill to fit in another head: Katherine could see the size of it even from where she sat. The small gas-fire was burning her legs, but she did not move them away.

The drilling started again, and the little quavering moans. This time there was a definite crackling sound, quite audible. One of Miss Green's feet lifted a second from the iron foot-rest, then was jammed back again as quickly.

"Will you wash your mouth out," he said, ceasing. With a push he sent the drill back to its former position, like the sketched-in shape of a hooded bird watching the scene. Miss Green bent over the bowl, a glass of water at her lips, not at all as she had drunk at the fountain. As she spat out the fragments of the filling she slobbered ludicrously, and was instantly self-conscious, trying to break the hanging thread by feeble spitting movements, searching for the handkerchief that was in her bag, and at last clumsily catching it away with her hand. Katherine quickly crossed to her and put her own handkerchief in her lap. She took it blindly.

In the meantime the dentist was busy in a corner with a hypodermic syringe. Miss Green was watching him, and when she had collected herself sufficiently, asked

"Are you going to take it out?"

"Pardon?"

"If you are going to take it out, I want gas."

Her voice sounded on the edge of tears. The dentist advanced a few steps.

"Gas?" he said in his flat voice. The sleeves of his white coat did not quite cover the cuffs of his jacket.

"Yes, I want gas."

"I can't give you gas."

A short silence.

"Why not?"

"I can't give it you. My assistant isn't here, she doesn't come on Saturdays. I can't give you gas without an assistant."

"But I want gas."

"Pardon?"

"I must have gas."

"I can't give you gas." He stood looking down at her, holding the syringe. "My assistant isn't here. I am not allowed to administer total anaesthetic without an assistant present."

He sounded as if he were speaking into a telephone.

"But I can't——"

"An ordinary injection will do as well," he said, not heeding. "The pain——"

"But——"

Miss Green's voice broke in a sob. With the filling of her tooth broken down, she sounded near hysterics, as if she might scream. Quickly Katherine said:

"But surely you could?"

"Pardon?"

He turned, head dropped, to face this new attack.

"Surely you could give her gas. Dentists often do, on their own."

Her own voice sounded unnatural, raised to penetrate his deafness. He said slowly and bad-temperedly:

"Pardon me, but they do not. If——"

"They——"

"No ordinary dentist is allowed to administer total anaesthetic, without a qualified nurse or doctor in attendance," he said loudly.

"But surely it doesn't *need* two people," she argued, striking from a new quarter. "Surely you could do it."

"A local anaesthetic is all I can give," he repeated crossly, turning from side to side as if at bay.

"But why? What are they afraid of?"

He would not answer.

"There is no danger of heart failure, or that sort of thing. No danger at all. My friend has had gas before——"

He was silent, turning the syringe irritably in his hands. Miss Green was collapsed in the chair, seeming to pay no attention. The tap in the bowl clucked occasionally.

"There is really no danger at all. She has had gas before. But she is very sensitive—an injection might—that is, she might faint or——"

Whether she was speaking the truth or not she did not know. But she wanted desperately to move him, to make some contact. As it was, she could not even be sure he heard what she was saying.

"Well, I have told you the law, that is the law I have to obey," he said, refusing to add any more to the argument. Curiously, he had not grown more human during the exchange: once more the image of arrested development occurred to her as he stood outlined against the window. She had no idea what he might say or do next.

"But we never imagined there would be any trouble," she said, refusing to let the matter drop but carefully keeping her voice below any tone that might offend him.

"It's the law—the law of *this* country," he snapped. She took heart at this insult, knowing it to be a sign of defeat.

"But what are we to do? Surely, now you have started —now you have got so far——"

"I can't waste any more time," he grunted. He turned on Miss Green. "You have had gas before?"

She gave an almost inaudible assent. There was a silence.

Suddenly he put down the syringe and said: "All right,

will you come into the other room." His anger—if his semi-articulate abruptness had been anger—had sunk out of sight without being dissolved or forgotten: as he collected a few instruments together and led the way he was breathing through his mouth. As they followed, Katherine's triumph suddenly flagged. They passed through the blank doorway that had remained locked, and found themselves in a small, permanently blacked-out room, dingier than the first. A dentist's chair stood in the middle of the floor, with a washbowl and a few appliances, but there was no drill. In a disused rack on the wall were half a dozen old instruments, rusty and disused: in one corner were the long gas cylinders on a trolley. He gave this an impatient tug so that it rolled up silently behind the chair, and shut the door.

Miss Green took less kindly to this room than to the last. She stood by the chair, lifting her hands and dropping them; when he gestured that she should sit down, she balanced on the edge of the seat, and had to manoeuvre herself into the proper position by degrees. Most of the time she kept her eyes shut. The dentist filled a glass with water and dropped a tablet into it, which sank furiously to the bottom. There was no chair in here for Katherine to sit on, and she backed up against the wall.

He had finished his preparations, and turned towards Miss Green.

"You had better take your glasses off, and your necklace."

Uncertainly her hands crept to the back of her neck, unfastening a thin gold chain which drew into sight a small cross. This and the spectacles he laid aside.

"Now lie back, rest your head back, and fold your hands."

She lay back.

"Fold your hands."

She did so.

47

He put a roll of cotton wool in her mouth, then propped her jaws open with a sort of rubber gag. Unhooking the small, cupped, rubber mask, he twisted a small wheel slowly with his left hand. The needle on a dial gave a spasmodic flicker. "Breathe in through this," he said. Her eyes flew to it. It hid her mouth and nose. "Breathe in slowly. That's right. Keep on breathing in." There was a hush, that might have been the tiny sibilance of the gas. The dentist's voice continued, thick and expressionless. He did not remove the mask. It was impossible to tell whether Miss Green was conscious or not, but the gas seemed to be going on for many stretching minutes. The needle on the dial kept moving unsteadily. Katherine wished he would turn it off.

Yet when he suddenly hooked the mask back onto the trolley, and reached into the open mouth with forceps, gripping the tooth horizontally, she felt an upswerve of terror lest the girl should still be half-conscious but unable to move or speak. Her head stirred as he first pulled, and he put his free hand on her forehead, rumpling her hair, before giving another dragging wrench in the other direction. Katherine could almost feel the pain exploding beneath the anaesthetic, and nerved herself against a shriek. It seemed impossible for the girl to feel nothing. As the dentist levered and wrenched again, the muscles in his wrist moved, and as he withdrew the forceps she thought he had failed until she saw the long root in their grip, bright with blood. He dropped it in a silver casket, then tweaked out the wet and bloodstained roll of cotton wool, and removed the rubber gag.

These he put aside and stood watching her.

Katherine watched her too. Without her spectacles her face looked young, perhaps twelve years old, and quite peaceful: there was no hint in it of petulance or distress. She did not look at all the same: this was the face she had once had, but now had nearly outgrown, a face she would have soon quite outdistanced, that perhaps only her parents would remember. Her hands were still folded, as in prayer or death. She did not come round. The dentist picked up the golden cross, which swung to and fro in the electric light so that it flashed. The water in the glass had quietened to a deep crimson; Katherine found that step by step she had moved right up to the very arm of the chair.

The voice of the dentist broke the silence.

"It's all over," he said.

Miss Green's eyes were open, expressionlessly.

"It's all over," he repeated. "It's all right now. Would you wash your mouth round."

Slowly her hands began unclasping. She sat up, slowly, grasping for the arms of the chair. Her mouth seemed to move in a smile, or to speak, and a sudden thin stream of blood ran down her chin.

5

Katherine lived in Merion Street, though she had not said as much to Miss Green. She lived in a room on the top floor above the chemist's shop. Therefore when she got Miss Green out into the street again, she suggested they went up to her room, where Miss Green could rest.

Miss Green gave her to understand that she agreed, but she was not in an articulate condition. They had gone down the stairs one step at a time, Katherine holding the girl firmly round the waist: Miss Green's eyelids were drawn almost completely over her eyes, and the expression on her face was as if she had swallowed something decayed. Her footsteps were not steady.

Katherine hardly thought of the fact that to visit her room fell in with her own plans. Most of what she had been thinking had been wiped away in the last half-hour: she felt she had given Miss Green a bad time, yet it was hard to know if she could have suggested anything better. She was still desperately eager to help her. Outside the chemist's she propped her against the wall like a piece of valuable china, and hurried in to buy aspirins; then they pushed open the street door and began climbing the stairs. It was an old-fashioned building, with extinct gas-brackets on the walls, and no light on the narrow flights: carpets gave way above the first floor to linoleum. As they climbed higher, the walls looked bare and deserted, until on the top landing they emerged onto plain boards, an empty packing-case that had once held chemical glassware, a single door with a spring-lock, and a little room, at the end of the passage by an uncurtained window, that held a sink, and had been converted from a primitive laboratory to a primitive kitchen. It held a cooking-stove.

An electric-light connection hung from the ceiling, but there was no bulb in it.

Miss Green leaned against the banisters while Katherine found her key and pushed open the door onto inner blackness: they creaked slightly. A bottle of milk stood outside, and the door jammed momentarily on a letter that had been thrust under the door. These things she carried in and put down on an invisible table. A moment later daylight spread from a window inside and revealed a room beyond the door. Katherine reappeared anxiously.

"Come in," she said.

Miss Green detached herself from the banisters and moved like a sleepwalker through the doorway. Katherine helped her into a small easy-chair with wooden arms, and put a pillow behind her head: this was too big, so she fetched a woollen cardigan instead. She had no cushions. Miss Green's head rolled unstably, and then settled; Katherine shut the door and lit the gas fire, turning it up as far as it would go. She felt Miss Green's hands, and they

50

were cold, so she brought a rug off her bed and spread it over her knees. Miss Green stirred feebly as if in protest. Katherine stood up, and began to set the room in order. She felt surprised it was so untidy.

The attic was under-furnished, which made it look large: the ceiling sloped towards the window. On the side of the room opposite the door was a step up to a little curtained alcove—a doorway with no door—where there was a bed. Here she kept her clothes. In the main room were two tables—a square kitchen table, with the remains of her breakfast on it, and a small thin one along the wall, littered with all sorts of oddments—and also a large store-cupboard, two straightbacked chairs, the chair Miss Green was in, and a stool on one side of the fireplace.

Several shabby rugs overlapped each other on the floor, dingy enough to have been ejected from other rooms of the house. The window had no curtains except those of heavy black-out material. Over the mantelpiece a few cheap post-cards were pinned to form a semi-diamond, and the mantel-shelf was piled with empty cigarette boxes. On the side-table there were five or six books.

When Katherine had cleared up the surface disorder and made her bed, she lit a gas-ring fitted to the gas fire, and poured some milk in a blue saucepan to boil, absently licking the cardboard top of the milk-bottle. Then she carried the breakfast things out to the sink, and washed those that were not greasy in cold water, bringing back a clean cup and saucer. She looked at Miss Green. The fire was beginning to warm the room.

"I'm making you some hot milk," she said.

Miss Green turned her head from side to side, as if seeking to evade a dream. She said nothing. Her face was pale, almost yellowish.

Katherine felt really rather alarmed. Obviously the best thing for her would be to go home, but equally obviously she was in no state to go. If the visit to the dentist was

51

going to make her ill for a few days, and it had surely been disastrous enough, there was no use in her staying here for an hour or two: it would mean taking her home by taxi. That would be expensive. Perhaps she ought to go downstairs and ask advice of the chemist. Since she had forced Miss Green to the dentist, instead of letting her go home as she wanted to, all the responsibility fell on her that otherwise Miss Green's mother would have borne: really she ought not to have interfered. But since she had, it was up to her to do what she could despite the trouble and expense.

But perhaps she would improve with resting.

When the milk boiled, she poured it into the clean cup, holding the skin back with a spoon. Then she unsealed the bottle, crushed two aspirins, and stirred them in.

"Here's your milk," she said.

Miss Green did not reply. Katherine looked at her doubtfully, and stood by her with it.

"Don't you want it?"

Miss Green murmured something, shifting her head, and her eyes half-opened and shut again, like a doll's that is lifted and then laid back. Katherine knelt beside her and brought the cup to her lips.

"Drink some," she said.

Miss Green put out her lips, and took a sip; in a moment she took another, then licked her lips as if discovering there an alien taste. She breathed more deeply. At last she brought up her hands and took the cup herself, holding it against her shallow breast.

After five minutes she had drunk about half of it.

"Do you feel better now?"

"I——" Miss Green's voice was hoarse: she cleared her throat. "I don't feel as sick as I did."

"Did it make you feel sick, then?"

"That, and the"—she hesitated—"the taste of blood."

"Finish it up, and you'll soon be all right," said Katherine, vastly relieved. She walked away from her, smoothing her hair back over her ears, and suddenly came upon the letter lying by the opened milk-bottle on the table. It was quite obviously from Robin Fennel.

It was not that she hadn't noticed it the first time, but her mind had been so unreceptive that it had simply glanced off. Now it returned to exact its full impression. She picked it up with a hand that trembled slightly, noticing that it bore no stamp and an anonymous field-postmark. Her name and address were written in Robin's sloping handwriting, that had scarcely altered at all since he had written to her six years ago: each character was given its full shape, very occasionally two words would be joined carelessly, but never two words that did not look well when joined. It did not feel as if there were more than one sheet in the envelope.

She laid it down again. So here it was.

She would open it, of course; but not now, not while Miss Green was here. Though she thought she had prepared herself enough for its arrival, now she held it she was shy of opening it, as if it contained examination results. For in a sense it would be the verdict of the Fennels upon her. For whatever Robin said, it would be less his own individual opinion than the present attitude of the family put into his mouth. If he suggested that she visit them, she would know that they would like to see her again; but if he said no more than his mother—surprised you're in England, why didn't you tell us, hope you're getting on all right—she would know similarly that on the whole they preferred to keep her at arm's length and that she had done wrong to write. This letter would settle it one way or the other. Her forehead rested a second on her right palm, then her fingers trailed away through her dark hair. She shook her head.

"Some more milk?—do you like milk?"

"I can drink it," said Miss Green, looking like a crippled child in her rug.

"I thought it would warm you," said Katherine, hesitating with the saucepan.

"Yes, I'll have some more. Only I get a lot at home. Mother thinks it builds me up."

Katherine took the cup and tipped the last of the milk into it. Miss Green took it with a sigh.

"How do you feel?"

"Oh . . . better, I think. I don't feel I could walk yet, though."

"No, of course not. Stay as long as you like. Would you like to take your things off?"

"No, thank you."

Miss Green put her small nose into the cup again. Katherine sat on the stool by the fireplace, where she could not see the letter.

"Fancy you living in Merion Street," said Miss Green after a while. "I had an uncle in business here once."

"Oh yes," said Katherine vaguely.

There was a pause.

"Have you lived here long, then?" said Miss Green, presently.

"All the time I've worked here, yes. It was all I could find."

"Oh." Miss Green considered this. "I thought you'd have lived in a hostel, or something." As Katherine did not say anything, she went on: "It's nice to have a place where you can bring people."

"I've no-one to bring," said Katherine, scratching the parting of her hair with one fingernail. "You're the first visitor I've had."

"Oh!" Miss Green stared at her with her mouth slightly open. "Not really?"

"It's quite true."

"Don't they allow it, then?"

"Oh, they allow it, I suppose. I just haven't had anyone to bring."

"I expect you go out to other people's—it's different when they've their own houses."

"No. I mean I don't know anyone."

Miss Green stared as if Katherine were trying to deceive her.

"What do you mean?"

"I mean I don't know anyone—apart from the people at the library, of course." She smiled at the expression on Miss Green's face while she was digesting this.

"Don't you go out at all, then?"

"Not often. Usually I go to bed very early. Sometimes I go to concerts or films."

"Don't you dance?"

"I can dance, but I don't."

Miss Green considered her as if this was really too much to believe. Talking, Katherine thought, might do her good. Her face was already showing signs of animation, but she still had a yellowish look.

"Oh, but you must know *somebody*!"

Katherine refused to take up the implication.

"I don't know anybody here at all."

"Then somewhere else?"

Katherine gestured. "I did know one or two people in London, but I've quite lost touch with them now."

"Who were they?"

"People I worked with."

Miss Green was silent.

"Pardon me asking, but how long have you been in England?"

"Nearly two years now."

"You speak it awfully well, really. I mean, people would hardly know except for——"

"I learnt it at school, of course."

"But you hadn't been to England before?"

55

"Well, I had once, I suppose."

"When?"

"Six years ago."

"You mean you lived here?"

"No, I came for a holiday."

"All alone?"

"Yes. I stayed with a family I knew."

"Well, don't you know them any more?"

"I suppose I do," Katherine admitted. She moved her head as if her neck hurt her.

"Do they live round here?"

"No, in Oxfordshire."

"My grandfather lived there," said Miss Green. "What was their name?"

"Fennel. The father was an auctioneer."

"Fennel," said Miss Green. "I wonder if he'd remember them."

"They're still there," Katherine said. To speak of them made them more real, brought them into line, as it were, with the letter that lay on the table. "I haven't seen them since I came to England."

"Do they know you're here?"

"Yes, they do now. I'd almost forgotten about them. But I was in the Reading Room looking for the time a film started, and I saw something about them in a births and deaths column. It was pure chance, because I don't ever see a newspaper, hardly."

"What did it say, then?"

"Well, there was a daughter called Jane. She wasn't married when I knew her. Her little girl had died."

Miss Green shook her head in an incomprehending way that meant she was sorry.

"So I wrote, just to say the usual things."

"Were they friends of your family, then?"

"Oh no. That was the queer thing about it. I got to know them when I was at school." Since this seemed to

56

interest Miss Green, Katherine began explaining. "There was a scheme we all joined to improve our English. The idea was, you sent up your name, address, age, nationality, what you were interested in, and what language you were learning. Then they put you in touch with someone. Oh yes, and you had to put how much your father earned. Did you ever do that?"

"Oh no," said Miss Green, rather offendedly. "I've never heard of anything like that before."

"Oh. Well, that was the scheme. You were supposed to write to each other in the other's language, and correct each other's letters, if you were really keen about it. All they did was take your money—there was a charge, though I've forgotten how much—and then put you in touch with an English boy. We all said we wanted boys, of course."

"And you mean—your father and mother didn't say anything?"

"They didn't know till the letters came, unless you told them."

"How funny," said Miss Green, meaning it seemed hardly decent to her.

"We were very excited for a week or two. But it took so long to get started, we'd nearly lost interest when the letters began to come. And our English-teacher tried to make us do it properly—she asked to read the letters out in class, and that kind of thing. That took all the fun out of it. Most of us wrote a few times and then lost interest. One girl pretended she had stopped writing, but she hadn't. It was a day-school, so the mistress could never find out. They used to write each other love-letters."

"What, without knowing each other?"

"They sent photographs . . . they visited each other when they left school. In the end they got married."

"No! Where are they now?"

"In South Africa, I think."

Miss Green pressed her hand to her cheek again. Her thin astonishment made Katherine feel that she was telling her a fairy-story before sending her to bed. Her knees moved under the rug.

"And what about you?"

"Oh!" said Katherine. "Well, I was put in touch with the son, Robin Fennel. He was about my age. He'd said he was interested in books and music. Why, I don't know. He hardly said anything about them. In fact, I don't know why he was in the scheme at all. Still, I had said the same, so I suppose that was why we were linked up."

"Can you play the piano, then?"

"A little. I played the violin more. Then, when the summer came, he wrote and said would I come and stay with them for a holiday."

"You must have been thrilled," said Miss Green, almost resentfully.

"I was more scared," said Katherine. She took out a cigarette and was about to light it when she felt Miss Green's eye rather balefully upon her. "I'm sorry—do you smoke?"

"Only privately." Miss Green dived eagerly at the packet, and bending her head to the lighter-flame Katherine extended, put it out. Katherine relit it. "I say, do you think I should? Will it hurt my tooth?"

"I should be careful. How does it feel."

"Rather stiff and sore."

"You don't feel sick any longer?"

"No, not now." Miss Green wriggled in her chair, seeming to find it uncomfortable. "What was he like?"

Katherine was pleased she had cheered up this far, seeming to have forgotten her wounded mouth. The extreme paleness had left her and her complexion, although always rather sickly, had practically returned to normal. She flicked her cigarette and went on.

"Really quite nice. They were all very good to me. At first I didn't want to go. I'd hardly ever been away from home before. And I was terrified of going all that distance —wouldn't you have been?"

"I should!" Miss Green was whiningly emphatic.

"He said he'd meet me at Dover. But I was afraid he wouldn't. I was terrified I should have to ask my way. It's hard to understand English at first, you know: you all speak so carelessly." She frowned. "Still, I needn't have worried. Everything turned out all right."

"And did you have a good time?"

"Pretty fair. I was sorry to go back."

"I suppose you asked him back, the next year."

"Oh, yes. Yes, I did, but he couldn't come. I've forgotten why—he was ill, I think. And by that time we'd more or less stopped writing."

"What a shame."

"Oh, not really. We were never very great friends."

"But they're still there, are they?"

"Yes. I expect they'll be asking me to go and stay with them, or something like that."

"Won't that be nice," said Miss Green with an approach to enthusiasm. "Perhaps you'll pick up with him again. And auctioneers get lots to eat and that, surely."

"Well, yes, but would they want me?" Laughing, she added: "They haven't asked me yet, but it's the kind of thing they would do."

"Well, if they ask you, you needn't worry."

"No." Katherine considered for a moment, moodily. "You English are all so polite."

Miss Green bridled slightly, as if in the presence of somebody above her station. "I don't know," she said. "I'm sure it's nothing to complain of."

"No," said Katherine more lightly. "It isn't, I suppose. And I shall go to the Fennels if they ask me, and probably have a very good time. How are you feeling now?"

Miss Green put out her cigarette messily, and cautiously got up, leaving the rug in the chair. She patted her hair with care and complacence, and went to look at herself in a mirror.

"I don't feel too bad," she said. "Where is he now—the one you know?"

This brought Katherine up to the present moment with a start. She went to the table and picked the letter up again, nerving herself to open it.

"I don't know yet," she said. "But this is from him, I suppose." She took up a table-knife and cut open the envelope; withdrew the crested sheet, and gave it a shake to flatten out its folds. Then she read down the two paragraphs of Robin Fennel's unambiguous handwriting.

The first said how surprised and glad he was to hear that she was in England: the second that he would try to call and see her on Saturday sometime after midday.

Miss Green, who had turned to watch her, did not see any change in her face. All she did was to look quickly at her wristwatch. But within her, an extraordinary dread began crawling. This she had not expected. Whatever else he had said, she would have had time to think, to make herself ready: but at this moment it was nearly twelve-fifteen, and Robin Fennel was coming towards this room and her like a bead sliding on a string. Why this alarmed her she had no idea. But she was nearly panic-stricken.

"I must go back to work," she said, going to the door for her coat.

"You're off at one, aren't you?" said Miss Green, puzzled. "It's hardly worth while. What does he say?"

"Oh—" Katherine struggled with her sleeves. "He says he'll pay me a visit some time. He doesn't give me an address—just his regiment, care of the Army Post Office, whatever that is."

"He's in the army, then?" said Miss Green, looking at her reflection again. "That sounds as if he's going abroad.

That address is so that you won't know where he is, you see." She turned, glancing about the room. "Where did you put my bag?"

"Oh—" Katherine went to the side table. "Here."

Miss Green did not stretch out her hand to take it.

"But that's not it."

Katherine stared at her.

"It is, isn't it?"

"No—" Miss Green's voice rose to an incredulous whine. "Where's mine that I gave you?"

"That's it."

"It's not!"

"It must be." Katherine picked her own up. "Here's mine. There aren't any others."

"But this isn't mine." Miss Green inspected it, worried and petulant. "It's the same kind. I got mine at Hanson's. But this isn't it."

"Oh dear." Katherine took the brown handbag impatiently from her, and opened it. She felt in no mood to be hindered by accidents of this sort: she wanted to get away, as if this room were the scene of a crime. But for Miss Green's sake she controlled herself. The lining of the bag was shiny and worn, and in addition to a purse and mirror and other oddments there were a few papers and letters. She drew one out, and stared frowningly at the address.

" 'Miss V. Parbury'," she read aloud. " 'Fifty, Cheshunt Avenue'. You're right." She stared at the address longer than was necessary.

"But what have you done with mine?" insisted Miss Green, in a thin, apprehensive tone.

Katherine replaced the letter and snapped the bag shut. "Let me think. I was taking care of it in the dentist's. And I'm sure I brought it away with me." She looked round the room. "The only thing I can think of is that I left yours in the chemist's, when I bought the aspirins, I was

61

in such a rush. I can't remember. Perhaps someone took yours by mistake, or I took hers first. Shall we go down and ask?"

"This is a nuisance," Miss Green said grumblingly.

Katherine switched off the gas fire, and they went down to the shop, Miss Green holding onto the banisters and peering at the dark stairs. They questioned the chemist, who was kind and fussy, but could do little to help. He thought there had been someone in the shop when Katherine had been there, but he could not remember anything about her, nor had anyone come back afterwards to tell him of the mistake.

"Well, this other person must have your bag," said Katherine when they were outside. "What a bother. I'd better have some lunch, and go and call on her. Then I'll give it back to you."

Miss Green was fretful. "I wish it hadn't happened . . . there were keys . . . if they aren't honest——"

"It's my fault, I know." Katherine wanted to get away from this doorway. "I'm terribly sorry, I am really."

"And I've no money or anything——"

She opened her own bag. "How much do you want?"

"Well, Miss Lind, I owe you ten shillings already, for the dentist——"

"Yes, that will do any time. Will half-a-crown be enough?"

"Oh, yes, but—" Miss Green looked timidly from the coin to Katherine. "Could you give it me in change, do you think? They're so rude on the buses, nowadays, if you haven't the right money."

"I've no change——" Katherine hurried back into the shop, growing more desperate. She came out again with some coppers and sixpences, and also a bottle of mouth-wash tablets she had bought to avoid asking the chemist for nothing but change. "Will that do? And I bought these for you, in case you haven't any at home."

"Oh—" Miss Green looked ɪoo bewildered to be gracious. "I'll pay you back——"

They moved up the street together.

"Are you sure you'll be able to get home all right?" asked Katherine, with more compunction now they were away from her address. "Shall I come with you?"

"Oh, I can manage." Miss Green achieved an almost friendly smile, touching her mauve scarf.

"And you will go home and rest? I think you ought to."

"Well, I feel I should," said Miss Green pitifully. "But don't you think I ought to go back to work? I've missed a whole morning——"

"Oh, don't worry about that," said Katherine. "I'll tell them how ill you've been. There won't be any trouble." She smiled. "Go back home and lie down, or sit by the fire. And keep your mouth shut, you don't want to catch a cold in your mouth."

"Well——" Miss Green still seemed indecisive.

"There's no point in working this afternoon if you're going to be away on Monday, is there?"

"No." They stopped on the corner. "Well, I think I will, then. I'll go now."

"I'll see you on Monday."

"Thank you for—for the milk," said Miss Green confusedly. "I hope you get the bag back."

"I will."

They parted, Miss Green going off in one direction to the bus-stop, her pink nose high in the air. She was soon lost in the crowd. Katherine walked slowly the other way, her hands in her pockets, wondering if she could possibly be mistaken in thinking that the address on the letter in the strange handbag she was carrying had been written by Mr. Anstey.

PART TWO

I

The morning when she came to England for the first time had been still and hot: not an accidental fine day, but one of a series that had already lasted a week. Each had seemed more flawless than the one before it, as if in their slow gathering of depth and placidity they were progressing towards perfection. The sky was deep blue as if made richer by the endless recession of past summers: the sea smooth, and when a wave lifted the sun shone through it as through a transparent green window. She walked to and fro across the sharp shadows on the deck, noticing how the deck and all the ropes had been drenched in sea-water and then whitened in the sun.

It was incredible that she should be there at all. Walking on the deck that morning was a direct result of a day she could hardly remember, when they had all filled up their application-forms with much giggling and speculation. It seemed absurd. It was like taking a ticket in a sweepstake, or drawing a package from a bran-tub; no, it was less pleasant than that: it really was one of the silly things one does in company and regrets afterwards. For although Katherine was easily moved by a crowd she was not a person to make friends carelessly, and this was exactly what they had led her to do.

After that day, for some weeks she had gone about in subdued dread, but as no more was heard of the scheme this gradually passed. There were other more immediate things to take her attention, so that when one of her friends arrived at school brandishing the first of the letters it came as a shock. Several correspondences began, and as Katherine listened to the boys' letters being read aloud at sporadic intervals her alarm returned: she felt herself quite incapable of keeping her end up in this kind of exchange. In the hilarious search for double meanings she sounded as light-hearted as anyone, but inwardly she hoped her application would have gone astray. It was really not her sort of amusement at all.

She need not have worried. When Robin Fennel's first letter arrived, she was relieved to find it very formal. He described his home and school and daily life as if writing an exercise. Even her friends were hard put to it to find anything funny or thrilling. The only tangible thing he seemed to do was go bicycle rides, and so they called him "the bicyclist". In every subsequent letter when he innocently began a paragraph "The other day I cycled to" they shrieked with laughter. But the joke passed; other correspondents were far more interesting, and soon no-one bothered about her letters from England unless to say: "Well, and how's the bicyclist? Still bicycling about?"

Incongruously, her relief changed slowly to disappointment. She felt slightly annoyed with this Robin Fennel for letting her down: she did not mind their laughing at him, but she resented the patronizing verdict that Katherine had drawn a blank. She kept on writing, although the exchange affected her no more than an interminable business correspondence, and after a while began trying to draw him out. She started writing only half her letters in English, and filling the other half with more personal likes, dislikes, and enthusiasms, hoping to lure him into following suit. He did: but the two halves of his letters (divided by a short ruled line) remained equally dispassionate. He had been here, gone there; he had walked, fished, swum; he had read this, heard that. As a last attempt, she had begun writing in diary form, with alternate (and usually shorter) entries in English, wondering if he could be persuaded to adopt this form and so become more intimate. But he stuck to the half-and-half arrangement, starting, invariably, "Dear Katherine" and ending "Robin Fennel". This was all very exasperating. Fundamentally, as she knew well, she did not want a close friendship with

68

him. He sounded harmless but dull. But it would have made the task of writing to him much more interesting, and in any case she disliked failing in anything she attempted.

So after these vain attempts, she gave it up. She got into the habit of leaving the familiar letter with the English stamp lying about unopened for days, or she read half of it before being momentarily interrupted and then forgot to finish it. Her answers were shorter and less prompt. What now became so annoying was that he did not take this hint any more than he had taken her first one: though he could not be drawn on, he could not be shaken off. To Katherine's disgust, he sent her a card on her birthday—a woodcut, not displeasing. His letters always arrived nine days after hers were posted. From annoyance she passed to alarm: "But I shall never get rid of him!" she thought, panic-stricken. Her friends prophesied a life-time of writing serious letters to England, and receiving in return lengthy descriptions of bicycle journeys: "but perhaps it won't always be so bad, perhaps he will buy a motor-car one day. Then he will go much faster and much farther, and will have lots more to tell you, and he will write much oftener. Once a week he will sit down with his dictionary and grammar-book, with a clean sheet of blotting-paper and a razor-blade to scratch out his mistakes, and write simply sheets. Of course he'll be married. And his wife will say: 'Who is this Katherine you are always writing to? Leave your letter and take me to a music-hall.' And he will say: 'Later, dear, later: I have still to describe Canterbury Cathedral.' And then she will be very sad, and cry, and they will quarrel and part. You will stop writing, perhaps you will move, perhaps you will die—it will all make no difference. He will go on writing about his punctures and the watercress for tea." Several times Katherine vowed that she would just stop writing, or tell him gently but firmly that she found herself too busy to continue the correspondence. But somehow she never did. And so they kept it up for over a year.

Then, on the first of June, another letter arrived. There was nothing remarkable about the outside of it, and she carried it about unopened with her all day, for she made an affectation among her friends of being completely indifferent to him. Late in the afternoon, on the way home from school, she opened it: it contained an invitation for her to spend a holiday in England. She felt as if she had been holding a live hand-grenade without knowing what it was. It was unbelievable. Sitting in her bedroom, she scanned it for any trace of insincerity, but found none. The invitation was in perfect good faith.

She sat trembling for a while, and swallowed several times. It never entered her head to accept it: that was the only saving point in the whole business. She had never spent a holiday away from her family in her life, and if she did, the companion she would choose would be a really close friend. The best line of action seemed to be to say nothing about it, simply refusing the offer when she wrote back. But incautiously she mentioned it to her parents, who congratulated her on her luck. Not everyone, they said, has a chance to go to England.

"But I don't want to go to England!"

There was a great deal to settle: dates, routes, questions of luggage, clothes. After a short conclusive argument Katherine sat down to write a letter of acceptance and thanks. Rebelliously, she wrote it on the house notepaper, and not on her own lettuce-coloured kind she kept upstairs. This made it seem unreal, but the reality rushed back as soon as she had irrevocably posted it, and for the next few days she grumbled incessantly. Her father scolded her for ingratitude.

"But I want to spend my holidays with you," she argued. "I'm terrified of going abroad! And I'm afraid of the journey."

He said: "Rubbish!"

To her it seemed an ordeal; to her parents, a privilege; but to her friends it was a farce. She could not help laughing when she admitted it, and they all lay back and shrieked together. No-one suggested that there was anything romantic or even exciting about it. It was generally agreed that Katherine was in for an exhausting three weeks, the greater proportion of which would be spent on the rear seat of a bicycle made for two, pedalling miserably through the rain (it always rained in England) in search of bigger and better cathedrals. No doubt he would ask her to give him language lessons. There would be huge, badly-cooked meals, based invariably on roast beef: she would come back looking enormous.

Yet as she thought it over that night in bed, her apprehension returned, and with it a certain wonder. After all, it was a gesture of friendship. It startled her that this unknown boy in England should think of her, adding month by month to the conception he had of her in his mind, until now he proposed that arrangements should be made and machinery put into motion so that they could meet. It was fascinating. How little she had thought of him, and how shallow her ideas had been: she scrambled up, put the light on, and took out his letters from the drawer she kept them in. Sitting up in bed, she read them through critically. The first thing that struck her was that they really said very little about cycling—or cathedrals, for that matter. And in any case the English were very reserved. What was really important, she thought, dropping them on the counterpane, was that he should have kept on writing, promptly and indefatigably, even after her own interest had worn thin and her letters grown perfunctory. How kind he had been. What did he think of her? For almost the first time she pictured him sitting in the lamplight at dusk, in a room in a house at the end of a lane in England, writing to her. How strange that he should want to bring her to that room.

She picked a letter up, and brushed his signature with the tips of her fingers, imagining that she could feel the roughness of the ink.

She travelled light, her one large suitcase standing by a ventilator. It contained all her best clothes, freshly cleaned, washed or pressed, as if she were passing into another life and were concerned that only her finest things should go with her. Everything was in order. In her handbag she had keys, tickets, papers: the sea was so placid that only an occasional heave, a tiny hinting at illimitable strength, showed she was not on land: at Dover Robin had arranged to meet her. He had been thorough about this. He would stand just past the Customs, wearing a grey suit, a white shirt, and a blue tie: as for recognizing him, he had enclosed a photograph to help her. This gave her another shock. At times she had wondered what sort of appearance he presented: it was not a question to which she gave much thought, and she had assumed he was a variant of the red-hair, freckles and projecting-teeth English face. In this she had been wrong. The photograph showed him looking at the camera with his hands on his hips, lit by brilliant sunlight, wearing a cricket shirt. There was a swing in his body that suggested he had been called and had turned momentarily back while the picture was taken. He was dark and slight, with long eyelashes. The expression on his face was evasive in the sense of not being fully captured by the camera. Rather to her surprise, she had shown it to nobody except her parents: in return, she had despatched a conventional portrait of herself, dressed in white for the occasion, dark hair drawn severely back. She did not imagine it would be much like her after she had spent a night travelling.

All had been arranged so precisely. Yet she could not

help stirring uneasily as they neared Dover. Slowly the white-cliffed island drifted nearer. She knew very little about it: only enough to know that by this crossing of thirty miles of water she would land in a completely different country. As time drew on, the quality of the early morning, like paper-thin glass, grew deeper and more clear; high above the harbour an aeroplane, like a tiny silver filing, climbed and tumbled in the sky so that an enormous word drifted on the air, emphasizing the stillness of the day. The gulls met them, blindingly white in the sun, wheeling and screaming as they escorted the boat slowly towards the stone jetty, and their cries added to her mistrust. She did not want to land in this foreign country. Cables were thrown out and made fast: the boat shuddered to a standstill. She looked over the rail at the bare stones of the quay, terrified. Then she joined the large bunch of passengers that had begun to go down the gangway, possessed of a sick feeling that Robin Fennel would have failed to appear and that she would be left tongue-tied and helpless, unable to explain her business to anyone. She found it impossible to understand the chatter around her—odd words rose irrelevantly to the surface: "dear"; "punctual"; *Daily Mail*. The porters and customs officials spoke a language as intelligible to her as Icelandic, but to her great relief they took no notice of her, simply chalking her bag without comment, so that she could follow the main press of people up a concrete passage out onto the railway platform. Robin Fennel was standing under a notice-board which said: "To the Boats."

They saw each other simultaneously.

"Katherine?"

She held out her hand, smiling.

"So glad you could come. Did you have a good journey?"

"Yes—good."

73

"Let me take your bag—we'd better get seats."

She followed him up the platform. He had a very clear voice, and she was thankful to find that she could separate his words without difficulty. A soft grey hat shaded his eyes and face. They got into a first-class compartment and he put her bag onto the rack and let down the window as far as it would go. The carriage was otherwise unoccupied and filled with dusty light.

"Would you sooner face the engine?"

She blushed. "Please——?"

Without embarrassment, he made an effort to translate, slowly, with an accurate accent.

"Oh!—no. I never mind."

They sat down, Robin throwing his hat and a copy of *The Times* on the seat by him.

"We'll have lunch on the train. I expect you are hungry. Did you have anything to eat on the boat?"

"I had some coffee."

"Oh, then we'll eat on the train. We should get to London before two, and meet my father. He will drive us home."

"In a motor-car?"

"Yes, then you'll be able to see the country." He sat opposite her composedly, his arms folded, speaking as if they were old friends. "You haven't been to England before, have you?"

"Never."

"I hope this fine weather will hold. It will be too bad if it rains all the time."

The photograph had not been bad, but it had not quite done him justice. The thing it had failed to capture was the contrast between his severely-cut features and the gaiety conferred upon them by his youthfulness and fresh skin. Although he was only a boy, it was already quite plain what he would look like as a man—stern, with strong nose, chin and forehead. The muscles round his mouth would become prominent, and his cheeks hint at concavity. The dry black hair would appear on his wrists, and with constantly shaving his jowl would be dark-blueish. But this was all in the future: at the moment his mature look was counterbalanced by the almost feminine gentleness of youth, smooth as the skin of a pear and as delicate as linen.

She had been greatly afraid that they would find nothing to say to each other. This was well-grounded as far as she was concerned, but Robin seemed to feel no constraint. His manner was unhurried: he wasted no words or gestures, and this calmed her: he explained that his father and himself had stayed the previous night in London, and while his father had gone about some business, Robin had travelled down that morning to Dover, and spent the time wandering about the town until her boat was due. He said that it was a perfect day for seeing across to France. She remembered how she fancied she could see large patches of weed dark through the lucid water, but dare not try to explain this. No-one else got into their compartment and after a while the train started, easing forward with a surprising absence of shock: as they moved steadily out Katherine noticed two posters by the station bookstall: "Heat Wave" and "Lunchtime Scores". She wondered what they meant but did not ask. Robin went on talking quietly about nothing in particular: at one point she was disconcerted to learn he rode horseback.

"Is your case locked?" he asked as they rose to go along for lunch.

"Locked? . . . Yes. . . . I leave it here, don't I?"

"Oh, yes. It's safest to lock it, though."

"The keys are safe."

The dining-car was not full, and they had a table to themselves, with a vase of flowers which Robin moved aside. Clear soup swayed to and fro in the deep plates.

Katherine realized that she was very hungry. She took a roll from the wicker basket.

"People say food on English trains is very bad," Robin observed. "I can't judge. There usually isn't enough of it, but that's a different thing."

Katherine straightened this out in her mind, and made an appropriate remark.

"I hope you'll like English food, by the way," he added. "That again is supposed to be very bad—like the climate. But you can see what the climate does when it tries."

The midday sun wheeled backwards and forwards across the bright white cloth as they sat eating. Napkins on other tables were folded into mitres. After the soup they had ham and tongue, with salad in dishes, and glasses of colourless fizzy lemonade. She helped herself to salad with a wooden spoon and fork.

"Where are we now?"

He looked at his watch and told her.

"It's Kent, is it? The county Kent? But there are so many houses."

"Well, a lot of people live here."

"I thought that Kent . . . was farms."

"Hardly that," he said, rolling ribbons of lettuce expertly round his fork. His fingernails were cut bluntly and brushed very clean. "There's a lot of hop-growing. And there's a lot of fruit and vegetables, for the London markets. The lorries go up every night, before dawn."

"But there are factories," she objected. "There! And another one."

"Not many, though. This isn't anything like an industrial region. Most of south-east England is like this."

They finished tiny moulded jellies, and had cheese, celery and biscuits, with coffee. Katherine wondered if he would offer her a cigarette, but he didn't: he paid the bill with a new pound note and tipped the waiter directly. Then they went back to their compartment along the swaying corridor, Katherine catching glimpses through the bucking glass-panelled doors of English people awake or asleep, in many attitudes. "I expect you'll be wanting to change some money," Robin said as they resumed their seats. Her suitcase was still there. "Do you understand it? Or do you find it confusing?"

"Money?" Katherine had spent some time studying a handbook for travellers in England, so she was prepared in this respect. "Twelve pence are one shilling, twenty shillings are one pound. But I have never seen any."

He withdrew a handful from his pocket. "They're pennies. And that's a shilling. But there are also two-shilling pieces and half-crowns—they're two shillings and sixpence."

"And these?"

"Sixpences—worth six pennies."

They fell to talking about the rate of exchange and the vacillations of Katherine's own currency. The sight of the money depressed her, because in such small familiar things the foreign country around her was best expressed. Thinking how lonely she was, she suddenly found herself near crying: she looked unbelievingly at Robin. It was impossible to imagine what he was thinking: he seemed perfectly adjusted to all his surroundings—including her—and able to withdraw his real personality elsewhere. This was not at all as she had pictured him. She had thought of him first as dull, then as inarticulate: both conceptions were wrong. In either case she had imagined that she would be well able to hold her own in the impact of their characters, because she thought herself wise for her age, and because English boys were traditionally uncouth. In fact, he was a good deal more at his ease than she was: she was disconcerted to find herself deferential. For the moment silent, he glanced out of the window. The expression on his face was cool, as if travelling alone: he raised his hand slowly to draw one strand of his hair back into place. At first she had thought he was shy and was playing at being grown-up: now it occurred to her that he was simply being natural. Accustomed to sizing up and judging people at once, she could find nothing about him to fix on. Blinking, she looked out of the window too: they were on the edge of London. It was a Saturday afternoon and the rows of new brick houses were brilliantly shadowed in the sun. Once she caught a glimpse of a straight road, where an unattended baker's van was being amblingly led by a horse, following the baker as he went from door to door. Gone in a moment, it filled her with a sense of relaxation, and she watched the roads and gardens curiously. After a while the ticket-collector passed along the train.

It was intensely hot at Victoria, where according to plan Mr. Fennel met them. The station was crowded. "You've brought the fine weather with you," he said as they shook hands. "Had lunch?"

"On the train," said Robin. "Katherine would just like to send a postcard home, to say she's arrived safely."

She liked Mr. Fennel. He was short, spry, elderly and courteous, with close white hair and a felt hat the colour of oatmeal which reminded her that he was a country auctioneer. He did not wear spectacles, but a worn spectacle-case protruded from an upper waistcoat pocket. He was very slightly bow-legged. As she scribbled the postcard that she had brought specially with her she wondered if father and son were exchanging brief appraisals and condemnations, and in her confusion pushed the completed card through the slit marked "London and District" without noticing. As she rejoined them Robin said: "They had some good animals there once."

Their car was an old-fashioned model, very dusty about the wings, and Mr. Fennel handled it with the extreme care of one who has learned to drive late in life. "This is your first visit to England, then, is it?" he said to Katherine who sat beside him, Robin being in the back with the bags. "What do you think of it, so far?"

"Oh, I like it."

"Katherine was disappointed with Kent," said Robin with a chuckle. "There were too many houses."

"Well!" said Mr. Fennel. "I agree with her. She's perfectly right. But it's the same all over England—good arable land being turned into pasture, pasture turning into housing estates. It'll be the ruin of us."

"England is an industrial country, isn't it?" said Katherine, determined to keep up the conversation when she was able.

Mr. Fennel snorted. "It'll be the ruin of us," he repeated. "Suppose there's another war? What are we going to live on? Christmas crackers and ball-bearings?" He glanced from right to left, turning the wheel. "It's getting very hot. Are the windows all open, Robin?"

"Shall I open the roof?"

"Well, a little way, perhaps. How are you, Katherine? You must be warm with that coat on."

"Yes, a little."

Robin leaned over them and slid back the roof, so that a simultaneous breath of sun and wind struck in. Katherine felt her hair streaming, and resigned herself. "I dare say I'm not going fast enough for Robin," Mr. Fennel continued pleasantly. "To tell you the truth, I don't greatly care for cars. But everyone runs one these days. Still"—he sounded the horn—"when I do drive, I drive slowly. If there are any mistakes to make, the other fellow can make them. Really, the road accidents are nothing to laugh at. What were those figures in the paper the other day, Robin?—something to show it was no more dangerous to go through the war than cross Piccadilly?—something like that."

"Well, you won't get gonged for speeding, dad," said Robin with placid irony.

"The roads are crowded, certainly," agreed Katherine. Mr. Fennel's voice had suggested he was speaking to an invalid who did not properly take in all he was saying. "Saturday," he said.

When they were out of London, she sometimes looked about her for the England she had expected. It was difficult to see it. The main roads were full of cars and cyclists, the garages were all open, and every so often they would pass a teagarden with a sign, or a chalked board saying that fruit was on sale, plums or pears. There was no end of the cars. They streamed in both directions, pulled up by the roadside so that the occupants could spread a meal, formed long ranks outside swimming pools. Also there were innumerable hoardings, empty petrol drums and broken fences lying wastefully about. Occasionally she saw white figures standing at a game of cricket. These were the important things, and because of them the town never seemed distant. Only infrequently did she see things that reminded her of landscape paintings—a row of cottages, a church on rising ground, the slant of a field—and she preferred in the end to watch the road and feel the wind play around her. Everything seemed enshrined beneath the sky.

"Could I take a turn, dad?" said Robin once.

"I'd as soon you didn't," Mr. Fennel replied equably, and the matter was dropped. Instead, Mr. Fennel talked slowly and explicitly about ordinary things so that Katherine could understand and answer what he said. Already she found she could relax her classroom eagerness, and this cheered her. She was only afraid that it was tedious for him, and listened in dread for the resigned note that would mean: well, we've got her for three weeks and we'd better make the best of it. In the meantime, Robin busied himself in the back seat with a crossword puzzle. When she looked into the driving mirror above the windscreen, she could see his eyes dropped towards the page, or sometimes turned distantly out of the window. Once they were looking at her. She glanced quickly away, knowing that at present she had no idea of how to meet them.

At length when afternoon had become late afternoon and except for the continued brilliance of the sun would have been evening, they arrived at the village whose name she had so often written on envelopes, and there sought out a short gravelled slope, where a long gate was hooked open, and halted by a circular lawn in front of a large unimposing house built of red brick.

They got out into the sudden silence. Mr. Fennel removed his hat and wiped his forehead: "A job for you, my lad," he remarked, indicating the dusty body of the car.

Robin nodded, taking out the bags.

The front door stood open, and they went in through a small porch to a large hall, that had stairs ascending round two sides and the landing banisters running round the third. From windows set high up at the turn of these stairs sunless light came, making the hall seem like a well. There was a blue bowl of flowers on a dark chest, a few pictures in elaborate frames. Almost at once a door opened and Mrs. Fennel came out to meet them.

"Here's your guest, delivered safe and sound," said Mr. Fennel. Katherine advanced to shake hands.

"Very pleased to meet you, my dear. You must be tired out. Is it as hot in London as it's been here?"

"I should say, myself, it's hotter," said Mr. Fennel, smoothing the sides of his head with his palms. There were some letters lying on a salver for him and he picked them up. "It's breathless in London—simply no air at all."

"I'll show you your room," said Mrs. Fennel.

They went upstairs, Katherine looking wonderingly about her. The house was rather larger than her own. Her room was at the end of a long passage, and was reached by two steps down that Mrs. Fennel advised her to watch for. Her hostess was a strong, grey-haired woman. Her face was not beautiful but expressed great good-humour and tolerance. Robin had already taken up Katherine's bag and it lay waiting to be unstrapped on a cane chair, so when Mrs. Fennel had left her she did this and took out a few of her things. As soon as she had started she stopped to stare round the room. It faced south-west, and was decorated in cream and white, with a blue carpet and curtains; these furnishings contrasted coldly with the warmth of its aspect. There was a grey marble washbowl in the corner, with bright silver taps and white towels, and an expensive, low dressing-table with a stool to match in front of it: when she pulled open one of the drawers to put away a handful of clothes she found it lined with English newspapers, which gave her an unreasonable shock. It was like the money: unfamiliarity where she was not prepared for it. But she liked the room; crossing to the window, she looked out from the side of the house onto a small lawn edged by poplar trees, where two striped deckchairs lay empty in the sun. She thought dimly she could hear the sound of water, but decided after a few moments that it was only the unfamiliar hush of silence in the country.

She went very slowly down the wide staircase, keeping one hand on the banister. In her dark brown skirt, white shirt and dark brown tie pinned with a small Olympic badge, and with her hair newly brushed and drawn back, she looked severe and foreign. They had gone into the lounge, leaving the door open so that she could see where they were. "This is the untidy room," said Mrs. Fennel, from where she sat sewing. "The children do as they please with it." It was a long, low room at the back of the house with french windows opening onto a terrace, low, chintz-covered furniture and a grand piano. Robin snorted at the deprecation. "It's the comfortable room," he said, getting up politely. "There's lemonade, if you'd like some, Katherine."

"Oh, thank you."

He filled a long, hand-painted glass from a jug and handed it to her, first removing with a silver spoon a pip that floated on the surface.

"I hope it's cool enough," said Mrs. Fennel. "The refrigerator has gone wrong again."

"There's one thing about Jane," said Robin, tasting it critically. "She can make lemonade. I think it was what she was put on the earth to do. Jane is my sister," he added to Katherine, who sat down by Mrs. Fennel on the sofa.

"She won't be in for dinner, I'm afraid," said Mrs. Fennel. "I expect you three are hungry. By the way, Katherine, do we talk too fast? What do you think? Should we speak more slowly?"

"Oh no." Katherine blushed. "I can understand what you say. But I don't speak English well."

"That's all right," said Mr. Fennel, rising with his opened letters in his hand and folding away his spectacles. "We shall just ramble on as usual. You just do as you like —don't trouble about making conversation. We want you to be at home here. If you feel you are, we shall be satisfied."

But Katherine did not relax. They ate dinner in a dark-panelled room around a polished table, and it was served by a maid. She was so alert to behave properly that she hardly noticed whether she enjoyed her food or not, but thinking it over decided that she had. It was not imaginative, but of fine quality and well cooked. She was served first and pressed to eat more than she wanted.

Robin's face derived from Mrs. Fennel; the stern, serene features and regular teeth became too definite in later

83

years to be handsome in a woman, but it was easy to see that he would always appear good-looking, even when the delicate quality of youth had disappeared. She watched how they behaved to each other: they were courteous, as though conscious a visitor was present. Mr. Fennel served the second course with a ceremonial flourish, and they helped themselves to vegetables from dishes held by the maid. Katherine found it all rather trying and hoped as time went on they would be less formal.

Afterwards the maid brought coffee into the lounge, and Mrs. Fennel took the lead in asking her about her journey, but she tactfully confined herself to questions that Katherine could answer with a yes or no if she liked. Robin sat attentively and sometimes interposed a sentence. They were willing to laugh if she was flippant, and she tried to be as amusing as she could: gradually she was relieved to find the atmosphere becoming easier. Mr. Fennel smoked a cigarette with a deliberation that suggested he did not smoke as a rule. Later on Katherine found she had no handkerchief and rose to excuse herself.

"Can I go?" said Robin, getting up.

"Of course not," said Mrs. Fennel, waving him back. "You can't go rummaging round Katherine's bedroom." She rested an amused eye on her son.

"I shall have to look for them in my case, also," said Katherine. She sped upstairs.

The maid had turned back the bed and laid her night things ready, and although it was only nine o'clock the curtains had been drawn. She pushed them partly back and undid her suitcase, searching for handkerchiefs. Just as she found them she fancied there was a knock at the half-open door. She listened, but could hear nothing so shut the case with a sharp click. The door swung inwards silently, and in the dusk Katherine could see a girl standing on the threshold.

"Oh," she said.

The girl looked at her. She wore a lemon shirt and pale, shapeless skirt and no socks: her height would be the same as Robin's.

"I'm sorry," she said abruptly. "I didn't know if—I mean, I thought I heard you. I'm Jane. How do you do."

"How do you do," murmured Katherine.

They shook hands.

"When did you get here?"

"About seven."

"Good journey?"

"Yes, thank you."

Katherine knew that Robin's sister was over twenty. But she would not have thought there was more than a year's difference in their ages.

"Are you coming down now?" asked Katherine, shaking her handkerchief from its folds.

Jane had withdrawn to the door, her eyes still searching Katherine's face as if waiting for her to take the lead.

"No," she said. "No, I'll see you later." And with a brief smile she went. Katherine heard a door close along the passage.

When Katherine returned the other three were as she had left them. Robin suggested they went out onto the terrace, and held the french window open for her. Beyond a rockery and some rose trees there was a tennis court, sunk below a gravel path that led to a door in a wall running across the bottom of the garden. "Do you play tennis?" asked Robin. "We must have a game. You see, we decided to have a proper hard court instead of a big lawn; a lawn looks very nice, but it takes some keeping up, and in any case there's the little one at the side—under your window—if we want to have tea out or anything. Below the tennis court is the kitchen garden"—he pointed to the wall—"and then the river."

"The river? I heard it," said Katherine, pleased.

"Did you? Would you like to see it?"

They went down the steps and along the high gravel path. Robin ran his finger along the wire netting. "The apricots are ripening," he said, indicating some trees spreading against a wall. "Last year we got fifteen pounds."

He opened a door and they passed into the kitchen garden, meeting a profusion of lettuces, peas, runner beans, cabbages and rows of feathery carrots. In the corner were a small toolshed and a glass-house, where she glimpsed some tomatoes. A tap dripped slowly, wrapped in sacking, making a perpetual green stain on the cobbles.

"This is a wonderful place for growing things," said Robin. "See how sheltered it is, with the high wall on one side and these fruit trees on the other. And then you see it slopes pretty well due south down to the river, and catches all the sun." He pulled down a branch and fingered one or two plums; when he found one that rolled off into his hand he gave it to her. The bloom bore his fingerprints.

"Does the river——?" She failed to finish this sentence in English; however, he understood her to ask if the river ever overflowed? "Sometimes on the other side, where there are water-meadows. Come and see."

They went through golden clouds of gnats to a high door with faded blue paint, and when he opened it Katherine was surprised to see a broad river drifting by, as it seemed, on the very threshold, though there was ten yards of bank that had been scythed and mown, leading down to the water and a set of wooden steps.

"This is beautiful," she said, tossing the stone of her plum into the water, where translucent fish rose momentarily at it. "You are very fortunate, aren't you?" Looking up and down the river, she saw they were at the middle point of a slow bend lined with willow trees, at the foot of which were hoofmarks. Just opposite, the sweeping branches of a weeping-willow tree made a tent that a canoe could lie in. Further up the river, the sunset flashed off the water, showing hundreds of insects borne on transparent wings.

"It's nice," said Robin. He leaned against a noticeboard that said "Private. No Landing Allowed", and looked across the water at a field scattered with golden-fleeced sheep. "Do you go boating?"

"Yes—have you a boat?"

"We have a punt," said Robin, pointing to the end of a wooden landing-stage where a small boathouse had been built. "I didn't bring the key, I'm afraid. Can you punt?"

"Punt?"

"Yes, with a pole."

She pondered the image. "No! But I can"—she made rowing motions—"and"—she made paddling motions—"do you see?" She ended with a half-nervous, half-excited laugh, foreign and gleeful, that she thought might attract him. He shoved himself away from the post with his shoulders. "Well, we'll teach you to punt," he said. "Look, there's a water-rat. See it? Under the opposite bank." He pointed to a small brown head travelling steadily along, accompanied by a diagonal ripple, until it vanished under the weeping-willow tree.

"I saw it."

He led the way back, locking the blue gate and hanging the key on a rusty nail. She was alert for his mood. But his actions rarely had anything stronger than the flavour of a motive around them: in this case, he was at ease among his inherited surroundings. He took it for granted that she would find it interesting to look over them, but no more.

They went up the terrace steps to the now-lighted lounge. "Been looking round?" asked Mrs. Fennel. "Has he shown you our river?"

"Yes. You must like it."

"It is nice," Mrs. Fennel admitted. "But I think it makes the place rather damp, do you know? And it's mournful in winter."

This last remark, spoken as it was in a foreign language, came to Katherine with something of the impact of a line of poetry. She sank quietly to a seat, looking around her, and thought of the time she would be no longer there. Mr. Fennel, wearing his spectacles, was turning over the stiff, close-printed sheets of the local paper. Jane had at last come in, and was lying on the sofa, a book balanced on her chest, with a picture of mountains in it: she did not say anything to Katherine but was paying attention to her. In the electric light Katherine could judge her better. She had the angular, chiselled, Fennel face, but with neither the flickering beauty youth cast on it nor the good-natured repose of maturity. Instead she looked pale and irritable, rather like Robin after a long illness. Katherine wondered if she could be mistaken in thinking she was much older than her brother; she had none of his poise: she was not even dressed as well. Her clothes had a shabby look, and in addition she was not made up, nor were her hands attentively manicured. Robin dropped onto the piano stool and fingered a few notes.

"I expect Katherine would like to go to bed early," said Mrs. Fennel. "She must be very tired. Did you stay at an hotel last night?"

"No, I slept on the train."

"That isn't a proper sleep, is it," said Mr. Fennel, removing his spectacles and scratching his nose with the steel earpiece. "Sleep is more than rest for the *mind*. The *body* must lie down—every muscle should be relaxed——"

"Horses sleep standing up," said Robin vaguely. "Well, Katherine, do go to bed if you are tired."

"Oh, I will not go for a little while. I am not tired."

"You can sleep as long as you please tomorrow," said Mrs. Fennel, biting off a thread suddenly. "We shan't disturb you. Oh, Robin, what's that on the ceiling there? Is it a moth got in?"

Robin bestirred himself, and examined the immobile wings spread in the rose-coloured light on the ceiling. "It certainly is," he said. "Isn't there a duster somewhere on the bookcase? Can I stand on this chair?"

"Put a paper on it first."

"Be careful," said Jane. Robin looked round at her with amusement. "It's quite furry," he reported. "Have you suddenly taken a fancy to them?"

"You can handle it carefully."

"Yes, dear, don't crush it," said Mrs. Fennel. "Gather it up firmly but gently. Put it out of the window."

They all watched while Robin's head and reaching hands shut out the light, and Mr. Fennel looked up resignedly as the shadow fell across his paper. Katherine felt that at this moment it was at last natural for her to be there, yet at the same time there was no intimacy among them: the whole thing resembled a scene in a hotel lounge. But she dismissed the comparison in a moment, telling herself that three untouched weeks lay ahead of her. Her head reeled suddenly with fatigue: it was certainly time she went to bed. Robin reported that the moth had flown into the creeper.

Yet when, after saying good night all round, she was at length lying in the darkness, hearing nothing but tiny unfamiliar sounds from the trees outside and from other rooms in the house, she found she was not ready to sleep. Her thoughts were like a tangle of live wires: she would choose one and try to follow it to its source, but almost immediately she would be swept away again by one travelling in the opposite direction. Any circumstance she picked on changed disconcertingly to something else. Her mind was like a puzzle in which many silver balls have to be shaken into their sockets; it was her thoughts that were rolling free, and she moved her head from side to side as if to settle them. Then, abruptly, she succeeded: and her uneasiness faded as she knew what she was thinking.

When was Robin going to start behaving naturally?

So far he had stood insipidly upon his party-manners, even when they had been alone, as if playing at grown-ups. When would he drop that, and be more friendly, and put her at her ease?

Because she had nearly stifled herself trying to be polite, none of the visit so far seemed quite real. It was all a little insincere, like a school prizegiving. The parents, of course, might always behave like that. But Robin seemed to have taken his cue from them, so that she had now met all four of them, one after another, and was left with the absurd feeling that the most important person, her real friend, had not yet appeared. There seemed nothing in their greetings so far to warrant their inviting her so many expensive miles. They welcomed her undramatically, even casually, as if she had come from the next village. She found this a disappointment.

Was he, perhaps, shy? She pondered on his face, which she already knew well, and his attitude. It was impossible to think that. And she could not accuse him of being bored with her, either, because his attention was always on her and his manner was solicitous. Really, he acted as if he had long ago made up his mind about her, and had brought about this meeting simply in order to check and correct one or two trifling points. There was no constraint in his manner at all.

Then why should she assume he was not behaving naturally?

This was a facer.

Oh, because he just couldn't be. He was only her own age. It couldn't be natural for anyone of sixteen to behave like a Prince Regent and foreign ambassador combined. It just wasn't possible. Besides, if (ghastly thought!) by the thousandth chance it *was* natural, it would mean that he would never have asked her. They would be so entirely opposite in every way that—— And again to be so independent, yet so gracious—and Robin's movements were always beautifully finished and calm—well, it would mean that *people*, mere friends, mere other personalities, would hold no interest at all for him.

And consequently he wouldn't have invited her.

But he had.

And therefore this reserve, this sandpapering of every word and gesture until it exactly fitted its place in the conversation, this gracious carriage of the personality—this was not natural, or at the most it was a manner, so familiar by now that his thoughts and motives could change freely behind it. Somewhere behind it was a desire to see her, which would now alter into something else. At the moment she could do nothing but watch. But in time she would know. The time would come when he would let her see.

But after this period of order, her thoughts broke their pattern once more and recommenced rocking to and fro, so that she became too tired to follow them any more and sank into half-consciousness. At this, half-effaced impressions rushed upon her, details of the journey and passengers, the shine of the sea, the lifting of the waves that was the slumbering of strength, the gulls at Dover, and above all her surprise that after so many miles and hours and different vehicles, after threading her way along so many platforms and quays, through ticket-barriers, entrance-halls, customs-houses and waiting-rooms, she should have reached the point she set out for, successfully encountered Robin Fennel, and have been taken along so many un-named roads and lanes until they reached the house where he lived. Finally, her mind gave one last flicker of surprise, as a sail gleams for a moment before going over the horizon, that she should at last be lying in this house, surrounded by strangeness on all sides to a depth of hundreds of miles, and yet be feeling no anxiety of any kind.

2

No-one called her the next morning, so she had her sleep out, waking up to find it half-past nine by her wristwatch and the sun already high, the heat spreading over the countryside like a huge green tree. She was uncertain what was expected of her, so washed and put on a linen dress. Then she stole through the corridor and down the stairs. Bedroom doors were freely open, and she heard a rattling of saucepans from the kitchens, and an unabashed voice lifted in song. All the carpets in the house were thick and soundless, and the doors shut precisely with a click. Blinding gold swords of light came obliquely from the landing windows, which stood open. She was relieved to find on opening the dining-room door that Robin and Jane were still sitting at breakfast. Robin put down the morning paper instantly, and rose to manipulate her chair.

"Good morning," he said. "Sleep well?"

"Yes, thank you. I am late, I'm afraid."

"Not at all," said Robin. "We breakfast at any old time on Sundays. Besides, you were tired after your journey." He pushed the sugar across and she began sifting it on her grapefruit.

"And we were tired after our lack of journeys," said Jane obscurely. She reached over and hooked the paper away from Robin. They were both eating toast and marmalade. Grapefruit was a luxury to Katherine, and she scoured it with enjoyment until it spat in her eye. After that she went more slowly. Her subtleties of the previous night no longer seemed at all plausible, and she was left once more shy and uneasy.

"What would you like to do today?" asked Robin, after he had rung for bacon and fried eggs by pressing a bell concealed under the carpet with his foot. He motioned that Jane should pour out a cup of coffee for her.

"Why, I don't know." Katherine was wary, suspecting there might be a concealed answer to this that etiquette required her to give.

"You wouldn't like to go to church?"

"If you go, I will."

Jane looked up, her elbows on the table, and gave a short chuckle. "We are a godless family," she said. "But we respect your principles, if you have any. There was some speculation as to whether you'd be a Roman Catholic or not."

"Oh no. I'm not Catholic."

Robin looked relieved, and felt for the newspaper, which was not there. Jane threw it back to him and rose, lighting a cigarette.

"But I should like to see some of your churches, all the same," said Katherine hastily. "They are very fine, I believe."

"Oh, we'll have a regular orgy of that," said Jane. "We'll go to London and Oxford and Salisbury and all the other places. Robin will tell you all the dates." The cigarette looked unusually large in her small mouth as she lounged on the window-seat.

Robin drew a silver pencil from his jacket pocket and flattening the newspaper down more firmly, pencilled a solution in the crossword puzzle. Then he rested a glance on Jane. "The question is," he said, "what are we going to do this morning?"

"I suggest we show Katherine the village. What there is to show."

"Not a bad idea."

"And the river."

"She's seen that."

"She can see it from the other side, then."

"Rivers," said Robin mildly, "look much the same from either side."

Jane glanced round sharply. "Well, there's nothing to see in the village. You could walk through if you didn't know it was there and never see it. And that'd be a good thing, too." She sounded inexplicably cross.

Katherine gathered that Jane was co-host, so to speak, and this disappointed her, because she wanted to get Robin alone. Further, she had taken something of a dislike to Jane. She was short-mannered and irritable. Her hair was cut rather outmodedly into an Eton crop, and her figure was small, bony and unemphatic. When all three of them set out she wore a raffish check shirt that contrasted with the Sunday sedateness of the other two. The front door was open, and as they passed through the tiled porch the sun seemed simultaneously to lift up at them from the ground and to press down on their heads and shoulders. Robin appeared to straighten himself against it, looking round at the trees that ascended on all sides towards the sky. He looked handsome to the point of sleekness.

They went up a lane to a secondary road, which led them to the village. As Jane had said, there was not much to see: nothing but one street of cottages, a tiny toolshop and garage, a combined general shop and post office, and an unpretentious public-house with a bench outside it. At the end of the street was a pond, and standing back on a slight rise on the right was a church. The cottages had brief front gardens blazing with flowers, and the air was full of the noise of birds.

Undistinguished as it was, Katherine found it fascinating. She looked curiously round the sides of cottages, where small ugly children were fussing, and at old people who sat on kitchen chairs in the doorways. When she saw their hands lying in their laps, or on the wooden arms of the chair, she thought it was strange that these husks, that had poured out their lives so distantly and differently from her, should for a second look at her with their bright eyes. From occasional doorways came dance music from Radio Luxembourg, and she could see dimly through the lace curtains on the windowsill mass-produced china figures and Sunday newspapers, read by men in shirt sleeves. A white dog looked at them and then lay down. They walked together through the pouring light, which so far was not balanced by such heat, but which promised that the two would reach equal intensity at perhaps three in the afternoon.

"Well, now you know all about it," said Jane, after Robin had finished some rambling anecdote about the Civil War. "Don't you think it looks nicer than it sounds?"

"It's very nice," said Katherine.

"Yes, it is, for what it's worth. It palls with time." Jane yawned with the heat. "But tell me"—as the yawn abated, her voice assumed by contrast unnatural clarity— "is it as you'd imagined it? All this, I mean?"

Katherine looked at her, caught off her guard. This was the question Robin ought to have asked—the one she had rehearsed. Yet Jane obviously expected an answer. She hesitated. Did Jane mean simply the village, or the whole visit? Robin, she guessed, would have meant the former, unless she had got him very much wrong: with Jane she was not so certain. But she did not like Jane sufficiently to treat it as a personal question.

"It's smaller," she admitted. "I did not know what to expect. I had looked in some books about England to see if I could find anything of it, but there was nothing. Really, I suppose I thought there would be—white cottages, a very old church, grass——"

"A maypole, and everyone going hunting and eating roast beef," Jane finished, throwing off the remark without deflecting her watchfulness. "Didn't Robin tell you about it?"

Katherine thought guiltily of long passages of description in English impatiently skimmed through and tossed aside. Words that baffled her she had not troubled to search out in a dictionary.

"I had a shot at it," Robin said. For some reason he carried an ash walkingstick with which he cut at nettles and peppery cow-parsley. "But I'm not very good at that sort of thing."

"Robin favours the guide-book style," said Jane. "Although I don't think we are in any guide-books."

"Jane's favourite literature," Robin retorted, with the nearest approach he made to sarcasm, "is written by people who travel about with a gun and a typewriter."

"I like to *know* about places." Jane's voice took on a curious, younger-sister note of defiance. "All you care about is the birthrate and the standard of living. I want to know what I should feel like if I lived there."

"You'd be bored."

Jane addressed herself solely to Katherine.

"Does what you've seen of England fit in with what you'd read about it before you came? Of course, you've probably read a lot. But does it?"

Katherine was rather bewildered at this.

"Perhaps a little," she said. "Not very much."

"I shouldn't think so," said Robin. He came to a halt at the edge of the duckpond, and tucking his stick under his arm took a bread roll he had saved from breakfast out of his pocket and began breaking bits off to throw to the ducks. They hovered in an expectant semi-circle, rushing towards each new piece as it fell. "But you can connect it, you know. Take what you see now," Jane muttered impatiently, and pulling up a grass-stalk to nibble, lounged aside to watch the ducks. Robin went on, breaking the bread neatly in his fingers. "Small fields, mainly pasture. Telegraph wires and a garage. That Empire Tea placard. And you know, don't you, that Britain is a small country, once agricultural but now highly industrialized, relying a great deal for food on a large Empire. You see, it all links up."

Katherine looked at him doubtfully. The edge of his

96

voice sounded as if the gap between his inner and outer thoughts had closed up, and that he was speaking sincerely. She wondered why. The ducks gobbled and made slapping noises.

"That one at the back hasn't had any," said Jane. "Do you see? He makes little rushes but the others always get there first. Give him one to himself."

"He's not trying," said Robin. "He doesn't really want one."

Nevertheless, he threw a bit, so accurately that it hit the duck on the head. Before it could realize what had happened, the crust had been gobbled up by another, streaking in with a flurry of speckled feathers.

"Oh, give him another bit," said Jane.

"There's no more." Robin dusted his hands, and took his walking stick in hand again. "I don't suppose he was hungry."

The ducks followed them hopefully as they turned away, the one that had been hit swimming with dazed dignity away from its fellows. Robin suddenly and unaccountably brought down his stick on the end of a twig that lay on the ground, causing it to leap up into the air, and then, before it had touched the ground, knocked it ten yards over a hedge, where chickens rushed towards it. "Boundary," he said, looking at Katherine, who laughed, infected by his sudden irresponsibility. "Remember what day it is," said Jane in mock reproof, but looked at him with a sort of futile contempt. Katherine saw them both very clearly for a moment: Robin standing erect in the sun, looking about him, bearing the stick authoritatively; Jane sallow and irritable, wanting to get back indoors. "It's absurd," she thought. "He's not shy at all. But of course, why should he be?"

They climbed a path leading through the churchyard, where flowers and seeding grasses mingled with the graves and the sound of singing came from the church. The pure light picked out the distance of woods and hills, as well as

97

sharpening the immediate surroundings; the blue hare-bells, the roughness of the carved headstones, the insects half-way up the stalks of grass. At the end of the path was a wicket-gate, leading into a wide field that sloped down to the river, thickly covered with kingcups and butter-cups. A few cattle stood in the shade of trees, their flanks shining, and watched the three of them pass through the gate and down the scarcely-worn path. As she walked be-hind the other two, Katherine noticed that the shiny flowers threw a yellow reflection upwards to the shadows of their clothes, making it seem as if they walked in a kind of splendour.

It was on the first day, too—or, at latest, the second—that they started to play tennis. Afterwards there were few days that passed without a game. Jane objected that it was far too hot, and Katherine hoped that this would separate Jane from Robin and herself, for she wanted to see how he behaved when they were alone, but when she came down after changing her shoes Jane had lounged out onto the court, and was throwing her racquet up and catching it, the strings glittering in the sun. It was obvious that she did not want to play, and Katherine admitted a fresh problem to her attention—why Jane was attaching herself to them so persistently. When she said anything, particularly to Robin, she was derisive and (as far as Katherine could tell) bored. Robin treated her politely, but with just the suspicion of offhandedness that suggested that in his opinion he thought very little of her and had the whiphand. Yet though she didn't look it, Jane must be at least four years the elder. Katherine sensed that there was a subdued conflict between them, though of course it might be only an elaborate family joke. Her ear was not quick enough yet to catch such fine shades of meaning. But since this situation existed, why should Jane prolong it by hang-ing about with people so much younger than herself?

So far she did not expect an answer to such questions. All her attention was concentrated on picking up what was said.

Before they started, Robin wound up the net. It appeared by implication that he was the best player, and so the first game was between the two girls. They went to the ends of the court and Robin stood by a net-post to call the score. As soon as she started to play, Katherine realized that she was wretchedly out of practice, and her clumsiness was aggravated by Robin's presence. The racquet she had borrowed from Mrs. Fennel seemed unwieldy, and time after time her shots came off the wood. She tried to concentrate, knowing Jane to be an indifferent player, but only became over-enthusiastic, and lost the first two games. Then, as she made the first service of the third game, the court came suddenly into focus, and she was all at once confident. Six consecutive games went to her, giving her the set. She rejoined Robin and Jane at the sideline guiltily, wondering belatedly if she should not have allowed Jane to win a game or two more.

Surprisingly, Jane did not seem annoyed.

"Robin will give you a better game," she said. "I'm going for a deckchair."

"Would you like to rest a bit?" asked Robin, touching the rubber grip on his racquet-handle.

She refused, eager to see how he played. For she knew that in playing a game a person can display much of their character. To oppose her, even on the tennis-court, would force into action the personality he was concealing so well. Jane, for instance, had been quite different from what Katherine expected: not at all petulant or flashy. Instead, she had been timid and incapable of pressing an advantage until it was too late.

So on the dark red tennis court, sunk below the garden and surrounded by high, rustling trees that glowed and rippled in the sun, Robin and Katherine faced each other and began to play, Jane sitting with hands clasped at her knees and calling the score in a clear voice, and using the family tennis-balls marked with a purple F. Katherine determined to do her best. Clearly Robin was a better player than Jane: he hit hard and confidently, and the game was fast, for he swung the ball to and fro with long cross-shots. These kept her continually on the run and breathless. She began to panic. Robin won the first game, and the second, and also the third.

The fourth he allowed palpably though without comment to go to her, presumably to avoid the embarrassment of a love-set. This annoyed her, and she determined to make him regret it: she had been studying his play, and now began to see where it was lacking. There was something mechanical about it. The first thing she noticed was that he invariably returned her serve to her backhand, even after she had demonstrated that it was not weak. Then she saw that he rarely looked at her before placing his shot, and that his cross-drives were largely a matter of habit. Finally, his game was limited. He never chopped or made piratical excursions to the net. His style was fast, neat, open, and unvarying.

Once she had grasped this, it was easy to take the initiative and break up the pattern he imposed by soft centre-line serves, short returns, high lobs. This unsettled him, and he was soon rushing about as Katherine had done. After taking the score to five all she won seven-five. Jane clapped theatrically from her deckchair, a small sound in the afternoon.

"Splendid," she cried.

"Here, I say," said Robin. "What happened?" Coming up to him Katherine saw the disarrangement of his hair, his forehead wet with perspiration, and it pleased her to think she had caused it. Once more, as at the duckpond, she felt the opacity he presented to her was wearing somewhat thinner; she could sense his interest turned towards her, as a blind person might sense the switching-on of an electric fire.

"She used her head," said Jane.

"You see," said Katherine, "if I play as you play, I lose. So I play differently."

"Smart of you," said Robin. "It makes all the difference. But I never could bother to think: I just swipe about."

"Swipe?"

Jane explained, throwing a blazer over her shoulders, while Robin slackened the net. They went up onto the terrace where there were basket-chairs round a circular iron table. "Robin can still have his fresh air if we sit here," she said. "I'll fetch some lemonade. What a joke, your beating him like that."

"Will he be annoyed?"

"Oh no, that would be bad manners."

Katherine sat down. The three weeks of her holiday, still almost untouched, receded like brilliant water. Here with the Fennels, time had a different quality from when she was at home. She could almost feel it passing slowly, luxuriously, like thick cream pouring from a silver jug. As she wasted it, it added to her. She watched Robin loop the net, and come out of the gate of the court, carrying his racquet and a box of balls; it was typical of him, she thought, to clear up after the game. In some respects he resembled the perfect butler. Oh, but he was hopelessly muddled in her mind, for as he gave a bound up the steps towards her, his delicate, wary face struck again deeply in her, and his dark half-tousled head carried itself with such simultaneous independence and attention—attention, what was more, to her—that she herself felt like a servant.

"Staying here, are we?" he said, beginning to screw his racquet into its press. Her heart sank. She did not want to talk trivialities with him. She felt, as she had felt ever since she had first seen his photograph, that he could, if he wished, say something that would be more important to her than anything she had ever heard. What it would be she had no idea.

"The court is very good," she said.

"Not too bad, is it? It's wearing nicely."

Jane reappeared from the lounge, bearing on a tray the jug and glasses they had used when Katherine first arrived. "There's still no ice," she said. "And this is the last of the lemonade. There's a certain amount of pith and pips and what-not settled to the bottom, but it can't be helped. All comes from pure lemons."

"You didn't strain it properly," said Robin, holding up a glassful critically and then passing it to Katherine. "Why didn't you use muslin?"

"Couldn't find any." Jane brought a third chair to the table and sat on the other side of Katherine. "It won't kill us. You can make the next lot, if you're so fussy."

Robin smiled inattentively.

3

The house was surrounded by trees, and gradually she became accustomed to their continual whispering, and to many other things that had at first seemed strange. She came to know which rooms were behind which doors: Robin's room, Jane's room, Mr. Fennel's study, filled with shelves of files, a set of the Stud Book and other similar volumes. These were nearly the only books in the house: the bookshelves in the lounge held only cheap novels, picked up on summer holidays, while Robin kept what few he had in his room, and Jane seemed to possess none. Katherine had glanced furtively into Robin's room one afternoon, and noticed a small set of shelves, holding a dull assortment of accumulated birthday presents, school prizes, and books presumably self-chosen—the stories of great operas, a few paper-covered political works.

She grew accustomed to the early morning sounds, when she was lying awake: soft treadings to and from the bathroom, Mr. Fennel's car starting up outside. No longer was she shy of the housemaid, who usually passed some unintelligible remark to her in uncouth English when they met. She learned to be hungry enough by nine in the morning to face her breakfast.

"Everything is very solid and comfortable," she wrote in a letter to her best school friend. "In fact, rather like staying in a hotel. And one always feels on one's best behaviour. There are four of them—the father and mother, whom I only see at mealtimes, but they're very nice— and Robin and Jane. Robin is much better-looking than we'd imagined. I have a photograph I'll show you when I come back. I wish I could describe him, but at the moment he rather mystifies me. I can't understand why he asked me to come, because he doesn't take any interest in me at all. Of course, he's very polite and kind, and spends all his time with me, but you know the feeling. Like being conducted round a museum. He gives the impression of being miles away—not in a poetical sense, either. Jane is different. She must be twenty or so. She hangs about with us *all the time*—and does seem prepared to be friendly, but doesn't know how to go about it. Sometimes she's almost rude—as far as I can tell—but that's probably just nerves. I don't think I care much for her—and in any case I wish she'd find something better to do. If Robin and I were alone more, I might be able to find out more about him. There's not too much time, because there's someone else coming in my last week—a man this time. Some friend of the family."

Jane was a puzzle. Whatever they were doing—walking, cycling, playing tennis—she was with them, and she always seemed out of temper, but without the strength of character to propose any alteration in their plans. Robin made no comment on her presence. Gradually Katherine evolved an explanation, which was that Robin had definitely enlisted her help to deal with the visitor. It was hard to imagine him saying openly: "This girl is coming on Saturday for three weeks; will you help keep her amused, because I shall be bored stiff." But no doubt he did make the request in more equivocal language; Katherine felt sure there was another side to Robin's nature that might prompt such an appeal. And Jane had listlessly agreed.

This was not a flattering solution. One day when they came in from a walk on which Jane had developed a blister and a bad temper, Katherine thought of another one: in England it would not be proper for Robin and herself to go about alone together, and Mrs. Fennel had asked her daughter discreetly to act as a chaperon. This evaded the weak point of her other idea, which was that in her opinion Jane would not give two hoots for anything Robin asked her to do. And it was much more flattering. It made her feel warm inside, even though it was probably only a meaningless English convention; the English were, after all, very formal, she remembered, having once laboriously read half a novel by Jane Austen.

But Jane was still a puzzle.

One morning she brought Katherine her cup of tea. Up till then the maid had brought it regularly, and the taste of it on a clean palate had decided Katherine finally that she did not like the stuff. In fact, she had contracted the habit of pouring most of it down her washbowl when the maid had gone. Also it embarrassed her to be waited on. She tried to cover her confusion by looking as if she had just woken up.

"Good morning, and how are you this morning?" said Jane with mechanical sarcasm. She had a dressing-gown drawn shapelessly round her, not a smart one: it looked like a relic of childhood. She put the pale blue cup and saucer on a small bedside table.

"Oh, very well," said Katherine, struggling up dazedly into a sitting position. As she did so a disconcerting thing happened. The corner of her pillow pressed down on the rim of the cup and neatly overturned it, flooding the table-cloth and part of the pillow and sheets with tea.

She was speechless.

Jane, who had turned away, looked round at the noise. "What——" she began. "Oh, glory." She started to laugh, and once she had started seemed unable to stop. When she laughed, she resembled Robin much more and was, therefore, better-looking: the irritable expression vanished from her face and she looked attractive and carefree.

Crimson, Katherine floundered about in an effort to kneel up. "But it's awful—I'm so sorry. Everything is ruined——"

Jane sat on the eiderdown, gripping the end of the bed in order to laugh better. "That's funny," she gurgled. "Too funny. Forgive my manners. How did you do it?"

"But really I couldn't help it——" Katherine stared incredulously at Jane; then, convinced of the sincerity of her laughter, calmed down. "I don't know! First the cup was there—then it was—everywhere . . . But there's nothing to laugh at!" Jane had gone off again. "The bed all ruined——"

Jane, moaning, righted herself. "Mind, you're kneeling in it. You'd better take the pillow-case off—this thing, I mean." She shook it limply. "Give it me, I'll put it in water."

She took it away to the bathroom, and came back with a cloth to mop the table.

"Lord, that was funny."

"Funny?"

"Well, it seemed funny to me." She gave a subdued snort. "I like that kind of thing—do you know what I mean? Something really outrageous——"

"I apologize," said Katherine carefully. "I will apologize to your mother." She put on her own dressing-gown and shuffled her bare feet into slippers.

"Oh, nonsense," said Jane. "Don't you worry. Nobody will mind at all. There, that's got the worst off." She shied the cloth across the room into the washbowl, where it fell with a limp smack. "It's the kind of thing that makes life worth living."

"What do you mean?"

"Something that really upsets——" Jane made a gesture, which finished with her drawing a small enamelled cigarette-case from her pocket. "Here, you do smoke, don't you?"

In the circumstances Katherine thought it better to accept one. A box of matches lay in a candlestick on the mantelpiece, which was put there in case the lights fused.

"There." Jane lay back on her elbows and blew smoke at the ceiling. Her gaiety still seethed quietly within her. "Beautifully funny . . . I remember Robin once taking a photograph of us on a beach one holiday. He kept backing away to get us into focus. Very serious over the whole business. Back he went—didn't notice"—Jane began to wheeze—"didn't notice a little rock behind him. Over he went. Legs in the air! I nearly died. Can't you just see it?"

"I can, yes," said Katherine with guarded laughter.

"Lord, it was . . . Look here." Jane rolled onto one elbow, flicking ash impatiently onto the carpet·with her other hand. "What do you think of him?"

"Robin?"

"Yes, do you like him?"

The cigarette was making Katherine feel a bit sick. She laid it aside, composing herself to answer.

"Yes."

"You do." Jane rolled back again, considering this. "Why?"

"Why?" Katherine attempted to laugh, wondering if she ought to take offence. "Is he so bad?"

"Is he as you'd expected him to be?"

"Oh, no." This truth was out before Katherine thought to stop it. "At least——"

"How had you imagined him, then?" Jane rolled back again, the cigarette in her mouth: Katherine surreptitiously rubbed the ash into the carpet. Jane's questions had the bright quality of a child interrogating an adult— or (though Katherine did not think of it) an adult questioning a child. There was nothing personal in her curiosity.

"Well, I suppose I thought he would be . . ." Katherine searched for the English that would approximately express her feelings. "Rather ordinary."

"And so you think he isn't ordinary?" Amusement was bubbling again not far off. "Why not?"

She thought it better to be firm at this point, and said: "Because I have never met anyone like him before. I can't understand him."

"Robin is ordinary, down to the last button."

Katherine looked up at this. There was an emphatic note in Jane's voice that solicited belief, but she was not prepared to take it on trust. There was something behind all this.

"You think so."

"I know so. It's no good thinking you're twin souls, or anything like that. You're absolutely different." Jane yawned, and yawning, went to the dressing-table where she sat looking critical and fingering her hair.

"Why do you say that?"

"Because it's true, and you don't know it." She said this without any interest whatever, glancing along Katherine's dressing-table. Picking up Katherine's hair-brush, she said:

"This is very heavy."

"It's made of silver."

"And what is this pattern—a tree, is it?"

"Two trees," Katherine said deprecatingly. "It is meant to be the tree of knowledge and the tree of life. And on the comb one finds the serpent."

"So it is. That's most original."

"My grandfather was a silversmith," said Katherine, watching the former subject receding with only partial regret. "He made them for my grandmother."

"But they look almost new."

"Well, they have hardly been used. My mother kept them until I was fourteen. Then she gave them to me, and said I could keep them or use them, as I pleased."

"And you're using them."

"I use them at special times. But I think when I leave school I shall use them always. They were meant to be used."

Even so slight a conversation marked a step forward. To have broken personal ground with one of the Fennels was something she had begun to think impossible; now it had happened she became much easier in her manner, not only with Jane but with Robin and the others too. It had been just such a hint that she immediately warmed towards; a gesture of friendship she paid back tenfold.

She could be grateful and friendly to Jane, though, without necessarily believing what she said. The remark about Robin's being ordinary she distrusted on two counts: one, Jane was simply doing her job in squashing any incipient romantic feelings she might have towards him; two, from her own observation she thought it false.

Katherine had not known many sixteen-year-old boys, and the ones she had known had not been English, but she had heard the kind of letters their English counterparts wrote, and was certain that Robin was exceptional. In five years' time it was quite possible he would no longer be remarkable, but at sixteen his almost supernatural maturity suggested that he drew on some inner spiritual calm. Looking at him one evening when he happened to be fingering the piano, she was overwhelmed by a sense of barren perfection. He had reached, it seemed to her, a state when he no longer needed to do anything.

On their outings, since Robin remained unconcerned, she and Jane drew together more, and out of their good humour a sort of bantering front arose against Robin. One afternoon they went to a local gymkhana in a large field on the outskirts of the next village; this was Robin's suggestion, and Jane as usual was against it. She blinked crossly around in the strong sunlight and developed a game with Katherine, which consisted in pointing at people whose faces indicated a horse somewhere in their ancestry, along with other rudeness. Katherine laughed, but on the whole enjoyed the scene. A large inner square had been roped off for the parades and jumping, and the crowd mingled round the sides along with the horses and ponies, cars, a few traps, and a hastily-erected refreshment stall. Most of the spectators were local people and Robin was frequently drawn off in conversation with young men and girls in shirts and riding breeches. She was glad he did not introduce her to any of them. They would have nothing in common. Yet watching him talking to a tall, slender girl standing up in one of the cars, she could not help reflecting on the kind of life he led when she was not there.

She watched the jumping, only moving when one of the large hunters edged near her through the crowd. The event in progress was for children under sixteen, and the fences were proportionately low. Each entrant went round the field, over a hurdle, a double-hedge, another fence, a mock-wall, and finally a low gate. At the moment a girl was having an awkward time with a roan: already it had swerved at one of the fences, broken through the supports, and thrown her. A loudspeaker kept up intermittent encouragement as the roan refused at the wall and the girl lurched perilously. Katherine felt sorry for her. It was a slow business to manoeuvre the horse back again for the second attempt: then again it refused. Once more she turned and made another attempt: this time the horse scrambled over in a very ungainly way, and after clinging on a few seconds she slid once more to the grass. At this point she gave in and led the horse off without tackling the last gate.

She was followed by a little biscuit-coloured horse, with a white mane, ridden by a small, solemn girl, that was much more successful. It trotted docilely at the obstacles and suddenly hopped over them like a cat. This was done with such unexpected ease that the onlookers giggled slightly, but this did not disconcert the small girl or the horse, who together cleared each jump without displacing a single bar, and trotted off imperturbably. Katherine studied the programme. The entry was called "Cream Cracker", and under the heading "description"—bay, grey, chestnut gelding—the compiler had failed to put anything more imaginative than "cream horse". To her delight the judges announced that Cream Cracker and another competitor had tied for third place, and asked them both to jump again: therefore Cream Cracker came out once more. By this time it had interested most of the audience—particularly those who knew nothing about horses—and the loudspeaker tried to be funny about it. It circled the field again, picking up its heels impeccably behind it, and left the ring to a loud ripple of applause.

"Sweet little thing," said a woman nearby.

The loudspeaker announced that Cream Cracker had

been awarded third prize, and the three winners came out again to receive their rosettes. There was a curious custom, she noticed, whereby the riders held the rosettes in their teeth while they cantered round in order; when they did this there was another roar of laughter, for whether accidentally or not Cream Cracker led the parade. After circling the field twice they went out among renewed applause. The little girl in the saddle had never given the slightest indication that she was not playing on a rocking-horse in her nursery.

"This is an English crowd," said Jane. "They're quite unique. Their lowest common multiple is very low indeed."

Katherine smiled, but she was enjoying herself. The warm air was filled with the smell of grass and horses. Occasionally a whiff of pipe-tobacco sharpened it by contrast. A great good-humour filled the crowd, which was a local one from the surrounding villages. Every class of person wandered aimlessly about: village women, looking older than they were; knowledgeable farmers, who knew what neighbours had left at home in their stables as well as what they had brought to show; a tramp dressed in a long overcoat fastened with a safety-pin and with a wisp of grass drooping from his mouth, who stumped painfully round three sides of the field in order to buy a bottle of beer from the refreshment tent, and then retired to the foot of a five-barred gate to unwrap a large cheese sandwich. There were young men with raw, red necks and closely-tailored suits, young farmers' sons who pushed through the crowd on their horses, groomed and braided for the occasion; unplaceable men who stared from the open sunshine-roofs of their cars; the fantastic older gentry, hardly to be taken seriously, in archaic tweeds, with old sticks and fobs and hat pins that had been worn through season after season of this same company and pursuit; and then there were the young gentry, on holiday from school, rarely one in twenty with a face that was beautiful, but all having the fine texture of skin that good food and exercise automatically gave. A bevy of them was helping in the refreshment tent, charging extortionate prices for lettuce sandwiches and home-made cakes, and muddling the change that was kept in an upturned trilby hat. Katherine and Jane went there and bought a bottle of cherry cider each, very gassy, which they held as they strolled round, swigging occasionally. It was all very free and easy. Finally, there were village children, the elder ones minding the younger, busy with anything but what was going on in the roped-off arena. Little ones strayed about almost under the feet of the horses. Small groups of bullet-headed boys, who a hundred years ago would have been scaring crows for a few pence a week, lifted their bottles to the sun to see who could drink the most without stopping. It was strange that, islanded in the half-attentive, slovenly crowd, the horses seemed more highly strung, as if belonging to a higher breed altogether. Also many of them were reluctant to jump, as if resenting doing so before so many people.

As time went on they lost Robin, and Jane, by now tired even of being offensive, suggested they should go home and have tea in peace. "Or haven't you had enough yet? They'll probably go on all night: they're hours behind time already."

"I don't mind. We'll go if you like."

She was willing to leave before she became bored, and they crossed the littered grass to the entrance gate. As they walked off down the road the deep quacking of the loud-speaker followed them, along with the noise from side-shows. There had been a few stalls of amusements, tra-ditional games with backcloths grown shabby from being hawked year after year round such village entertainments. Eventually the sound died away.

"I enjoyed that," said Katherine.

"Did you really? I shouldn't have thought you would."
Jane kicked at the dust piled by the edge of the road as
she walked. "I should have thought you'd find it insuffer-
able. I do."

"But why? I liked it."

"I thought you were too clever for it."

Katherine chuckled. By now she was finding it easy to
understand English, and less difficult to speak it.

"Well, I don't know, but the sight of people enjoying
themselves in the mass always depresses me," Jane went
on. "Some people may take a pleasure in it."

"It's strange to me," said Katherine. "That's the reason.
It was very English and interesting."

"It's English all right," said Jane. "But then I am
English, more's the pity. And I know a lot of those people,
rot them, and they aren't at all interesting."

"Of course, I don't go to—horse-shows?—at home."

"No." Jane suggested they should take a shorter path
across some fields, and they climbed a stile. "What do you
do at home?"

"What do you mean?" Katherine was surprised.

"How do you spend your time?"

"I go to school. There's always work to do in the
evenings. But I read, go to friends' houses, sometimes go
to the theatre."

"Of course, you live in a town. There's always so much
more to do in a town," Jane said ruminatively. "Whereabouts in it do you live? I mean, what does your house look
like?"

Katherine recollected her home with difficulty.

"I live in a wide street with trees and seats . . . The
houses are much alike. High, white . . . fairly big."

"Have you a garden?"

"No. No, it is not like England, you know. There are
gardens near—the—I don't know what you call them.
Gardens—a park—with a café and a band."

Jane pondered on this. After a pause she remarked that it was raining. Large white clouds had hung about during the day, but had not interfered with the sunshine. Now they had coagulated for the time being, and a determined shower was falling, though another part of the sky was quite blue and the sun continued to shine. They went into a barn to shelter.

"Beware of the bull," said Jane, peering inside.

The barn was empty, and they stood in the broad open doorway and watched the glistening rain fall. Behind them the barn was like a whispering hollow shell as rain beat on the roof. Jane leaned at the side of the doorway, folded her arms, and stared out across the veiled meadow. The small shoulders of her check shirt were wet.

"What are you going to do?" she said. "When you grow up." She inflected the last two words sardonically.

"I haven't thought," said Katherine. "I hope I shall go to the university."

"Robin has his career all planned out, down to the Order of the British Empire," said Jane. "He wants to go into the Diplomatic Service. Haven't you really any ideas?"

"Not many."

"What does your father want you to do?"

"Oh, he doesn't mind," said Katherine, laughing. "I don't think he has ever thought of the question." She considered. "There is always being a schoolteacher. I thought once I should like to work on a newspaper."

"Yes, that would suit you."

"But I hope privately that something more exciting will turn up."

"Something more exciting," Jane echoed, and the rain echoed behind her. It was falling now with astonishing vehemence, making the grass dance, whirling across the field in sudden silver ghosts. "Do you mean you want to get married?"

"Oh no!" Katherine was truthfully surprised. "No, I

114

meant some work I had never thought of—I might meet somebody at the university who would offer me a really good job—to be a secretary, perhaps——"

"Well, but you might get married," said Jane. "Hadn't you thought of that?"

Katherine had indeed discussed it for hours on end, and so had her answer ready. "One should act as if one was not likely to," she said. "Though as you say there's always the possibility."

"I didn't say that exactly," Jane murmured. "It isn't a thing one can include in any plans, though Robin does. He will marry at thirty—I can't remember for the moment what post he'll be holding then."

Katherine did not quite follow this, so remained silent. After a time she said curiously:

"What about you?"

"Nothing about me," said Jane. The hiss of the rain slackened abruptly, and it fell gently in front of the open doorway, running in tiny rivulets in over the stone flags, that were dusty with chaff. The clouds had huddled over onto one side of the sky and separate rays of sun forked obliquely down, making the distant tree-tops shine; from somewhere nearby they heard the liquid croaking of a full stream. Jane stepped out and looked about her.

"We can get home in this, though our shoes will be soaked," she said. "There ought to be a rainbow somewhere about." She squinted upwards. "I can't see it."

4

Katherine realized one morning that half her holiday had gone. This surprised her, for so far her visit had been unremarkable, as if the three of them had been wandering in a green maze, getting no nearer the centre. How had it passed? Most of the mornings they spent at the house, setting the afternoons aside for excursions; these were slow and leisurely bicycle rides around the many south Oxfordshire villages, to Nuneham Courtenay, to Dorchester to see the church and its windows, and round a dozen smaller places, Toot Baldon, Marsh Baldon, Berwick Salome, Ewelme, Benson—names Katherine never remembered, that remained in her memory as a composite picture of cottages built of Cotswold stone, church porches, oaks and beeches, and the river, with its locks and bridges, always close at hand or just out of sight among the trees. It was August and the reapers were out, saying cautiously that it had been a middling year. Also they had made two longer excursions—one to London, where Katherine had been exhausted by sight-seeing and would have preferred to look at the shops; and one northwards to the Midlands, to see Banbury, Warwick, and Stratford-on-Avon. She reported all this to her friend, who had been very sceptical about her first letter. "I don't understand cream cakes, but I eat them."

Indeed, she had grown rather sceptical about it herself. The time passed so easily, with cycling and tennis, cutting sandwiches and eating them under trees, or simply lounging about, that she no longer felt aggrieved that Jane was always with them. It seemed simply that she had nothing else to do. Mrs. Fennel and a maid took care of the house, and the few duties that Jane undertook were more to keep her amused than anything else. Katherine wondered if all English girls did as little as she did. As she seemed to have no proper work to do, Katherine half-expected her to lavish unnecessary attention on something else—needlework, her clothes, perhaps even work in the village. She did not. Except for her cigarettes, she was like a discontented schoolgirl on perpetual holiday. No-one suggested that it was her place to do anything; in fact, the subject was never mentioned; and in consequence she had all the time in the world to tag along with them, sometimes silent, sometimes argumentative. The only times she paid willing attention were when Katherine said anything about her own home, how it differed from theirs, and so on.

Robin's manner did not alter. They were friends, but he was the host, and she was the guest. He treated her as he might a boy of his own age whom he wanted to impress. Her assent was asked for everything they did: he never left her alone without making sure she had something nominally to amuse her. And this began to exasperate her. She was used to striking a quick response from people, to jumping from track to track of intimacy until either she tired of it or they reached a stable relationship. With him she simply could not get going. And this annoyed her, because he was attractive. If he had—well, if he had only laughed and paid her openly-insincere compliments, which was the lightest kind of flirtation she knew, that would have satisfied her. It would have shown he was human, at all events, and having exacted such tribute she would probably have forgotten the matter. But when he held her chair for her at meals, when he sketched out excursions on a map with the point of his pencil, when he met one of Jane's sarcasms by pushing back his hair slowly and looking at her with faint surprise, when he was unexpectedly flippant, as if he had flicked a new halfpenny into the air, when he talked about Norman lead fonts or suddenly announced he was tired and would not leave the grass where they were lying— these and a dozen other things he did so composedly that he might only have been rehearsing them in his room. When she spoke to him he listened seriously to what she was saying; as it was often incoherent and usually trite she would rather he had looked at her while she was saying it. She became confused and embarrassed. It kept her attention on him too much: she brooded on what he might be thinking, or how she should meet a strangled avowal of love if he made it. A score of such fancies would occupy her mind, usually in the early afternoon or in the early evening, for the air in the river valley was so soft that there were times when it slackened all her muscles and she could only lie by an open window or out on the veranda, her mind suspended sensually above herself and the people round her.

But most of the time it seemed less important than at first. One morning a letter from home was waiting for her on the breakfast table, and this so delighted her that she paid little attention to what the others said. When they went into the lounge afterwards she realized Jane and Robin had been having a mild quarrel, something about Robin's swimming before breakfast in the river, which Jane seemed to resent. Or perhaps there had been another reason that Katherine had missed. It had not fully died down when Jane listlessly opened a small blue portable gramophone and put on a record. She sometimes did this when she was alone, for Katherine had heard it; there was a small pile of records on one of the window-ledges. They were all about eight years old and Katherine wondered how they had come to be bought. All of them were ten-inch dance records.

Robin shifted irritably when the music started. "Can't you put in a new needle?" he said with some self-control, as if the very fact of a gramophone fitted with a used needle annoyed him.

"There aren't any," said Jane. He grunted, and sat down. His hair had dried brittly on his head, and he wore a blazer and rubber shoes. Jane had on a grubby white dress.

The record was old-fashioned, and had a tinny quality only partly due to the needle. The tune it played had been popular for perhaps a week or two, or perhaps for even as long as a musical comedy had run in London, but was now quite forgotten. The orchestra that played it did so in what had been the fashion of the moment, with little empty tricks of syncopation that recalled the outmoded dresses of the girls that had danced to it. It was strange to think it had once sounded modern. Now it was like an awning propped in the sun, nearly white, that years ago had been striped bright red and yellow.

As if to prevent Jane playing any more, Robin got up when it finished.

"Let's go on the river," he said.

"Always the river," said Jane. "First you swim in it, then you want to float on it. You'll turn into a water-rat." She turned over some other records wearily.

"Coming?" said Robin, more or less to Katherine.

Jane shut the lid of the gramophone.

"Why do we always do what you want?" she inquired.

Robin stared at her as if he thought her rather ill-bred.

"I'd hoped we were always doing what Katherine wanted."

Katherine, who had taken out her letter again, looked up when her name was spoken.

"Are we?" said Jane. She looked out of the window moodily at the sunlight. A milkman was going round to the side of the house.

Robin turned almost elaborately to Katherine.

"Would you like to go on the river?" he said. "You haven't been yet, you know."

"I should," said Katherine.

This was the first time she had had the chance to show him whom she was prepared to side with. She had only just realized that the quarrel might result in their being alone. It depended on whether Jane took up the challenge.

She did not. When they went down to the boathouse, she was with them, carrying cushions, a book, and dark sunglasses. Robin led the punt out of the boathouse by the painter, as if unstabling a patient beast, and Katherine settled in the seat facing the way they would go. He dexterously swung the boat round, and they started off against the slow current, with the water drifting past Katherine at shoulder-level, covered with dead may-flies, twigs, and fallen tree-blossoms: here and there water-beetles sped on the bright surface. The morning had an almost-mocking quality of peace. On either side of them stretched the fields, with sometimes a garden coming to the water's edge where a house stood, and once they passed a row of riverside cottages, and a bare-armed woman came out with a pail. She set it down with a clang and stared at them.

Robin addressed his remarks to Katherine, who sat with her back to him. "I'm not splashing you, am I?"

"Not at all." She glanced round. He had dropped his blazer and rolled up his sleeves. At every thrust he made at the riverbed, the satisfying impulse forward lilted inside her. Some drops did sprinkle her occasionally, but this was more pleasant than otherwise. "I've never been in a boat like this one before."

"Haven't you really? They're great fun. Plenty of room, and you can't upset them. Slowish, of course, but they're not built for speed."

"There's no other boat you push along like that, is there?"

"I don't think there is. A gondolier has an oar, I believe. There are people who can pole canoes. Jack can."

"Who?"

Jane muttered something, and turned on her side.

"Jack Stormalong, a friend of ours. He's coming next week. But it's a mad thing to do, unless you're wearing a bathing costume."

It looked a very easy thing to do. After each stroke Robin threw the twelve-foot pole carelessly upwards before negligently slipping it back into the water. It whistled through his hands. He stood easily but quite still, not seeming to shift his stance in the slightest.

Katherine trailed a hand in the water which, to her surprise, was quite warm. There had been a mist in the early morning, but this had now disappeared, and the sun was climbing unhindered. The heat-wave during which she had arrived had broken up, but not disastrously; each day was now a mixture of sunlight and cloud, and the air remained humid. At present the landscape stretched luminous and detailed.

As they passed under a bridge, Jane, who had been lying with her eyes shut behind the sun-spectacles and her rough-skinned ankles close to Katherine's right hand, stirred in the cold bar of shadow and looked up.

"Where are we going?"

Robin whisked the pole in and out of the water a few times before saying: "Just up the river."

"What do you mean by just up the river?"

"What do you think I mean?"

"Well, I know you," said Jane. "You'll probably make us late for lunch."

"I thought we might go up to the Rose for lunch," said Robin, with an indifferent air. "It's a good place."

"Have you said we shall be out?"

"We can ring up once we get there."

"I don't know about that. It'll be too late then. We shan't get there till half-past twelve."

"We shall get there long before half-past twelve," said Robin with an edge of contempt in his voice. "I can put on a bit of speed." He gave an extra-hard push as illustration.

"If you wanted to go to the Rose you should have let them know beforehand," said Jane.

"I didn't think of it beforehand."

"Well, then, you'd better leave it till another time. You can't go messing all the arrangements up like this. Have some thought for others," said Jane, rather angrily. Robin poled on without altering their speed or his expression.

Katherine awkwardly studied the scenery. She could understand most of what they had said, and their tone of voice told her the rest. It was as if Robin was trying to push Jane down from the place she had assumed during the last few days, and Jane was refusing to be pushed.

He poled on, but gradually diminished speed. When he spoke it was lightly once more.

"I thought you'd appreciate the idea. Aren't you always saying we never do anything on the spur of the moment?"

Jane did not say anything, but looked red. She had taken off the dark glasses, but now replaced them.

"But if you don't really mean it, you ought to explain that first."

She threw down her book. "All right, go to the Rose if you want to. Only I've warned you, that's all."

"What do you think, Katherine?"

"Me?" Katherine had been afraid they would draw her into this. "I don't know where the place is." She struggled between supporting him and being sensible. "But if we had given your mother trouble—it would rather spoil it, wouldn't it? We can go another day." And she added, leaning backwards to smile at him: "Won't you teach me how to do this? You said you would."

As he stood against the sun, she could not see how he took the question, but she thought he was pleased. Jane glared indifferently out of the boat, and Katherine felt balanced between the two conflicting wills. So far she had given one vote to each. She hoped he would see whose side she was on: there had been a curious note in the way he had asked his last question.

"Well," he said at last, "perhaps Jane's got some objection to that, too." He could say these things in a level way, that sounded far removed from any bickering. Jane defiantly crossed her ankles.

"As long as I don't have to do anything," she said.

"And as long as you don't want more than one admiring spectator."

Robin let this pass. "Well, if you're prepared to risk it," he said to Katherine. She stood up uncertainly. "The point is, you might fall in."

"Oh, but I can swim."

"Yes, but we should get into a row for not taking care of you. It's tricky till you get your balance." He brought up the pole again. "Stand where you are till you get the feel of it, and watch what I do."

"Till you get sick of it," said Jane. She was watching them sharply, as if expecting entertainment. Katherine stood self-consciously in the middle, lurching occasionally, and watched while Robin poled with text-book correctness for some distance. "I can see what you do," she said eventually. "But I don't know whether I could do it."

"Come and try," said Robin.

She picked her way cautiously to the end of the boat, and joined him, it seemed in perilous isolation, above the surrounding river. Edging away to allow her room, he laid the pole in her hands. Taken unawares by its weight she dropped it, with a fearful clatter and splashing, and an exclamation from Jane. Robin picked it up, and gave it back to her. It was very cold and wet. The punt slowly came to a halt against the sluggish current.

"Now," said Robin, briskly. "Stand facing the way you're going."

"If you're lucky," said Jane. Her mouth tightened contemptuously.

"Feet about a foot apart, so that you won't fall in. Strictly speaking, a good punter never moves his feet at all, you see. You'll soon be more surefooted."

Katherine doubted that. The punt had stopped and had now begun to turn round in a slow circle. She prodded ineffectually at the water, nearly overbalancing.

"Wait a minute, I'll turn her round," said Robin, reclaiming the pole and standing on the very end, while Katherine watched him uselessly. "We'll turn back, since we're not going anywhere, it seems."

"How beautiful to watch you," said Jane.

When the punt was once more pointing straight down the empty river, Katherine tried again. She positioned her feet and on Robin's instructions lifted the pole vertically, so that water dripped down her arm. It would take very little to send her into the water.

"Now, point it slightly towards the way you want to go, and drop it in. Drop it, don't push it down. As soon as it touches the bottom, grip it as high as you can reach and haul on it. Fairly hard, of course, but don't fall over backwards. Now, try it."

Katherine tried it. She tried to drop the pole in slantwise, and only sent it diagonally under the boat. When she hauled on it, the punt surged forward in a crablike way, and ended up travelling towards the bank. Her next stroke was really not too bad, and sent the bow crashing into the rushes. As she dragged the pole up, it became entangled with the alders overhead, and she staggered as if in a nightmare.

Jane, shaken by the bump and showered with leaves and twigs, began to laugh. "End of Act One," she said.

Katherine furiously did not look at her.

After Robin had restored the boat to midstream, she tried again. This time she forgot to slant the pole, so that when she was ready to haul there was nothing to haul on, and she could only give the river-bed a frantic poke to justify the stroke at all, and this did not contribute to their progress.

Robin explained how to straighten a boat by wagging the pole in the water behind it, and as the punt was again drifting as if by instinct towards the bank, she at once tried this out. To her surprise it was successful.

"That's right," said Robin. "You're doing very well."

She looked at him with dislike, and as she brought round the pole for the next stroke nearly knocked him in the water. He saved himself by catching it with one hand, and this sudden interruption nearly upset Katherine. Jane was heaving quietly with laughter. Katherine viciously dropped the pole into the river again, and felt the splash swamp her right shoe.

"It's a good thing the current is with us," said Jane.

Having to keep her feet still made Katherine feel as insecure as if she were carrying a long plank along high scaffolding. Somehow she had imagined punting to be a gentle pastime, rather resembling croquet. She could not remember feeling so silly since her early schooldays.

"I can't do this," she said.

"It'll come to you all at once," Robin assured her. "Try again."

Their voices sounded flat on the water. Katherine, summoning all her determination, poised the pole and slid it (the hardest part, she decided) down into the river at exactly the right angle. Cheered, she hauled on it with all her might. It grew suddenly rigid in her hands. Carried on by the impetus of the stroke, she tugged wildly for a second, then at the last moment overbalanced by trying to improve her grip. Robin (who must have been watching her closely, she decided later) took a step forward, caught her neatly round the waist, and pulled her upright again. She stumbled and put her hands on his shoulders. A cow standing with its forelegs in the water lifted its head and gave a long bellow.

"End of Act Two," said Jane. "Love will find a way." She leant back and fished out a couple of old paddles from the front of the boat. The pole, stuck in the mud, drew away from them.

Katherine sank down on the cushions, trembling from rage, fright, and embarrassment. The bright, almost metallic contact when he had gripped her sharply wiped away all traces of self-deception. She knew she wanted to lie with her head in his lap, to have him comfort her: she knew equally that this was not going to happen partly because he had no interest in her, and because Jane was specifically there to prevent it. She sat blushing.

When they reached the pole again, Robin stood up and with a smart double twist drew it, dripping, from the water: he swished it in the river a few times to clean off the wet black mud, then with a slight smile offered it to her again.

"No," she said. Her voice shook. "No, I won't try again. I can't do it. I only make a fool of myself."

"You don't." Robin sounded surprised. "Not at all. You were doing well."

"I tell you I don't want to."

She stared down at the cushions.

"Well, of course, you can't do it," cut in Jane coolly, "if you try Robin's idiotic way. Nobody could, first shot. I wonder you didn't go into the water as soon as you started. Look here, try again. Go on, take the pole and try again." Katherine obeyed, seeing no alternative but an open quarrel. "Now forget all about your feet and doing it with one hand and all the rest of it; the important thing is that you want to drive the boat along by pushing the pole on the river-bed."

"I thought," said Robin, drying his hands on a handkerchief, "one might as well do a thing properly."

No-one answered him. Katherine worked off her fury by poling as best she could. Jane was right. Once she felt that her feet were no longer glued down and she could turn about as she pleased, it became much easier, and she 'drove them along in an ungainly but decided way. Robin, who had thus been defeated twice that morning, watched her with a subdued expression on his face which suggested to her when she once happened to catch sight of it that he would not be content to leave it at that.

At some untraceable point she had fallen in love with him. Her curiosity and his fascination had brought her to the brink of it, she knew, but she had fancied that love needed two people, as if it were a lake they had to dive in simultaneously. Now she found she had gone into it alone, while he remained undismayed.

Because Katherine was so young she had hitherto thought love a pleasant thing; a state that put order into her life, directing her thoughts and efforts towards one end, and because she found it pleasant she thought it could not be real love, which by all accounts caused suffering and was to be feared. Perhaps because she had lived always in her parents' house, making no effort to have a life of her own, she had not stirred up any but the surface of the passionate emotions—sentimentality; devotion; perhaps too it was because she had so far loved only women and girls. So she would have thought that to love Robin would have done no more than set a seal on her visit, to frame it, to enclose it in a glass sphere. Here, where he could not leave her, they would spend the long days in each other's company, with every romantic background ready to hand, deep cornfields, the burning-glass of the sky, the willows by the river, the white lanes.

But this was not what she felt. Being so far from home, it was natural for her to assume at one blow what was due to her sixteen years, that before she had shunned a little. When he had touched her, every nerve in her body had snapped as if with electricity, and the desire she felt for him was cloudy and shameful. It put a curious constraint upon her; at first she thought it might be the heat that made her flesh tingle at the touch of her clothes, and her ears alert to every sound in the house; it might be due to the weather, that she could not eat, and felt as if she had just left her bed after a convalescence. And to be with him was no pleasure, for she could not be satisfied with words, and the sultriness put such a hunger upon her body that sometimes she was driven almost to desperation to know that there would be nothing easier than to lay her hand on his bare arm, and yet also to know that this was a thing she could never do.

It was a strange, disturbing time, lasting a few days. It made her bitter and miserable. She was frightened to think that this feeling was something she would meet again, that love would henceforward have something of this manner, for it was not a sensation she rejoiced in. If this was love—even this tiny shudder caused by his holding her waist for a second—it made her feel guilty, for it did not change him in her eyes: he did not grow admirable, more noble, not even more likeable, as the girls had that she had loved. Simply she thought him beautiful, against her will, and nothing would have excited her more than to kiss him and to make him love her too. But then she would have had to be different, and he would have had to be different also, and it would not happen. Knowing this, she drew her curtains back and opened each window as far as it would go, hoping as she lay bitterly among the hot bedclothes that whatever stillness there was in the summer night would come to her and still her restlessness.

One morning she could not sleep after five o'clock, so got up and went out quietly into the clouded daybreak. The fields were wet, so she kept to the lanes: rain during the night had freshened up the bracken and pale wild-flowers until, with an over-reaching sky logically ribbed with clouds, they made a landscape of half-tones such as she had not seen before. There was a tang of damp wood from the fences. After a time she leant on a stile and watched a tiny stream running along a ditch, over a bed of white sand; she stooped and flicked her hand in it, finding it very cold. She noticed a small frog in the grass, struck to immobility by her presence; when she tickled it with a straw it crawled away. There was watercress growing under the hedge. She dried her fingers on her skirt.

It was little use troubling. She could not pretend to herself that he felt towards her one-tenth of the interest she felt in him, or that the house held her more securely than a pair of cupped hands may hold a moth for a few seconds before releasing it again. She could only hope that the burden of this new love would be taken off her before it betrayed her into actions she would regret.

"We thought you'd run away," said Robin.

He sat watching her eat. She had stayed out longer than she meant to, and come in a little late for breakfast. A cup of cold tea had been waiting for her in her bedroom, and she drank it guiltily. When she went down Robin and Jane had nearly finished, and now Robin remained in his place while Jane inspected the flowers in a bored way, picking out any dead blooms before changing the water.

"I couldn't sleep," she said. His tie was knotted carelessly round his throat, his shirt-collar not fastened.

"Bad luck," he said, pouring her some more coffee. She needed plenty to drink to force down these impossible breakfasts. He watched her, lightly bouncing a knife-blade on his plate, then suddenly laughed and said in her own language:

—And so you rose up to see the dawn.

—I did, she answered, surprised. But there was nothing to see.

Outside it was raining. He pushed back his chair and got up with his hands in his pockets. "Yes, that's rather a good idea," he said. "Why should Katherine talk English all the time? Let's return the compliment a bit. Two hours every morning, say."

"Rubbish," said Jane. She peered into the flowers. In short sleeves her elbows were very sharp.

"Why rubbish? It would be a graceful act. From ten to twelve every morning."

"She came here for a holiday," Jane said rudely, "not to give you lessons."

"But think what a strain it must be, talking English all the time."

"Robin's the perfect Englishman," said Jane to Katherine. "Everything is for somebody else's benefit."

"Well, if it's unpopular, I won't press it," said Robin. He regarded the point of a pencil and began to sharpen it onto a newspaper. "I just thought it would be rather fun. What do you think, Katherine?"

That question again. And Katherine was just about to temporize when she guessed the important point, which was, of course, that Jane spoke nothing but English. She nearly choked.

"I don't mind," she said faintly.

"There you are, Katherine doesn't mind," said Robin. He shook the paperful of sharpenings into the empty grate. "It would be rather a lark. Even you might learn something."

Katherine was alarmed. Jane could do three things. She could throw up her task of chaperon and leave them together, or she could give in and stick it out. Or, if she got angry (and Robin seemed careless of that), she could sail in and smash this younger-brother impertinence, so that no more would be heard of it. Katherine looked at her.

"Well, that's very kind of you," Jane said. "Are you sure you wouldn't like to make a small charge?"

"Well, you needn't listen if you don't want to—you needn't come if you don't want to," said Robin reasonably, tapping the end of his pencil on his teeth.

No, don't say that, Katherine was shouting, you'll spoil it all. She took the thinnest piece of toast and a spoonful of marmalade.

"I didn't know we were going anywhere," said Jane. She collected up the dead wet stalks, and from the sound of her voice, once again listless, Katherine knew she was giving in once more. "You'll pretty soon get sick of it. You say, Katherine, when you've had enough. You'll be teaching him irregular verbs before you know where you are." She dropped the dead flowers in the wastepaper-basket.

Where they were going was no more exciting than into the village. Yet Katherine was more expectant than she had been for a week—since she had first arrived, in fact. Apart from this bold attempt by Robin to get Jane out of the way, she had not foreseen how it changed her position. Hitherto Robin had been in command, with Jane second and Katherine herself third. Now she led, and Robin and Jane followed. When the rain stopped they walked down the drive, and she gave way to a silly impulse to quote a verse of romantic poetry that she had once admired, with no prefacing explanation. They gaped at her.

"Here, hold on," said Robin. "Let's all start level."

"I reserve the right to talk English," said Jane obstinately. She was wearing sandals that showed her small, perfectly-formed feet and was thereby the smallest of the three. "And if I ask what you're talking about, you've got to tell me."

"Then you must ask properly," said Katherine, and sweeping ahead under Robin's eye she told Jane how to ask for a sentence to be repeated or translated. Jane repeated the sentences dubiously.

"Well, shall we start?" said Robin. "Katherine had better begin."

There was a pause. It was hard to know what to say first. Finally she asked Robin why he was going to the village. He replied solemnly that he was going to buy some postage stamps and a packet of envelopes.

Did he write many letters, then?

No, but he had no more postage stamps or envelopes.

Whom did he write to?

School friends, relations.

Any girls?

Only one.

And did she write nice letters back?

Oh, very nice.

Where did she live?

Robin repeated Katherine's address, and they burst out laughing. Katherine could not help blushing. It was really too easy. Jane gave a suspicious and unconvinced smile.

"Are you talking about writers?"

"Yes, about writers," said Katherine.

Jane, after much warning and preliminary inquiries, managed to ask what English writers Katherine liked the best. Obviously she was doing her level best to stand her ground.

She had read very little. Shakespeare. Byron.

—What about Dickens, asked Robin.

She had read no Dickens.

That was a pity. Many English people liked Dickens.

—Ah.

But he was, perhaps of all writers, the most English.

Katherine turned out of a sort of distorted kindness to Jane and asked her if she liked Dickens. "Eh? Was that something about Dickens? Do I read Dickens?"

"Like."

"Do I *like* Dickens? No, I don't. He's too dull."

Robin observed that Dickens made a great deal of money by his writings.

—And you? Are you a writer?

—Eh?

—Have you ever written anything?

—No, of course not.

—Not ever?

—Not ever.

—One might think you had the artistic nature.

Robin's face wore a baffled expression, centred round a small frown similar to the one he had worn when she had started to win at tennis. Then he laughed, not at all put out.

—You're always very sarcastic.

—Think so if you like.

—What is an artistic nature then?

—One that cares nothing for other people.

—Cares nothing for other people, he repeated, as if to fix the precise meaning. And I care nothing for other people?

"This seems a very important point," said Jane. "What's it all about?"

"Katherine says I have something of the artistic nature," said Robin. "I'm trying to decide if it's a compliment or not." There was even a suspicion of guilt in his voice.

"She's pulling your leg," said Jane, as if relieved it was no worse.

At this point they arrived at the small post office, and Katherine unwarily entering with them, was formally presented to the old woman who kept it, who had of course heard that the Fennels had a foreign lady staying. Katherine was quite at a loss with the Oxfordshire dialect, and could only say "oh yes" and smile. The Fennels had been on the whole very considerate with her, but they had not been able to avoid some such introductions, which made Katherine feel like some rare animal in captivity.

When they were out once more in the puddled road, Robin said in a lingering, thoughtful tone:

—But I care for other people.

"Oh, don't start that again," said Jane irritably. "It's

stopped being amusing. For heaven's sake let's talk English."

Katherine saw the corners of Robin's mouth draw slightly back "We're still walking," he pointed out. "Is it boring you, Katherine?"

"Oh, no. I like it."

—My sister is not a scholar, Robin said with faint contempt. She did not learn very much. I have the brains of the family.

—Oh, obviously, said Katherine warily.

—It is a question of application. If she could learn by wishing, she would know everything by now. But she is incapable of sitting down and starting in real earnest. A pity, because——

"What are you drivelling about?" said Jane angrily.

—Although she is lazy she is not completely stupid.

—Whereas you are stupid though not completely lazy, retorted Katherine in a desperate attempt to finish the conversation.

He smiled.

—She wastes her time thinking about what she might do one day if she tried. But she knows she never will try, and that makes her silly and irritable. I don't know what we are going to do with her.

"What is this?" said Jane sharply, and immediately, "Tell me! What are you talking about?"

"A mutual friend." Robin's voice had never sounded more courteous, more placid and exact than at that moment.

Jane went very red, and before Katherine could find enough words to speak, had broken into:

"I see. Well, don't let me stop you. I should hate to interrupt. I'll leave you to get on with it."

With that she turned and went off.

"My dear Jane," Robin said, as a complete sentence. Small and almost ridiculous in her sandals, she disappeared along the narrow lane lined with hedges, in which the autumn berries had begun to appear and were now beaded with rain.

"Shall I fetch her back?" Katherine burst out desperately.

Robin shrugged his shoulders. "She'll be all right, she's just got one of her moods on. I must apologize for her."

"But she thinks——"

"No, I tell you, don't trouble. There's nothing the matter. She often flies off the handle like this——" And because Katherine could not understand that phrase her mind was free to come upon the appalling success of Robin's manœuvre, staring her in the face. For a moment she felt almost frightened, as if although this was what she thought an impossible hope, it had turned, when realized, into something she did not altogether like.

But there was nothing to say. Robin, with an abstracted air, broke off a cornflower growing through a gate and drew it deliberately into his buttonhole. They continued their walk.

There was no more bother from Jane. During the rest of that day, they only saw her at mealtimes, when she was as uncommunicative as usual. Otherwise she avoided them as a singed cat avoids the hearth.

But Katherine had returned from the walk puzzled. Nothing notable had happened after Jane left them. If she had expected an onset of personalities, she was disappointed: he did not as much as refer to the fact that they were at last alone, alone without merely awaiting a meal, or a bus, or Jane herself. They had certainly kept up a sort of bi-lingual banter, but it had got them nowhere. Robin would ride boldly up to a subject, like one of the entries in the gymkhana, and then stop dead in front of it; nothing she could say would bring him a step further forward. She was bewildered. What was he playing at? He had invited her. She had come. For two weeks out of the three he had submitted to the uneasy threesome. Now he had got rid of Jane, so that they could be alone. She had consented, at the risk of seeming unpardonably rude; she laid herself open, ready to follow any pace he made. What was he waiting for, then; why the aimlessness, the tentative explorations of the already-known, the advances that weren't worth making, the sudden full stops?

As it happened, they were not alone much the rest of that day. Some visitors called and they were required to meet them; Robin played whist in the evening. Katherine was pinned for a time by a woman belonging to something called the League of Nations' Union, which gave her enough to think about. In the intervals she looked at Robin longingly, even while annoyed admiring his flexible company manners, that never for a moment, not even when handing round sandwiches, degenerated into servility. Occasionally she smiled at him ruefully, and he smiled back at her, only with a certain lack of edge that suggested he did not quite take her meaning.

But when the visitors had gone, and the noise of their car died away, he strolled back into the lounge where Katherine was shuffling the cards together and studying the unfamiliar patterns, the knaves, queens, and kings. The room was littered with glasses and ash-trays, and there was plenty of smoke in the air.

"What a fug," he said, looking round. He unlocked the french window and opened it onto the still night, so that a mild coolness drifted in, and a faint weedy smell of the river. There was still a streak of yellow in the west. She sat on the sofa watching him.

"Look," he said, with a small toss of the head that suggested his collar was too tight. "We've never taken you to Oxford yet. After all, that's the real show-spot. Shall we go, tomorrow?"

136

"Yes, I want to go very much."

She remembered how Jane had mentioned this on her first morning—Jane, who would not now come with them. As he stood against the open window, Katherine felt a moment of delighted thankfulness that he was accepting her love. For a second or two she had been puzzled, uneasy. But it seemed to her now that his odd behaviour was no less than the working-out of some pre-arranged plan, in which this last visit had a ceremonious place, depending on a chain of emotions she had not detected in him. She should not regard him as insensitive: there might be much she had not noticed. And because he was too shy to say he liked her, he was letting his actions speak for him till he should have the courage to do so himself.

She went to bed feeling satisfied for once.

There was a bus at ten to nine the next morning, and another at ten to eleven. They decided to get up rather earlier and catch the first one, and in consequence breakfasted with Mr. and Mrs. Fennel. She did not see Jane till she was on her way downstairs ready to go, and then Jane came out of the breakfast room dressed oddly in a white high-necked sweater, a freshly-lighted cigarette between her lips. She slightly resembled a doll. They eyed each other silently. Then Katherine said "Good morning" and Jane nodded.

She was glad to get away from the house: it was a relief to take her seat by Robin on the upper deck of the bus. He was dressed in an open-necked shirt, and a biscuit-coloured jacket; a light canvas haversack hung from his shoulder, as if he were bringing their lunch with them, although there was no need for it. Diffused sunlight gleamed on the outhouses and farmyard walls built of local stone; it was just another week-day morning, with shoppers travelling with them, and shirt-sleeved men working in the yards, building ricks.

She had resolved that morning to let Robin handle the outing as he pleased, and to attend not to her own wishes but to his suggestions. For now there was no hurry. They had all the day to themselves, and for the moment she was content just with his company. She would let him arrange things. The bus ran on.

Mainly to make conversation, she said:

"Jane is rather a strange person, isn't she?"

"Sometimes," he answered, briefly and lightly.

"Is she much older than you are?"

"She's twenty-five."

"As old as that!" Twenty-five was practically middle-aged. "No!"

"She's nine years older than I am, yes," said Robin. "I know she looks younger."

"What does she do?"

"Do? Nothing much. At one time she used to help Father, but I fancy she was more trouble than she was worth. She went to evening classes for a bit."

The bus swooped along, branches scraping on the windows.

"There is nothing she wants to do, then?"

"There may be, I don't know." He struggled into a more upright position. "She is strange, as you say. I don't know much about her. If you watch carefully, we ought to be seeing some of the spires from here."

She obeyed. But the one or two visionary glimpses she caught over the tree-tops were swiftly rubbed away by their eventual approach through very matter-of-fact streets. They were set down on a wide pavement by an antique-dealer's shop, whose freshly-scrubbed step had not yet dried. The pale sun was just warming the fronts of buildings, and there was plenty of traffic; the air smelt fresh and clean. Katherine, who was by upbringing a town dweller, felt her spirits rise.

"And where is the university?" she said.

Robin laughed. "Everywhere. Everything you see or touch."

She stared. They strolled slowly up the street while he explained the collegiate system, and then as they automatically began the rounds of the graceful triangles, squares and circles of the college buildings, he began to tell of what she saw. Though he knew probably no more than one-fiftieth of what a standard guidebook contained, it was enough to keep up a continuous quiet chatting that she found restful. Actually she was disappointed with the city, for what she had heard about it led her to believe that to enter it would be like stepping back into the Middle Ages: as it was, she found so many shops and taxicabs that she thought there were more medieval towns in her own country. But, as he continued to recite the litany of monasteries, kings, noblemen and prelates, she realized that every century had left accretions, and though she did not trouble to follow his details, she was impressed by the uniqueness of the place, where such variety was controlled within a single atmosphere. In the intervals he allowed her she did a little unpremeditated shopping, buying a small bowl with a map of ancient Oxford in the centre, a handbag, a cigarette-case, and an elaborate ring from an antique shop that was reassuringly expensive. Since coming to England she had spent hardly any money. The other things she would take back as presents, but she decided to keep the ring herself.

Robin was in the best of humours. She could feel that he was as proud of Oxford as if it belonged to him. It was almost irritating, the way he kept informing her that this or that building was three or four or five hundred years old, from the reign of James or Henry or Edward, as if extracting whole plums from an over-rich cake. The very public-houses, where old men held curling matches to their pipes, had stood for centuries: this dated from Tudor times, here Shakespeare had often slept on his way from

Stratford to London. He was not simply trying to impress a foreign visitor: he was more like a millionaire who cannot refrain from saying how much everything that he owns has cost him, with a certain fascinated awe. For his sake she tried to feel as he did. But she found that when they were walking down a broad, tree-shaded avenue, lined with hurdles, she did not much care that these meadows had been given to the cathedral to maintain a chantry by a noblewoman whose tomb he had pointed out to her. It pleased her more that they could walk together in such a pleasant place, going towards the river and hearing the cattle tearing up grass nearby, and when they sat down eventually to rest at the side of the water, she leaned back and thought that as far as age was concerned, sheer age that was almost timelessness, the sound of the trees was more impressive. The surrounding tree-tops settling and unsettling with an endless sifting of leaves reminded her as she lay with closed eyes of the unceasing wash of waves round the shingle of an island. They filled the air with whispering of eternity, or as near eternity as made no matter, making this place, famous as it was, like all other places. Like all other places, it was both temporal and eternal, and she found that degrees of temporality did not interest her—while in eternity, of course, there were no such measurements.

She sat up and looked at Robin. He had relapsed beside her with his head on the haversack, eyes closed; his face wore an expression of patience. She leaned over and stroked a lock of his hair into place, at which his eyes, in the shadow of her arm, opened wide.

"Wake up," she said.

"I wasn't asleep." He sat up quickly as if it had begun to rain. For a moment they sat side by side, then he scrambled to his feet. "If you've rested, we might perhaps be getting on."

Katherine realized at once—though too late—that she

had made an advance he would not receive, and she scrambled up blushing—blushing and bewildered. He had behaved almost as if she had scared him, and it had shaken the whole day off its course. What was the matter with him? Was she doing any more than she had done, showing him that she loved him? And if at that moment he didn't want her to, hadn't he enough poise to treat her better than this? Almost she was pushed back on the fear that he was indifferent to her, but then, why ask her, why manœuvre so that they were alone?

She followed him sulkily on their solemn pilgrimage. The whole day was being spoiled.

But there was worse to come. They finished their tour just before lunch by climbing to the top of the Radcliffe Camera. They climbed in silence, coming out onto the balcony from which they could see the whole elaborately chiselled and buttressed panorama of Oxford spread out beneath them, like the decorations on an enormous iced cake. Robin said something vague about James Gibbs, and leaned on the balustrade. Together they looked at the slate roofs, the spires, and the hills in the distance, backed with clouds.

The sun had gone in, and a light rain began to fall in the wind. Robin straightened up regretfully, and, looking round the sky with a knowledgeable air, said: "I half expected this." He swung the haversack to his hand, and drew out a thin mackintosh, folded small, which he held while she put it on. "Lucky I did. Shall we go and have lunch, and give it a chance to blow over?"

"All right."

She was fumbling in the pockets: there were gloves. When they emerged at the bottom of the dark stairway, she pulled one out and inspected it casually. It was old and wrinkled, and one of the fingers had become un-stitched. Looking inside, she found the neat red-and-white tab "Jane R. Fennel".

It was silly to mind. But she could have thrown it at him.

For there seemed something supremely callous in the situation. Robin was quite indifferent to both of them, showing that he had no notion of the battle he had contrived and won. This showed that he was not alert to every stir of emotion around him, as she was; showed in fact that she had been constructing an elaborate pagoda out of nothing, and the shame she now felt was a punishment for this. In fact she could not have made a bigger fool of herself if she had tried carefully. At that moment she hated England and everybody in it—this would never have happened if she could have understood all the foreign inflexions and shades of meaning. The idea of the afternoon still untouched made her sick, and the conversation at lunch she could anticipate so well: Robin, composed and unconcerned, was turning up his collar against the rain, to reveal a strip of plain lining under the lapels. All she could think of that she would welcome doing would be to make some sort of apology to Jane, who had offered far more friendship and had been treated very poorly. Otherwise she would have been glad to go home. The rest of the week did not bear thinking about.

6

She found Jane in the garden when they returned shortly after six. It had rained steadily until half an hour ago, and now the sun shone again. Robin had gone upstairs to change, having got rather wet waiting for the bus; Katherine passed through the empty lounge, came out on the terrace and saw Jane's bright shirt moving among the lupins. She was tying up a peony that had broken in the force of the shower.

Katherine hesitated a moment to watch her, as she worked with sullen persistence. Now she was actually here, she felt less eager to apologize; the desire had come in the first place from a longing to set everything right, so that she could extricate herself, as one might pay a bill before leaving a hotel. But it might lead to nothing of the sort. She contemplated Jane's neat shoulders, her small head made to look smaller by the tidily-brushed dark hair. More likely it would precipitate more entanglements, more commitments, clumsy and unsatisfying because she could not fathom what these English people meant. But if it only meant publicly dissociating herself from Robin— and it meant more than that—she would have to do it.

So she went down the steps and turned across the lawn. Jane looked up without any surprise or pleasure.

"Hallo," she said.

"We came back," said Katherine. "It rained all the time."

"It rained pretty hard here." Jane did not seem interested enough to avoid the obvious.

"All the afternoon. We went to a cinema."

"Oh yes? What did you see?"

"I really don't remember."

She waited till Jane had finished tying the raffia and cut off the loose ends. Other flowers brushed beads of water onto her skirt as she worked. It was quite plain that she would go not a step towards meeting her.

When Jane had got off the flower-bed, Katherine took a deep breath.

"I want to apologize for offending you yesterday."

Jane glanced at her with mixed surprise and boredom. Her face had become slightly sunburned, and there were a few untrimmed whiskers round her mouth.

"Oh, that's quite all right," she said.

"I truly did not mean to be rude."

"There's no need to apologize."

Jane looked so small and sensible standing there that Katherine almost believed her.

"But you were offended, weren't you?" she asked uncertainly.

Jane made a slight distasteful gesture. "Can't we let it drop?" she said.

"But I never meant to be rude," Katherine persisted.

"There's no need to worry," said Jane, with a hint of sarcasm. "I accept your apology."

Having brought herself to apologize, Katherine was irritated by Jane's bland refusal to accept it. In spite of herself, she said: "You behave like Robin," which was an insult according to her present mood.

"How do you think you're behaving?" said Jane, so softly and swiftly that Katherine hardly heard what she said. After a moment she went off to mend another peony. The heavy crimson head shook water over her hands.

Katherine was taken aback by this sudden attack: she would have found it difficult to deal with in her own language. Now she stood helpless. The rain had brought out the snails, and there was one crawling tenderly over the base of a stone bird-bath, turning its horns from side to side.

"I will explain all we said," she re-began weakly.

"It doesn't matter," said Jane. "It doesn't matter to me just exactly how rude you were."

"I was not rude—I did not say——"

Jane shrugged her shoulders.

"You shall understand!" exclaimed Katherine. "We said——"

"I understand you wanted to get me out of the way," said Jane, and Katherine stopped speaking, to give her every courtesy. "But I must say it didn't occur to me. Two is company, of course."

Katherine flushed. However right Jane was, there was no excuse for this hypocrisy. "Well, that was your business."

"But that isn't the way visitors usually——" Jane stopped, pulled up by Katherine's answer. "It was nothing to do with me."

"Oh, wasn't it? I am not as stupid as all that."

"What do you mean?"

"You needn't worry that your valuable Robin will be——"

"What do I care about Robin?" asked Jane, speaking from sheer wonder.

"Oh!" said Katherine irritably. "Shall we forget all about it? It's rather a boring subject. I only want to apologize."

Jane looked at her evenly, narrowing her eyes in the strong light. "Wait a minute," she said. "I don't understand. What has Robin been saying about me?"

"Nothing."

"Then where have you got this notion?"

"What notion?" said Katherine, obstinately.

"That I was supposed to keep an eye on you and Robin."

"It was so clear I could see it for myself."

"But do you think we should ever . . . But why?"

Katherine disliked being thus cross-examined.

"You are older than we are," she said. "You came with us wherever we went. And you found it boring, so there must have been another reason."

"It's almost laughable," said Jane. She turned away.

"I'm sorry to mention it," said Katherine, wondering if it had been an error in taste. "But you made it plain to me."

"You mean you couldn't see what I was doing here at all?"

"No, I couldn't."

"And why should there be an explanation—why shouldn't I go about with you, seeing that this is my own house?"

"Why should you," said Katherine. "You don't want to. You're older than we are. It's a waste of your time."

"Well, you've got a pretty low opinion of yourself," said Jane, with a breathless snatch of laughter. She wound the raffia in her hands. "Don't you think your company worth keeping?"

Katherine said nothing, being ignorant of the phrase and suspecting it was sarcastic.

"Well then, I'm sorry to have plagued you," Jane went on after a moment. "I'd no idea I was turning into a maiden aunt already. Thank you for telling me."

"I didn't mean that!" said Katherine. "I'm certain that I don't want to be with Robin all the time, and I expect he feels the same."

"What's the matter with him?" said Jane casually. "Isn't he as extraordinary as you thought?"

"*I* never——" Katherine then caught the reference, and felt rather silly. "He's all right. Why did he ask me, though? For the pleasure of improving my mind, or to get some language lessons?"

She said this recklessly, to make her own feelings clear, and thought afterwards that Jane might take offence. However, she did not. She looked at Katherine with weary amusement.

"Don't you know?"

"Know what?"

"That Robin asked you because I made him?"

Katherine stared at her. She repeated the sentence to herself several times, wondering if she had failed to shake out the right meaning.

"What do you mean?"

"Robin invited you because I asked him to," Jane repeated. She leaned against the back of a garden seat.

"But why?"

"I thought it'd amuse you, and it'd be fun to have you here."

"Do you mean that he didn't want me to come?"

"Oh no!" Jane released the seat, and smoothed her hair, lifting her sharp elbows. "Just that he didn't think of it."

Katherine was beginning to see the light. At first she had thought Jane was telling a desperate lie for some reason or other, because she could not believe it. But as soon as she had thought twice about it, she saw how fatally obvious it all was. For two weeks she had exercised her imagination in building up theories based on the fact that Robin had invited her, and trying to hide from herself the dissatisfaction she felt with them. This was what was wrong with them. Robin had not asked her at all.

"Well!" she said. "This is very extraordinary. I wish you had told me earlier. May I ask, then, who did invite me?"

"I've told you," said Jane. "I did. Which incidentally is why I was such an efficient chaperon. Glory." She chuckled slightly. "Like chaperoning the British Museum. How marvellous."

Katherine looked at her closely. "Then why did you ask me?" she demanded. "To see what the savages were like?"

"No. I wanted to meet you."

"But you knew nothing about me."

"There were your letters."

"But I only wrote——" Katherine stopped. "You read them?"

"Yes, I did."

"Did he show them to you?"

"If I asked him, yes."

"Oh!" Katherine struggled to speak through her annoyance. "You had no right!"

"Why not?" said Jane. "There was nothing personal in them." She picked a grass-stalk and began nibbling it.

"That does not matter—if—— He should have told me! It was wrong of him—and you too."

"Don't worry. I was a far more appreciative audience than he was."

"I wanted no audiences!"

Jane looked at her meditatively, and blew a piece of husk from her mouth with a crisp sound.

"I'll explain," she said. "We seem to have been at pretty fair cross-purposes all along."

"I am not to blame for that."

"I was interested when Robin began writing to you," said Jane. "It was about the only thing he's done I should have liked to do myself." She was silent for a moment. "I think it would be fascinating to write to somebody who didn't know you, who'd never seen you, even, and who didn't even live in the same country. You could tell them anything, and it wouldn't matter: you could make out you were all sorts of things you weren't, and they wouldn't know any different. Or you could tell them the truth, and see how they took it. I suppose it would be rather like confessing to a priest." She looked at Katherine, as if prepared for her to laugh.

"Well, it isn't," said Katherine, simmering down. "It's rather boring."

"You're thinking of Robin," said Jane rather impatiently. They began to walk up and down the small lawn. "Supposing by chance you'd struck someone different— someone you really liked—someone you felt understood what you said. Don't you see what I mean?—how wonderful it would be to be able to tell them everything, and be certain that they'd never—I mean, that they'd be so remote and away from it all."

Katherine said she understood. She was doubtful if she did.

"Well anyhow, that was what I thought when Robin began writing to you. I didn't think for a moment he'd strike anyone worth while." She paused to rattle a poppyhead, full of seeds. "But as a matter of fact you turned out rather well, not that Robin noticed it."

"In what way?" said Katherine sarcastically, cross with this last remark.

"I mean, what you wrote was so interesting. I read the parts in English, and Robin translated the rest," she added as explanation. "It interested me no end. What you did, how you lived, what you felt about things —just ordinary things—all as if you'd known us— Robin, anyway—for years. Yet so strange." She paused to think, as if conscious of giving the wrong impression. "You didn't write pages of description—Lord knows what drivel Robin was sending back—but for all that I felt I knew you perfectly well. And it was all so natural; you weren't trying to make an impression."

Oh, wasn't I, thought Katherine. Wasn't I!

"So you see," Jane finished, "I couldn't help thinking that just by accident Robin had—well"—her casual tone became harder and she spoke as if afraid Katherine might laugh at her—"well, that Robin had struck exactly the kind of person I should have liked to know myself."

"Why didn't you write to me, then?" said Katherine, catching her self-consciousness.

"I couldn't, really." Jane gestured. "You'd have thought I was mad. I thought the best thing to do," she went on, speaking quicker as if to get out a discreditable confession, "was to get Robin to ask you here for a holiday. Then I could meet you and see what you were like and if we got on well I might have written when you got back. I hoped we should get on well," she ended, raising her eyebrows and looking downwards. They had reached the seat again. Katherine kicked it softly. Even she could connect the last sentence with what had happened the previous day.

But she felt bound to make some protest. She found what Jane had said hard to believe, partly because she had never felt anything of the kind herself, and partly as one is not moved by even a poem in a foreign language. And as Jane spoke almost dispassionately, she found herself unconvinced.

"But——"

"You think all this sounds very silly."

"No. No! but—but what did Robin think of all this?" This was not the question she meant to ask, but it would gain time.

"I don't think he knew. I never mentioned it." She looked downwards again. "This seat isn't dry enough to sit on. Shall we go indoors?"

"If you like."

They went up the steps to the still, close lounge. Dust sparkled in the sunbeams. The clock said five to seven.

Katherine sat on the sofa. She was bewildered. When she had written her letters she had barely known that Jane existed, and now she was asked to believe that the nets she had contrived so cunningly to capture Robin had succeeded down to the last syllable in snaring Jane. Apart from not believing it, she found the suggestion absurd. She had no feelings for Jane at all. And it was ridiculous that she should affect a person she did not care about. Besides—the impossibilities thronged upon her—she was sixteen, while Jane was twenty-five, middle-aged, and foreign, too.

"But I can't see," she said haltingly, "why—*you*—bothered."

Jane was leaning against the piano lighting a cigarette.

"I suppose it is rather difficult to understand," she said. The weariness had come back into her voice. "I wonder if I can explain."

She shut her eyes a moment. "Put it this way," she said.

"I get so bored that things are apt to get out of proportion." She looked at Katherine, to see if she understood.

"You get bored," said Katherine, to show she did.

"Yes, bored!" said Jane, with a sudden flash of temper, flicking her cigarette needlessly, and moving to the bookcase. "And that sounds silly, too. What have I got to be bored about? I'm healthy, I'm not starving, I live in a perfectly good house. Silly, isn't it? I don't know. I've only been doing it ten years," she ended with a touch of juvenile sarcasm.

Katherine realized at last with relief that Jane was going to talk about herself. That explained it. She had had these conversations before, when people had caught her interest by paying her compliments, and then had held her to confess their self-centred immaturities. This was like all the rest. She settled down to listen, a little disappointed, nevertheless, that they were not going to talk about herself.

"Tell me," she said.

Jane moved from the bookcase to the gramophone, and fingered a record as if she half-intended putting it on.

"I don't know if I can," she said at last. "There doesn't seem anything to tell. I left school when I was sixteen, because it seemed no use staying on there. As you've no doubt gathered, Robin has the brains of the family. So I came back and lived at home." She put down the record, and played with a little brush kept to clean them. "They stuck me for about a year and a half. Then it was decided I ought to do something. So I went to a technical college to learn shorthand and that sort of thing. We typed for hours. When I was considered to know enough, Father got me into an office of a friend of his, an insurance office, and I worked there for nearly a year." She drifted on to the fireplace, and tapped ash into an ornament. "Then they said politely but firmly that they had to reduce staff, and I had to go. I wasn't very surprised, as I was quite

hopeless, but it was rather a slap in the face." She
laughed. "They were probably only speaking the truth,
because of the slump, but I didn't realize that at the time.
So I went and messed around in Father's office while he
tried to find me another job. That was worse than the
insurance place, because I hadn't anything definite to do,
and people felt I had no business there. Of course, he
didn't pay me much. In the end, he couldn't find anyone
silly enough to take me—who would take a half-trained
nincompoop?—so I said I was sick of the whole thing
and came back to 'help mother'. Since then I've gone on
helping her."

She finished, rocking to and fro on the fender.

"But your father—he would help you to do anything
you wanted to do, wouldn't he?" said Katherine uncertainly.

"Oh yes. But you see there isn't anything I want to do."

Katherine said nothing. Jane moved on, straightening
some flowers on the window-sill. A petal fell off.

"Careers for women," said Jane. She took up the petal
and tore it. "What about women that don't want careers?
In the old days, I suppose, we should have an enormous
family and I should quietly turn into a sort of unpaid
housekeeper. Aunt Jane and what-not." She threw the bits
of petal into the coal bucket. "But nowadays nobody
forces me to do anything like that, and there's nothing I
want to do, so the answer's simple. I don't do anything.
Now understand this," she added, as Katherine seemed
about to say something. "It's the whole point. I'm not
lazy, I'm not even scared of the big world and all the rest
of it—and heaven knows I should like to pay for my keep
instead of just sponging. I can even kid myself for as long
as three weeks that I'm thrilled with something and want
to go on doing it—though I don't know if I still can, I
haven't tried lately. But then I get so sickened—" She shook
a curtain straight. "And then I sometimes hear of people

I was at school with, getting fresh appointments or being married or something. I can remember some of them. They weren't very special. But at least . . . And then there's Robin. He appals me sometimes. Or rather, he makes me appalled at myself—because I know they're right, you see. They've got this desire to—well, it's hardly that; I mean it seems quite natural for them to peg along and do things, they don't give it a second thought. But I don't see any *point* in it," said Jane, giving the piano-lid a soft blow.

"You might get married," said Katherine tentatively.

"No, you don't understand," said Jane in an irritated voice. She put her hands on her hips. "I mean everything, all the things I might do. I might get married, I might start shorthand-typing again, I might even go in a factory or be a waitress, I might even stay on here. Don't you see? Just because I don't see any point in doing anything, it doesn't mean I see any point in doing nothing. Oh——" She turned as if tired of her own voice, and sat on the piano stool, the sun coming in over her shoulders. The smoke from her cigarette was grey in the sunlight.

"Besides," she threw out as an afterthought, "if you don't see any point in getting married, nobody's going to marry you. I know that all right. They'd as soon marry a Zulu."

"The question to ask yourself," said Katherine carefully, after a long pause, during which Jane tossed her cigarette through the open french windows, "is: what would you do if you had a million pounds?"

"Sounds pretty stupid," said Jane. "What should I do if I lived on the moon?"

"It might help you to make up your mind."

"But I haven't got a mind to make up—oh well," said Jane, rising and starting to rove round the room once more, "I might travel, I suppose. I might like that."

"Where would you go?"

"Europe, Russia, America. Nowhere hot. Move on as soon as one got bored." The idea did not seem to attract her much. "I don't know," she said. "It beats me. You know, I thought once before you came that if we became friends, I'd tell you all this, and ask you what you thought about it. I suppose I should have told you anyway." She sighed. "What do you think about it?"

Katherine had an extraordinary idea. She did not know where it came from, unless for the last few minutes she had been taking Jane seriously. It was that she should suggest that Jane came back with her, to her home. She could stay there for six months or even a year as a paying guest; live with them, learn the language, make friends, do more or less as she pleased. Her parents, who were intellectual and given to strange actions, would probably not object. There was a room for her. Even if it made no lasting change, it would amuse her till the novelty wore off. For a moment it seemed brilliantly sane. Then all at once it appeared melodramatic. Jane would turn down the suggestion at once; it was presumptuous to think that she could play the fairy-godmother like that. Jane was not seriously asking advice of her: she simply wanted to talk. If there were anything to be done, her father would do it, for he had money enough. Or at least, it would be silly to make the offer straight off. She would have to ask her own parents first; it would be far better to wait, and then perhaps suggest it in a letter. It was not a thing to blurt out. She collected herself.

"And you really have no money?"

"About a hundred pounds."

"Then it's quite clear," said Katherine, laughing. "It's marriage or nothing."

"I suppose so. But who?"

"Oh, a foreigner," said Katherine, stretching her legs. "To take you away. Someone opposite to you."

"Well, we'll see," said Jane, as if bidding farewell to the subject. "That is, if you're serious."

"Of course I am. Aren't you?"

"Deathly," said Jane, laughing too.

7

And here matters came to a halt, no longer puzzling, no longer leading on her imagination. She found herself suddenly in unremarkable surroundings, friendly with two unremarkable young English people, at her leisure in their well-appointed house. When Jane had been speaking to her so sincerely and desperately, she had supposed that they would naturally become more closely dependent on each other, but Jane never referred to the subject again and Katherine had no wish to bring it up. She knew that these confessions are their own reward, and imagined Jane was now at ease. Her voice had been like that of a chess-player, explaining after defeat the tactics with which she had intended to gain victory: her manner had all the sterile quality of one who has never lain open to another. Nor was Jane's anger mentioned: the three of them went about together as before, though Robin still insisted in talking to her in her own language.

It was odd to find Robin's manner warming towards her. At the beginning of her visit he had been reserved, making sure his dark rambling hair was always carefully combed, springing to hold doors open, making sure everything they did was to her liking. Now he relaxed, and, when her interest in him had nearly died out, became unceremonious, casually bold. He lounged around in dirty trousers and no socks. He no longer had a special voice for her—articulate and precise—and he no longer treated her like royalty. Because her daydreams were over, and her over-heated fancy extinct, she paid no attention to this, but occasionally she could have sworn he had taken on a half-flirting tone. He had a trick of laughing at her, not looking away, and of taking her arm familiarly now and again, that she could not but notice.

Well, it was nice of him, but a little late. She thought fantastically that he had caught the tail-end of her four-days' love and was manfully doing his best. She was more concerned with trying to forget her embarrassing behaviour when she had been trying to coax him out into a non-existent open. That made her blush deeply, and was something she would never tell her friends.

But what was she going to tell them? She could already imagine the scene. After a decorous tea-time, the three—or perhaps four—of them would retreat to the bedroom, where there would be chocolates. The nightdress-case, shaped like a woolly dog, would be stuck rakishly on the mantelpiece so that at least two of them could sit on the bed. And then: "Well, Katherine dear, let us have the whole story." What was she going to tell them? "We played tennis, and I won." "We went on the river, and I lost the pole." "We went to Oxford, and it rained all the time." And what would they say? "Did you go lots of bicycle rides?" Well, as a matter of fact she had been a fair number. "And you saw St. Paul's Cathedral and Westminster Abbey?" That was true, too. "And he made you give him language lessons?" She could not deny even that. "And of course you never went near a dance-hall or a theatre or a beer-garden all the time you were there!" No, it was really rather appalling, how terrible they would make it sound. Yet had it been terrible? On the evidence, yes. On her own feelings? She was not sure.

For not all the holiday had depended on how Robin had behaved, or what he had said, or how Jane had acted. There were moments when she was alone that compensated for them. There was a time when she could not sleep, so she had leant out of her window to look at the moonlight, and the smell of the stocks and wallflowers had made her dizzy. In the mornings she liked to hear the men calling to the horses, and the explosive threadbare calls of the roosters. She loved the extraordinary soft greenness of the landscape, and the way hills were capped with dark green woods. She remembered with pleasure how she had found a child squalling in a lane, and had stopped its crying by talking to it, though it had probably been as much dumbfounded as comforted. But it had laughed eventually. And there was a grave in the churchyard that fascinated her, ornate and Jacobean, with four angels, an urn, and a grinning skull, all worn away by the continual weather that had beaten it for three hundred years. She did not ask Robin whose it was, and dreaded lest he should tell her. But there had been an evening or two when she had sat by it in the deep grass, able to look down towards the village on the one hand, and down towards the river on the other. The moon had risen not with freshly-minted brightness, but with almost a bloom, like a ripe fruit, and when the landscape was dusky touched the mist to pearl-colour. As she sat there she noticed a cat sitting ten yards off by another headstone, and sometimes the cat looked at her, and yawned, as if they both happened to be waiting on the same street corner. She had had to go home and leave the cat still there.

These, and other things that she no longer remembered, made her feel that in some way she had taken possession of that summer there. Once she had thought that for them, too, she would remain inextricably embedded in their recollections, and be referred to as a date—"the year Katherine came"; "the summer Katherine was here". But on the whole this was unlikely. For she had asked:

"Robin, do you have many people to stay with you?"

They were walking up towards the main road, where they would intercept Jack Stormalong's car. The weather was humid, a foretaste of autumn. The blackberries were ripening in the hedges, and earthenware bowls of red and yellow plums stood in the kitchen, ready for jam-making. Jane had stayed indoors because of this—or had it been something to do with moths discovered in the spare-room blankets? She had not been clear. At any rate, they were alone.

"Well, most of our friends are family friends, if you know what I mean," he replied. She did. The watered-down relationship was typical of them. "I suppose a fair number, by the end of the summer."

"And this Jack we are going to meet—has he been here before?"

"Rather. We've known him for ages. His father and my father were in the army together."

"He'll be surprised to find me here," said Katherine.

"No, why should he? He's used to finding other people here. And you're almost one of the family."

"It would be amusing if I were," said Katherine absently. "Don't you think families with a foreign side are more interesting? They become much stronger. And the one branch can help the other."

"That's what the Jews think, isn't it," he said rather distantly.

Jack Stormalong was in high spirits. He had driven from somewhere—Tewkesbury? Newbury? Aylesbury?—in sixty-five minutes by his shockproof wristwatch, his dashboard clock being out of order like all dashboard clocks. The engine of his dark crimson sports car roared hoarsely as he whisked them back home again, explaining to Robin that he was using a new kind of juice. He had no difficulty in making himself heard above the noise of the engine.

His introduction to Katherine was not fortunate. He greeted her loudly and asked her a question she could not follow: she realized suddenly that her conversance with English depended a good deal on being accustomed to the Fennels' voices. This made an awkward gap in the conversation till Robin straightened it out, and Katherine found herself blushing. He looked at her with an expression of arrested benevolence as if she had said something improper. She noticed that his two middle top teeth pushed each other outward and formed an *arc brisé*.

His arrival put her rather into the background, and for the moment she was not sorry, finding it amusing to see another guest welcomed as she had been. Also she had subconsciously been waiting for this new visitor ever since she heard he was coming. Her sensation that there should be somebody else had never quite left her. But she did not know what she had expected, and certainly Jack Stormalong made very little appeal to her. When they assembled in the lounge before dinner to drink some sherry in honour of his arrival, she expanded her initial rebuff into dislike. He would be about twenty-five, with short, oiled hair that waved slightly in front, a face neither handsome nor ugly, that spoke of little but a sense of his own authority—a military face, such as she was used to seeing above the high collars of cadets in her own country, offering peace but not friendship on certain terms. He was over six feet tall and very strong. He shook hands warmly with Mr. Fennel, whom he called "sir", and, carrying a glass of pale sherry to Jane, said "Hello, Jane" in a low, affectionate voice, gripping her right arm momentarily just below the shoulder, which caused her slightly to stagger. Katherine kept out of his reach, sitting quietly on the piano stool.

With increasing annoyance she noticed however that his arrival put the Fennels in good spirits. With her they were attentive, kind, relaxed: now, matched with a different partner, they grew sunny, skilful, almost flickering as the conversation at dinner played lightly around garden-pests, even Jane joining in, and Jack Stormalong demonstrated that it was perfectly easy to eat and hold up one end of a conversation at the same time. There was no doubt that he was more of a success than she had been. He took it for granted that he was at home there: he embarked on long anecdotes, sipping at the wine, and after each sip redirecting his discourse to a different person. Only he never said anything to Katherine. When they brought her into the conversation he forced himself to take notice of her, blinking his cold blue eyes once or twice. It was not quite as if they had introduced the maid into the discussion, but all the same he seemed disconcerted.

Robin was very attentive to him. Perhaps by contrast, he seemed more boyish than usual; he asked questions about fishing and the sports car that Jack Stormalong answered with good-humoured superiority, as if speaking to a younger brother. Katherine, in whom Robin had never shown such interest, grew sulky, and let the babble go on without bothering to follow it. At the end of the meal Robin finished by suggesting that while they were all there a photograph should be taken, and Katherine knew that he would not have suggested it for her sake. However, she followed the party out onto the small lawn while Robin went upstairs to find the camera.

"There ought to be a couple of films left," said Mr. Fennel, flattening worm-casts with the toe of his shoe. "When did we use it last? At Easter, was it?"

"Robin took one the day we were held up by the sheep on the way to Reading," said Jane, from where she was standing with Jack Stormalong. "I thought he finished the roll then."

Jack then began describing an incident that Jane seemed to find funny. Katherine, momentarily abandoned, drifted towards the garden seat that had stood between Jane and

160

herself on the evening of their discussion, and where Mrs. Fennel was now sitting.

Mrs. Fennel looked up.

"Well, my dear, we are quite a party now."

"Yes, we are."

"Sit down a moment, won't you? I'm afraid I've seen very little of you since you came. Not very gracious of me. But I thought you'd sooner be with Robin and Jane than holding my wool for me."

Katherine murmured something, not understanding. But she was grateful to Mrs. Fennel. All the small embarrassments that were consequent on staying in a strange house had been smoothed deftly and precisely away by her, and Katherine had felt no hesitation in speaking to her. She now laid aside a novel by Sir Walter Scott.

"I'm sure it hasn't been a very exciting holiday for you, but we thought it would be best to carry on as we are. We were a little uncertain about what you would expect."

"I'm sure . . . everything has been wonderful."

"Well, I hope at any rate that England won't be a foreign country to you any longer," said Mrs. Fennel. "You will come again another year. We all like you very much."

"Oh, thank you——"

"And I think Robin has been very fortunate to make such a good friend."

At this point Robin ran down the steps carrying a folding-camera. Mr. Fennel, who was wearing a panama hat, stepped forward.

"Now give that to me. I'll be the man who presses the button."

"Oh, but we want you in the picture," exclaimed Jane, coming forward.

"Not a bit of it. Just you all get together. Ladies at the front, gentlemen at the back. Yes, round the seat will do."

"Is it all right for the sun, sir?" said Jack Stormalong

anxiously, looking as if he would like to take the camera into his own hands.

"I've taken dozens of photographs," said Mr. Fennel firmly, "without bothering about things like that. The secret is to hold it steadily."

"It'll do," said Robin, aside.

"You might hold it straight as well," said Jane. Mrs. Fennel was in the middle, with Katherine on her right and Jane on her left. "If you'd wait a moment, I'd put some proper shoes on," she said. "These aren't really fit to be seen."

"My dear, posterity won't be interested in your shoes, presentable or not. Now let me see. I can't see anything at all. Where are you?" He swivelled the camera plaintively. "Wave something."

Jane waved a hand.

"Ah. Yes, that's got it, thank you. The next trouble is going to be Jack's head. I'm afraid your head will be out of the picture, Jack."

"Well, that's a comfort," said Jane.

"Wait a minute. Nil desperandum. I'm afraid we shall have to dispense with the ladies' feet—you needn't have worried about your shoes, my dear."

"Perhaps if you stepped back, sir——"

"No, this will do very well. Now then. That's got it. Everybody smile. Remember this is a special occasion— where's the thing, the button on this thing? Where—ah. Now then."

And so the image of them standing and sitting in relaxed attitudes in the evening sun was pressed onto the negative for all eternity.

"One of Katherine," called Mrs. Fennel. "We ought to have one of her alone."

"Certainly we should. My dear, would you mind? Stand against the monkshood—the flowers there. Wait while I turn this film——"

"I don't think it's any good, dad," said Robin, coming forward. "There was only the one film left."

"Well, let me see. Oh yes, what a nuisance. I'm sorry, Katherine, there's no more film left—is there none in the house?"

"Not unless you've bought any."

"Never mind," said Mrs. Fennel, picking up the fringed cushion she had brought out to sit on. "We have one of you in the group."

Nevertheless, she did mind. It seemed to her that she was already embarked on her homeward journey, and watching their faces recede into a common blur. Robin was infuriating. At his suggestion the four of them spent most of their time together, and the brush with Jane was no longer referred to: Katherine's last two full days were spent in slack fourhanded pastimes—doubles at tennis (and if there was anything Katherine disliked it was doubles, particularly when partnered with Jack Stormalong, in a game of England versus the world: Jack Stormalong held a post in India), two hours wasted by moving chairs to the Village Hall. The weather, after the dash of rain, stabilized in a pleasant waxen sunshine, and in the evenings there was occasionally a chill in the blue shadows, an infinitesimal hint of autumnal frost, saddening in any circumstances. It was not that Robin and Jane disregarded her: they did not. But they assumed that she was contented, which she wasn't, and that anything done by four people was automatically more enjoyable than anything done by three or two. They seemed to assume, too, that she was never to leave them: an outsider could not have gathered that on Saturday they were to say goodbye to her and not see her again: her departure was simply not regarded as important. Katherine was disgusted, and she reserved a special corner of her disgust for Jane. Whatever else she had felt when Jane had told her all that stuff, she had respected the emotion behind it: she had rc-estimated her as the only Fennel with sensibility. If Jane had continued petulant or even hostile, she would not have minded, but now she behaved quite differently: the irritable languor had slipped from her as if by the very confessing of it. She contributed her full share of laughter and idiotic jokes. And Katherine summed her up bitterly in Robin's word: Jane's moods. Mood after mood after mood. Her crossness had been a mood, so had her friendliness, and it had amused her after that to pose as a person trapped and misunderstood. Now all that was over, and there was someone else to show off to, she had changed once more. Her emotions, thought Katherine, are as flexible as Robin's manners, and that's the only difference between them.

On Friday, her last full day, they fulfilled Robin's original plan and went up-river to the Rose for lunch. It was a heavy day, and the sun shone intermittently: at midday a few drops of rain fell, but nothing more. Katherine began with a headache too slight to be mentioned as an excuse to stay behind, but which nevertheless weighed on her throughout the trip, which was tediously jolly. Jack Stormalong poled them vigorously there, and theatrically drank a quantity of beer on arrival. Robin also had some, and there developed between them a masculine waggishness that aroused laughter at Katherine's expense, as she could not properly understand them. She struggled to take this in good part, but even Jane found it trying and began edging her remarks with sarcasm, which quietened them down somewhat. After lunch, they had some more drinks in the garden, where there was a skittle-alley: Jack and Robin played, and Jack won. The clumsy clattering got on Katherine's nerves, and she said as much to Jane, who sat with her. Jane, who had been drinking gin, replied: "This is, quite seriously, life itself," and such pretentiousness did nothing to soothe her. She was relieved when they took the punt home again,

Jack (who had paid the luncheon-bill) poling indefatigably. Robin fell asleep.

Between tea and dinner she went to her room to pack. First of all she held her face in cold water, opening and shutting her eyes, then sponged herself, and put on what clean clothes she had left. Everything else was dirty. She sat by her open trunk, remembering how carefully the laundered garments had been stowed the first time, layer upon layer, with great regard for relative weight and likelihood of creasing. It seemed distant to her now. Putting aside what she was to travel in, she began sorting and folding, carelessly at first, then with more attention as the pleasure of working alone came over her. She found the few presents she had bought to take home, and to turn them over and anticipate the thanks she would get made her eager to see her parents and friends once more. When she rose and looked round the room in search of things she had missed, it pleased her to feel that she had practically withdrawn herself from it, that she would leave it exactly as she had found it, that she would pass through this house and leave no trace behind, as all the others who had slept in this guest room had done. Disregarding the few hours that remained, she reviewed her visit and condemned it. She had come expecting to solve a mystery, and had found at the end there was no mystery to solve. From what she had been told, she had been invited partly out of politeness and partly to divert Jane's alleged boredom: Robin had played host with true English reserve, and had managed to slip in a few free language lessons on the side. She thought bitterly that it would hardly be out of place to hint that they might refund her fares.

Dinner was a little better. The beer and exertion had left Jack Stormalong subdued for the moment, and at her first mention of the word "packing" they were all solicitous. Mr. Fennel had been consulting a timetable and had written out a list of trains and times in an old-fashioned, delicate, ledger-book hand. The conversation ran lightly over the events of her stay, spinning them into a web of reminiscence that took only the pleasant colours for material. Both Robin and Jane contributed, treating her as if she were quite a different person, and her visit as if it had been one of the many meetings of established friends. It was the best they could do, she imagined, in the way of a happy ending, and she was grateful.

However, in the lounge afterwards Jack Stormalong awoke to conversation again, and a tactless discussion followed in which Robin and Jane tried to persuade him not to leave on Monday night but stay till Tuesday.

"Or do you find it so dull here, after all your tiger-shooting?" Robin added, putting an ashtray for him on the arm of his chair.

"Oh, we can't compete with tigers," said Jane, who for once was wearing lipstick. "Not that I believe you've been near one."

"I really ought to push off on Monday," said Jack, continually placing his cigarette between different pairs of oblong fingers. "I might stay if you could provide a tiger."

"We could ring up a zoo."

"They would be very expensive, though. Would you give us the skin?"

"Will you give us a skin anyway?"

Jack Stormalong wagged his head, grinning.

"I haven't any skins."

"I don't believe you've ever shot one at all," said Jane.

"Oh, he has, haven't you?"

"I've put a bullet into one, if you count that. But you have to stand down in favour of the senior man in the party—the Resident, in this case . . ,"

They talked a while vaguely about India, during which Katherine listened sourly. Their goodwill at dinner, allied with their resumed assumption that this night was like any other night, had once more awoken regret in her that she must leave them. Now that the surface of their relations had quietened in her mind, she saw that only her inquisitive imagination had prevented the holiday being like this from the evening she arrived—an untroubled expanse resembling a lake between hills. She wished it could go on. Although she was eager to return to her own life and country, she wished she could stay a little longer to watch the quiet procession of evenings, of meals on the dark table, of small presents of hothouse fruit from neighbours left wrapped in baskets in the porch with a note, of the river drifting southward. Now that it was too late, she felt that all the time she had been paying attention to the wrong things.

But Jack Stormalong, encouraged by the others, was deep in tigers. "Of course, you don't find them unless you go out and look for them," he said. "As a rule, they keep out of your way. If they start killing, it's different. If a tiger kills a man, you have to do something about it for the sake of prestige—and they say as well, of course, that once a tiger gets a taste for human flesh it won't look for anything different. I don't know about that. But obviously men are easy things to kill—we've no claws or horns or tusks . . . we can't even run fast."

"We're not much use when it comes to a fight, are we?" said Jane, looking at her own right hand.

"Not with tigers, at any rate," said Jack. He guffawed. "A man I met had a narrow squeak once—a perfect madman, mind you. He and another chap had been out, and they'd come across a tiger and put a brace of bullets in her, but she got away. What did they do but follow her. The prints were clear as day in the jungle, but when they came out into a clearing they lost them. So they separated to have a snoop round. This chap said that he was just bending down to take a look when there was an earsplitting roar and up comes the tiger from a ditch fifteen yards off, in a pretty savage temper, and went straight at him. He hadn't time to do more than put out his rifle with both hands—it was just as well he did—and then he was bowled over with the tiger on top of him. Luckily the other man noticed what was up and got a lucky shot in her brain as she was turning again. The shekarries were scared blue. He's still got the rifle, and he showed it me— it had caught the tiger's first swipe, and there were claw-marks a quarter of an inch deep down the butt, and the trigger and guard were bent flat." Jack leaned forward with leaden sincerity. "Absolutely flat."

Robin expressed amazement. "But you don't go on foot, do you?" he said.

"Surely when it was wounded——"

"On a formal shoot there's elephants. But even then it isn't all jam. You'd imagine you'd feel as safe as houses up on an elephant——"

"Well, I don't know," said Jane.

"Oh, you do. At least you do till our friend stripes comes along. But you see it's like this. The tiger goes for the elephant—I've seen a tiger spring right up on an elephant's head—clinging, you know, with the claws in. And then it all depends how the elephant behaves. It's liable to get bothered, and anything may happen. It may try to shake the tiger off, and only succeed in shaking the poor bloke out of the howdah. Or the other elephants may get the wind up. What it ought to do is stand still and let the guns pot the tiger till it drops off. But they don't always see it that way."

There was general laughter.

"Oh, it's a terrific thrill," said Jack Stormalong, sitting forward with an eagerness that suggested he was still a trifle drunk. "You've no idea. A tiger will go on fighting till it drops. You imagine yourself surrounded by elephants as big as houses, with fellows on top putting both barrels

168

into you. You'd leg it for cover as fast as you could. But I've seen a tiger with as many as eight bullets in it go on trying to beat the whole crowd till he drops. Absolute rage incarnate. You can't call it courage; it's more than that." He studied the squashy end of his cigarette for a moment. "And you look down, you know . . . if he got you he'd tear you to bits. You can't help feeling scared. That's where the fun comes in."

"I think it would go out, with me," said Jane.

In response to a question from Robin, Jack began to describe the particular tiger-shoot he had attended, and they fell into a discussion of rifles; calibres, velocities, bores. Jack's elephant had lurched, causing him to put his foot into the luncheon-basket and break a siphon: this had impressed him more than the destruction of the tiger. Robin asked if a tiger's stripes were really effective camouflage; Jack Stormalong lit another cigarette and began to tell him.

Katherine had had enough. Surely, she thought, Jane can't be less bored than I am. Experimentally she caught Jane's eye, trying to express resignation, and rather to her surprise Jane gave a little annoyed gesture, which Katherine found hard to interpret. She could not think that they were both annoyed at the same thing, because although listening to the half-intelligible ramble of this English Colonial Official was irritating enough, she could have borne it on any other night than this. What made her desperate was the invisible running-out of time; a stupid thing to resent, and yet it galled.

She jumped up. "I think I'll go out for a little," she said.

She was out of the french windows before anyone could protest, and a glance back from the foot of the steps showed she was not being followed. For this she was thankful. At the moment she wanted only time enough to calm herself; it was nothing serious. All she needed was a little space to look around her for the last time and accept the fact that she was going. When this was done—when she had made her peace, as she called it—she could return and mix with them on equal terms.

It was very solacing to be alone. She looked about her at the garden and the sky. It was after nine o'clock; the sun had set and the trees hung motionless in a barely-visible mist; down towards the west there ran a vast fan of tiny clouds, ribbed and golden. She walked slowly along the path by the tennis-court, looking at the broad bed of flowers. Many of them had softly closed. From here she passed through into the kitchen-garden, where the air was richer with a confused smell of vegetables; on an impulse she went over to the tap and tried to stop it dripping. Twist as she could, the drops still slowly formed and fell onto the stones, and at last she gave it up. Let it go on. A few grasses touched her bare legs as she walked on towards the blue door, and she shivered, although it was not cold. The key turned easily in the lock and she found herself again on the short mown bank, remembered so vividly from her first evening, at the edge of the river that moved contentedly past.

It was always bigger than she expected, and she sat down on the grass to watch it flow. Lazily throwing a twig upstream, she watched it drift slowly level with her and then pass on, and she wondered where the river rose, how many towns and bridges it passed on its course, and past what fields the twig would be carried in the half-light of next morning, before she was awake. She had never even found out its name. The line of trees on the bank were reflected in it, thin upflung branches being flattened in the reflection to dark gesturing masses. Underneath them she could see small erratic shapes flying. They dipped and swerved furiously, and she realized after a few seconds that they were bats. They were too far away to alarm her.

But she withdrew her eyes to the foreground again, and noticed that the fastening of the tiny boat-house—little more than a low shack—had not been padlocked. She got up and went to it, and looking in saw that the punt was there. Half-experimentally she drew it silently out, and climbed in. It rocked soothingly. She wondered if it would be wrong of her to paddle it a few hundred yards downstream and back: it was no use her unstrapping the pole, but she thought it would be quite easy to manage with a paddle that lay on the seat beside her. Would they mind? Surely not, on her last evening; and even if they did, there would be little enough time left for them to mind in. She picked up the paddle and dipped it in the water.

"Are you stealing our boat?" said Robin. He was standing on the bank behind her.

"Oh——" She dropped her hands. "You left the door unfastened."

"Did I?" He glanced towards it. "No, don't get out," he added as she prepared to rise. "I'll come with you. Or would you rather go alone?"

"Please come."

He sat beside her, taking the other paddle from the back, and, paddling together, they felt the punt draw away from the bank, rocking lightly on the sensitive water. She regulated her strokes with his.

"I hope you did not mind when I left you," she said presently. "I was a bit tired."

"Oh, there's no stopping old Jack, once he gets talking," Robin said. He smiled.

The evening was so still, it was like setting forth into silence itself, that sharpened the noise of their paddles stirring the dull river and of an occasional fish breaking the surface with a tiny liquid explosion. As they proceeded downstream, sending ripples towards either bank, the trees fell behind and fields opened around them. On one side the bank had been built up with bricks, now grown dull and mossy after much weather, and an iron ring fastened in them was rusty and disused. The water was the colour of pewter, for the afterglow had faded rapidly and left a quality of light that resembled early dawn. It had drawn off the brightness from the meadows and stubble-fields, that were now tarnished silver and pale yellow, and the shadows were slowly mixing with the mist. In this way the edges of her emotions had blurred, and they now over-laid each other like twin planes of water running over wet sand, the last expenditure of succeeding waves. There was no longer any discord in them: she felt at peace.

"Robin, what is this river called?" she asked after a while.

"Why, the Thames, of course."

"Not the real Thames?"

"Certainly." And then he added with mild amusement: "If we'd lived in prehistoric times, before England was an island, I could nearly have taken you home. The Thames used to flow into the Rhine."

She glanced at him. His expression was friendly but serious, as if concentrating; at the end of each stroke he gave the blade a twist sideways, to neutralize the fact that his strokes were stronger than hers. There was something formal about him, as if he were a figure in allegory, carry-ing her a stage further on some undefined journey, and she smiled to remember her discarded belief that he might at any moment say something she would never forget. She doubted if she would ever think that again of anyone: with this in mind, she stopped paddling, and after two more strokes Robin allowed his paddle to trail diagonally in the water, so that the punt's direction slowly altered, and it drifted towards the bank, about eighty yards from where they had started. In time the front of the boat crushed over the reeds with a dry crackle, and they came to rest, Robin digging his paddle in the mud to prevent their moving with the current. He folded his arms and looked in front of him.

It's come to an end, she thought. No matter what she thought might happen, or what she had done that she regretted, it was all now part of the past. Tomorrow she would undertake the long journey back to her normal life, and this isolated excursion to England would remain in her mind as something irrelevant and beautiful. For better or worse, it was over; it had been dull, perhaps; Robin had been less exciting than she had thought he would be, but that might be for the best. The parents had been tactful and quite uninterested in her, which had been a good thing. The house, so comfortable and unpretentious, would stand for many years yet among the trees, and she would not miss it. As for what she would tell her friends, she would distort her visit into something amusing. There was nothing sacred about it. Yet for all that as they floated there she wanted to add nothing more, not a word or a look. It was finished. Her mind was free to be diverted by the surface of things she had no need to remember— the sound of water, of birds close at hand, the remote sound of a train-whistle. Her attention rose and fell from these things as the shadow of a ball thrown against the side of a building rises and drops back again; they were, she felt, tiny decorative tracings on the finished vase.

Suddenly he took hold of her.

She gave a start and bit her tongue.

He ducked his head and kissed her inexpertly with tight lips, as if dodging something that swept above their heads. It was not a bit like lovemaking, and she never thought of it as such till afterwards. He kept his face hidden against her hair. At the end of this unfathomable interval, he shivered, and the shiver changed to a short scrambling shudder, almost an abortive attempt to climb on her; then he slowly relaxed. Still he would not look her in the face. In the end he released her, carelessly.

Neither of them said anything.

After a time he dragged up his paddle, washed the blade, and they turned upstream again.

When they got back, she went upstairs to her room, tenderly moving the end of her tongue to and fro without knowing what she was doing. She felt dazed, as if she had nearly been run over in the street. Sitting at her nearly-empty dressing table, she looked at herself, trembling. The evening whispered outside, the quiet evening that had suddenly risen up against her in one great stamping chord, like the beginning of music she would never hear.

There was a bang on the door. She turned quickly. It was Jane.

"Oh, you are here," she said. She hung onto the doorknob, swaying slightly as if drunk, and breathing hard. Then she put her hand to her forehead as if faint, and gasped with laughter. "What a life," she said. "Your tactful exit . . . glory." She flopped on the bed, then instantly scrambled up to say: "I've just had an honourable proposal of marriage!"

She stared at Katherine.

"Well?"

"I said I would."

PART THREE

I

But the snow did not come. The sky remained as immovable as a pebble frozen in the surface of a pond. The lights had to be kept on in offices, and some people worked in their coats; those who looked out of the windows of expensive centrally-heated flats still saw the bare, motionless trees, the railings, the half-obliterated government notices.

It was easier to forget about it in the city, however. For one thing it was Saturday afternoon, and by one o'clock most people were free to go home. They could turn their backs on the window, and the slab of garden, and read the newspaper by the fire till teatime. Or if they had no real home, they could pay to sit in the large cinemas, where it seemed warmer because it was dark. The cafeterias filled up early, and the shoppers lingered over their teas, dropping cigarette-ends into their empty cups, unwilling to face the journey back to where they lived. Everywhere people indoors were loth to move. Men stayed in their clubs, in billiard saloons, in public bars till closing time. Soldiers lay discontentedly in Y.M.C.A. rest rooms, writing letters or turning over magazines several weeks old.

And meanwhile, the winter remained. It was not romantic or picturesque: the snow, that was graceful in the country, was days old in the town: it had been trodden to a brown powder and shovelled into the gutters. Where it had not been disturbed, on burnt-out buildings, on warehouse roofs or sheds in the railways yards, it made the scene more dingy and dispirited. Women went round to the coal yards with perambulators and large baskets; elderly men picked up pieces of lath from heaps of rubble: there were no fires in waiting-rooms. Paper-sellers with the three o'clock edition stood well within the locked entrances of banks. The papers said nothing about the weather, but gave lists of football matches and race-meetings that had been cancelled.

On one of the stations, a crowd watched a porter come out and chalk up on a board that the Paddington train was eighty-five minutes late.

2

Katherine came out of a self-service café where she had lunched. The time was three minutes after one o'clock, half an hour after Miss Green had left her to go home.

She was angry with herself for behaving unreasonably and for the knowledge that she was still not quite controlled. What was wrong, to make her rush away from her lodging, leaving no message and making no arrangements? She would only have to go back again, and her steps took the direction of Merion Street as if walking to a scaffold. What was the matter with her? Her feelings were like a flight of birds that swoop over to one corner of a field and then stop, all trembling equidistantly in the air, and then come streaming back, like a banner tossed first one way, then the other. Had there been anything more exciting than the thought of this letter? Was she afraid of meeting Robin, as Robin? No, of course not. Wasn't such a meeting as Robin suggested exactly what she had anticipated as being practically unavoidable? Why was she acting so immaturely?

Yet she almost wished she had not written to Jane. The truth was, that she had set too much store on a meeting for it to happen so quickly. She was gripped by the reaction that follows the granting of a wish. Had she pushed herself forward, had she cornered them so that they could do nothing but make such a response? And was this proposed meeting a compromise between ignoring her and having to invite her to stay? At this construction her nervousness increased. She was again brought up against the fact that she might not, according to English standards, be acting correctly, and she would sooner be ignored than accepted unwillingly. Looking over the letter again, she had to admit that he did not sound overjoyed at the prospect. Conceivably Mrs. Fennel had directed him to meet her and fob her off in some way— for at this distance of time they were all strangers. If she met Robin now, in this street—it was an hour after twelve and he might well be on his way to her address—she would probably not know him. He would be in officer's uniform, deep-voiced, full-grown. She stopped on the pavement opposite Merion Street, and looked cautiously around her. Her fingers encountered a bent cigarette at the bottom of her coat pocket, and she meditatively put it into her mouth and lit it.

No, she decided suddenly, she would leave no message. This was somehow not the kind of meeting she wanted— inconclusive, on strange ground, brief, finding her unprepared. She would let things fall by chance, as they would; and in any case there was no need. If she left a note in her room or even on her door, he would not see it, and the only alternative was to tell the chemist's wife that she would return about half-past seven at night— which the chemist's wife knew already and would certainly tell him if he called. If he could see her then, presumably he would; if he couldn't, no messages would alter the fact.

In the meantime, then, there was this handbag. She would just have enough time to return it before starting work again. It seemed quite natural to her to set off on this errand as she made her way towards the Bank Street bus-stop once more. This day was already so unlike other days that it was beginning to resemble an odyssey in a dream: to find herself in strange places, looking for strange

179

people, following out thin threads of coincidence—it was almost as if an enchantment had been put on her to keep her away from the only two places where Robin knew she might be. But it would be awkward if she met him in the street.

Miss Green, she thought, as she settled down in the bus, would be home by now. The driver swung into his seat, and they began to move. Off once more. As long as she was travelling, she was safe.

But safe! safe from what? It was time she faced the question. What did she remember of the Fennels, plainly and without embroidery? There had been Robin, of course; he had puzzled her at first, because he was so very English—how English she never realized till she met more English people—but once she had got used to him he had been rather dull. She did not remember ever having been attracted by him. Now he would probably be even duller. Jane—well, Jane was indistinct to the point of anonymity. She had got engaged during her visit to someone she couldn't recall anything about except his surname, which was so queer. The parents had been kind and pleasant. What else? It had been very hot: she had not taken enough light dresses. Then afterwards she had told her friends that Robin was passionately, simply madly and passionately, in love with her. One had had to say something. Hadn't he kissed her once? Or had she made that up afterwards?

So it wasn't any personal attachment that made them so important. They had continued writing spasmodically for about six months afterwards: Jane had sent her a piece of wedding-cake. It seemed that once they had met they had lost interest in each other. Since then she had not thought of them; there had been other things to think of, a few pleasanter, the rest such that she kept them out of her mind. She had not thought of the Fennels again till she had arrived in England for the second time.

The first few weeks had been a nightmare. Luckily there was little for her to do about them: in a haphazard way, she was provided for, and had only to accept what she was given. She lived in a hostel, ate in a canteen, and shared a bedroom with two other girls. She had to attend interviews in hastily-furnished offices. Never in her life had she experienced such bottomless despair and loneliness: there was nothing familiar, nothing of her own choosing, nothing that she could turn to and grasp in the face of everything else. It was as if the world had been turned round, like innumerable bits of reversible stage scenery. Quite frequently she felt moments of stark terror at the strangeness of things, at the way all had collapsed, presumably as a cat will go mad upon the ruins of its suddenly-destroyed home. There was only one sure thing: she was still alive. The rest was like walking across a plaster ceiling.

It was then, naturally, that she had thought of the Fennels. Should she write to them or not? She had decided not, for several reasons, but as much as anything because she did not want to make a fuss. Most of all she wanted to be unobtrusive and disregarded. And so she had set herself to climb out of the slithering pit into which she had fallen, without success at first, but as time went on managing to re-establish herself gradually, to regain her willpower, to avoid the terrible moments that left her sickened. She did this by suppressing as far as she could every reference to her former life, and treating every day as complete in itself. She ate, slept and worked, and refused to compare what she did or ate, or where she slept, with any work or food or household she had known in the past. Everything had to be reduced to its simplest terms.

The trick—if it was a trick—had worked: she found herself gradually able to relax. After some months of sorting forms, or copying out new ration-cards, she had applied for several more ambitious jobs, and to her surprise had been appointed to the one she now held. It was only for the duration of the war, but it was a fraction better-paid, and she quickened her attention till she could do the work without embarrassment. It gave her a sense of independence. When she had left London to come here, her sense of desolation had returned, but less strongly than before, and she discovered she was well in control of it. It was affecting her no more than the discomfort, say, of a hard frost.

There was time now to look round, and take stock of her position, to mend what clothes she had, and buy new ones. She was reluctant to part with her old clothes and start wearing English ones. Nearly everything she possessed was a reference back to the days before she left home: her leather motoring-coat, for instance, was a relic of her student days. There had been a fad about dressing in accordance with the machine-age. But she hated to part with anything. Although she was not keen on mending, she spent many evenings darning stockings and underwear, with a sort of love for them. They were all she had left.

The truth was, she had not been facing the facts. To live from day to day, as she had been doing, shut out the past, but it shut out the future too, and made the present one long temporary hand-to-mouth existence. All the time she had been behaving as if everything would suddenly snap back to normal, if she could only hang on a little longer. Without admitting it to herself, she had been believing that in a little while the walls would fly back, and at a touch she would find herself back at home, or studying in the university, with her old life about her.

It shocked her to realize she had been believing anything so absurd, and it shocked her to realize that it was absurd. But a third fact shocked her most of all: that even if her old life had been waiting for her, she no longer wanted to return to it. And truly she did not realize this for a long time. In strange surroundings one was bound to have strange thoughts, that perhaps did not go very deep: such fancies as this she dismissed as wish-fulfilment: since she could not go back, she did not want to. But as time passed she could not ignore it any more than she could have ignored a dislocated bone. Somehow, without knowing it, she had broken fresh ground.

For she knew, now, that in most lives there had to come a break, when the past dropped away and the maturity it had enclosed for so long stood painfully upright. It came through death or disaster, or even through a love-affair that with the best will in the world on both sides went wrong. Certainly there were people to whom it never came: girls she had known had slipped cosily from child-hood to marriage, and their lives would be one long unin-telligent summer. But once the break was made, as though continually-trickling sand had caused a building to slip suddenly on its foundations so that perhaps one single ornament fell to the floor, life ceased to be a con-fused stumbling from one illumination to another, a series of unconnected clearings in a tropical forest, and became a flat landscape, wry and rather small, with a few unfor-gettable landmarks somewhat resembling a stretch of fen-land, where an occasional dyke or broken fence shows up for miles, and the sails of a mill turn all day long in the steady wind.

She knew—for such a break brings knowledge, but no additional strength—that her old way of living was finished. In the past she thought she had found happiness through the interplay of herself and other people. The most important thing had been to please them, to love them, to learn them so fully that their personalities were as distinct as the taste of different fruits. Now this brought happiness no longer: she no longer felt that she was exalted or made more worthy if she could spin her friend-ships to incredible subtlety and fineness. It was something she had tired of doing. And what had replaced it? Here she was at a loss. She was not sure if anything had replaced it.

She was not sure if anything would replace it.

For the world seemed to have moved off a little, and to have lost its immediacy, as a bright pattern will fade in many washings. It was like a painting of a winter landscape in neutral colours, or a nocturne in many greys of the riverside, yet not so beautiful as either. Like a person who is beginning to go physically colour-blind she was disturbed. She felt one of her faculties had died without her consent or knowledge, and she was less than she had been. The world that she had been so used to appraising, delighting in, and mixing with had drawn away, and she no longer felt she was part of it. Henceforward, if she needed comfort, she would have to comfort herself; if she were to be happy, the happiness would have to burn from her own nature. In short, since people seemed not to affect her, they could not help her, and if she was to go on living she would have to get the strength for it solely out of herself.

Perhaps there was nothing startling about that. But she shrank from accepting it. It was the only thing she could not conquer by accepting, because it was not a fancy or a new piece of self-knowledge that she could fit to her own vanity, but true, true in a sense she found horrible, like a medical diagnosis. Life was not going to be as pleasant as it had been. It would be more cramped, less variegated, more predictable. She was not going to be surprised any more. She was not going to trust anybody. She was not going to love anybody. And when the time came for her to die, she would die not only without having done anything worth while, like most other people, but without having done anything she wanted.

Once she had thought belief depended on inclination. But she fought against this new realization as hard as she could, trying to shut out the future as before she had shut out the past; yet still it gained ground. It mingled with her daily life, with the war, with the winter, until it scarcely seemed a separate thing at all, but merely a state of mind produced by living alone, living in England, and all the rest of it. She deeply hoped it was. There were times when it seemed a trivial and shallow depression. And there were times when the fear of it touched her as cold as wet steel: when she could see herself hardly aware that she was unhappy, because her feelings had so nearly atrophied, and receiving no compensations in return.

Was it silly to worry about such things? Weren't there enough material circumstances to trouble her? The answer was of course that she did not worry all the time. But when it came to the forefront of her mind, she did not dissociate it from the apparently meaningless disasters that had driven her to England. They seemed bound up together. And she had believed for a long time that a person's life is directed mainly by their actions, and these in turn are directed by their personality, which is not self-chosen in the first place and modifies itself quite independently of their wishes afterwards. To find her theory being proved upon herself increased her uneasiness.

So where did the Fennels come in all this? Simply, that she was lonely; more complexly, that they supported her failing hope that she was wrong to think her life had worsened so irrevocably. Since writing to Jane, those three nearly-forgotten weeks had taken on a new character in her memory. It was the only period of her life that had not been spoiled by later events, and she found that she could draw upon it hearteningly, remembering when she had been happy, and ready to give and take, instead of unwilling to give, and finding nothing worth taking. It was as if she hoped they would warm back to life a part of her that had been frozen, with the same solicitude she had tried to give Miss Green that morning—though she feared in retrospect that she had done no more than if she had handed her an elaborate basket of fruit left for weeks in a refrigerator, all frosted over and tasteless.

It was extravagant, even melodramatic. But she could hardly have cared more if her life had depended on them.

3

Cheshunt Avenue was on the north side of the city, in a district made up of rows of houses occasionally relieved by a grocery shop or the back of a laundry. Somewhere among them was a football ground. The bus ran towards it along a long road lined with shops, public-houses, and factories, called Balsam Lane.

Sick of thinking about herself, she crushed out her cigarette in the blackened ashtray and looked at Miss Parbury's handbag. It was brown and unremarkable. Out of curiosity she opened it and looked inside. It smelt of stale scent and peppermint, and the lining shone. In places the seams were fraying. Rather it looked as if Miss Parbury couldn't afford to buy a new one for everyday use.

There came back to her mind that odd conviction that she had found a letter addressed by Mr. Anstey in it, and she poked about among the papers till she discovered it again. As well as a purse and a handkerchief and some odds and ends, there were a few handbills giving the times of buses, a folded paper bag, a shopping list and an empty envelope that had come from the Inland Revenue Department. All these she had mistaken for letters, but in fact there was only one, and she drew it out and looked at it. If it was not Mr. Anstey's writing, it was extraordinarily like it. The mincing hand, the fine-nibbed pen: these she had seen often when at her work. The postmark was of the day before, posted locally. If it had been written at the library, the address would have been typewritten, but this looked like a private letter. Was it from Mr. Anstey? Strange: she thought she knew his writing well enough, but once she examined it closely half a dozen doubtful instances occurred to her. She grew less confident as she continued to inspect it.

If it was a private letter, of course, that still did not prevent Anstey's having written it; it was only that she had not imagined him as an individual who had friends like everyone else. The thought was as unfamiliar as meeting him in the street on a Sunday. But it tantalized her not to know. Should she open it? Quite honestly, she did not much care what was inside, only it would settle the argument one way or the other. She was not curious about people any longer. But then it was so strange, such a coincidence, if in truth it was from him. And Katherine was always disposed to follow coincidences to their fullest extent.

The envelope contained one sheet of paper, inscribed on one side and folded with the writing inwards, like her letter from Robin. It would be quite easy to glance at the signature without necessarily reading the rest, and this she did, finding not very much to her surprise that it was signed "Lancelot", Mr. Anstey's outlandish Christian name. This put the question beyond doubt. So she opened it fully to glance momentarily over it before slipping it back in the envelope, and remained reading it for perhaps half a minute.

There was nothing startling about it. But it puzzled her because she could not instantly pick up what it was about. Her eye fled from sentence to sentence, trying to break into the meaning. Accustomed to grasping any passage at once, she was baulked. Then she tried reading it slowly, sentence by sentence.

"My dear Veronica, (it ran)
"I received your letter this morning.

187

"You only say all over again what we have discussed many times, and seem no nearer deciding than you were last week. I have tried hard enough to show you I sympathize with your point of view, but surely you can see that what I suggest is the best way. If you do not agree, you only have to say so."

Then two sentences to make a final paragraph:

"At all events, I see no point in waiting any longer as you suggest. I say finally that if you cannot make up your mind one way or the other, we had better let the matter drop."

No more. She turned it over: the other side was blank. There was nothing else in the envelope. Once more she read through the shrouded sentences, feeling somewhere the meaning striking like a muffled drum, as in the procession of a funeral. But what was the meaning? It seemed no sentence carried a loose end she could pick up and thereby unravel the whole. The masked phrases—"what we have discussed many times"; "what I suggest is the best way"; "we had better let the matter drop"—were as smooth and heavy in her hands as stones. She could get nothing out of them. There were a dozen things such a letter might refer to: it might be the sale of some furniture, or a proposed illegality, or something dark and evasive like a will-making or disposal of property. Yet it sounded funereal, troubling. The chief point was this correspondent, this Veronica Parbury. Who was she, Katherine wondered. It could be that they were related, and that she was a cousin or an aunt. Their different names denied close blood-relation. Hadn't Miss Green said, for instance, that Anstey had been married, but his wife had died? This might be a sister-in-law, then. And family business might well take on such masked and muffled sadness.

But if they were not related in any way, and there was no evidence of this, what was left? The drums deepened, as if coming nearer, heading a wintry company that would tread her down. It was ridiculous to think of Mr. Anstey marrying anyone, but that was the first thing that would come to anyone's mind if they read the letter. No-one would write so guardedly unless their feelings were involved. But him! Had he any feelings? It was absurd. Yet she was not amused. She read through it again. If only it had been a simple, blurting letter, she might have been scornful easily: she had often thought it would be satisfying to get some handle against him, to give her dislike a vicious instrument. But as it was, the figure of him was blurring in her mind, no longer a sharply-cut target for loathing, and was beginning to waver like something seen under water, to wobble, and even grow for moments together to more than life-size, not so much menacing as monumental. Her compact hatred dissipated against it, like a herd deprived of its driver, pulled up, beginning to amble in all directions, grown purposeless.

However, she was not in the mood for further speculation on these vague themes that led her bemusedly round and round the outskirts of things. She replaced the envelope in the bag and snapped it shut; and soon afterwards the bus set her down by a glazed-brick tavern called The General Wolfe. She knew that Cheshunt Avenue was the first turn left in Cheylesmore Road, that opened into Balsam Lane a little way after this bus-stop. It was a little after a quarter to two, and she hurried, because there was not too much time. One and three-quarter hours after middle-day: would Robin have arrived yet? Would he learn that she had been there and read his letter, and be offended that she had left no message? This was the first time that had occurred to her. She half-stopped, wondering if at this eleventh hour she should ring up the chemist and find whether he had called, and if not, leave some sort of explanation. There was a telephone-box on the other side of the road. She hesitated.

But no. Something made her resolve to leave it to chance. If any good was coming to her, she preferred not to interfere. By stretching out a blind hand she might knock the cup over. And if he was offended, or had not sufficient interest to seek her out again, it was better that they should not meet, for she would sooner miss him outright than meet him awkwardly and fail. Instead, she went on. She had never been in this part of the town before. Through occasional grills she could see lights on in basements: a table spread with food, or an edge of hanging washing. And there were streets upon streets extending on either side of her, like a deathly stone forest.

When she turned into Cheshunt Avenue she realized that the mist that had hung undispersed since morning was thickening somewhat. She could not see to the end of the road, and it seemed like a cul-de-sac. On each side stretched two rows of quiet houses behind dirty hedges: all had secretive lace curtains and some had panels of stained glass let into the front door. They had iron gates and perhaps a yard of earth in front of them, now covered with snow. Like the rest of the district, it was not quite genteel and not quite common: through one window she saw a man in shirt-sleeves drinking tea, and outside a second stood a bicycle with a ladder tied to it, and a small signboard advertising a painter and decorator. A third had a card in the window announcing a make of corsets.

She rattled at the knocker of number fifty. After a while someone came down the stairs that rose inside flush from the front door, and opened it.

"Is Miss Parbury in, please?"

"Why, yes," said the lady. "I'm her."

Katherine had been wondering what she would look like, and was rather disappointed to find she looked ordinary. She was twenty-eight or thirty years old, and spoke with local accent. Rather tall, with a rosy complexion and fair hair, she looked like a large tea-rose gone well to seed.

She held up the handbag. "Is this yours, then?"

"Oh!" Miss Parbury, who had been holding the door defensively, as if suspecting that Katherine was canvassing for a refugee's charity, now released it in relief. "That is good of you. I couldn't think—but come in. Yes, please do. Everything is rather untidy——"

Katherine stepped into the house and followed Miss Parbury as she scuttled into the back room. The air smelt of cooking.

"This room—I would have asked you into the front, but there's no fire, and it's so bitter, isn't it?" Miss Parbury was snatching things up, newspapers, and a library book with a knitting-needle to mark her place. She whisked away some object Katherine's eye could not catch, and bundled some sewing into a bureau whose lid already would not shut. "Do sit down. This is good of you, to come all this way. Everything is rather——" She completed her extempore change of scene, and motioned Katherine to the armchair on one side of the small coal fire. Katherine sat down, undoing the belt of her coat.

"Oh, I'm so pleased you've brought it back, I was in such a state . . . Until I came to pay my bus fare, I didn't notice I'd taken the wrong one. It was silly of me. And I knew I should put someone else to no end of trouble, I was so worried . . . I'm always doing these silly things. It was in the chemist's, was it?"

Katherine nodded.

"I was wondering how it happened. I had been shopping, you know, and I was just about to go home when I remembered I hadn't got some things for mother, so I was going up that little street—what is it called, now? I forget—and I noticed the shop and went in. After I'd paid—it must have been after—I put my bag on the counter, and took the things out of my basket to make more room, because I'd had a busy morning and I was just loaded—and I dropped a box of drawing pins and they went all over the floor." Miss Parbury laughed at herself. "So what with all that, and knowing if I missed the bus it would make me late, particularly on Saturday with all the crowds, and then with the dinner waiting, I just rushed away as fast as I could, and I must have taken your bag by mistake, not thinking."

"Not my bag," said Katherine. "It belongs to a friend of mine."

"Oh, I see. But you were in the shop, weren't you? I remember you, now I come to think."

"I bought some aspirins."

"Yes, you did, I remember. But how did you know who I was—who it belonged to, I mean?" said Miss Parbury. She took up the thin little poker that hung from an ornamental fireirons-stand and prodded a coal uselessly.

"The chemist said your name and address were in it. He told me where you lived."

"How lucky—because there's nothing in your bag— in the other one, I mean. There was nothing I could have done, except perhaps take it back there to the shop. I was in a stew about it. Still, all's well that ends well, though I shouldn't say that, should I?—the cause of all the trouble. I'll fetch your bag, it's upstairs. And you will have a cup of tea, won't you?"

"Well, I don't——"

"Oh yes! But you must. It's such a very cold day. I won't be a jiffy."

Miss Parbury went out, and Katherine heard her scamper up the stairs in her carpet-slippers. She was a quaint, sloppy person, and Katherine had been wondering increasingly how any such letter could have been written to her. Because it seemed so incongruous. In her woollen jumper and cardigan she was breathless and rather grotesque; her pale eyes bulged somewhat and her neck was too long. She was one of the people who do not look right till they are nearly fifty, when their eccentric appearance harmonizes with the caricaturing onset of age. But now, for she could only be thirty at the most, vestiges of youth still clung about her, and while she did not look as if she had ever been pretty, she still kept a gaucheness of manner that would have been suitable only in a very young girl. It made her laughable.

Left alone, Katherine looked round. Sometimes, when her own attic depressed her, she thought for comfort how miserable she would be living with a family, and looking round now she knew she sometimes forgot how ugly the English houses were. This room was overcrowded with gimcrack furniture, and the furniture overcrowded with trifling ornaments and photographs, fancy matchbox stands and little woolly dogs made of pipecleaners. On the wall were a few framed, coloured photographs, extraordinarily unpleasant to look at. On the small square table was a table-centre with a basket of wild flowers, somehow dried and coloured into permanency. But Katherine looked for other things than these. She wondered first who else lived there. There was nothing masculine in the room, nothing cross-grained; no pipes, or bottles of lighter-fluid, or textbooks on building construction or pigeons. In fact apart from the one Miss Parbury was reading, there were no books in the room except a small shelf in the window, and this was filled with dreary rubbish, such as a Holiday Haunts for 1928. This gave the room a slack, soulless air. Through the window she could see a depressing yard, with a bucket standing in the snow, and a high wall. Who else lived in the house beside Miss Parbury? She had mentioned her mother. Perhaps they lived alone together. What could be her "point of view"?

She yawned, and leaned back in her easy chair, which was less comfortable than it looked. Very faintly she could hear music, as if a wireless set were playing in the next house. Miss Parbury came flopping downstairs and went into the kitchen, where she could be heard rattling spoons and saucers and singing what sounded like a hymn. There was a small book of Common Prayer lying on the sideboard bound in crimson. Eventually she came in with a large tray, on which were two large cups of tea and another brown handbag.

"Here we are," she said, beaming. "And here's your bag. I hope your friend won't mind, but I had to borrow fourpence from her to get home. Here is the money." She gave Katherine the bag and four pennies from the pocket of her cardigan.

"Thank you," said Katherine, slipping them in and snapping it shut.

"Now we can have a quiet cup of tea before you go out again. It was really very good of you to come at all." She gave Katherine a cup, strong, and, as she discovered at the first sip, virulently sugared. "Have you far to go? Whereabouts do you live?"

"Oh, right in the city," said Katherine. She instinctively disliked saying where she lived. "I have a sort of flat."

"Oh, have you? I believe it's frightfully difficult to find rooms these days. Do you share it at all?"

"No. I've been here about nine months. I came from London."

"From London! It must have been terrible there while the raids were on."

"It could have been worse. London's a big place."

"Oh, but I'm terrified. As soon as those sirens start, my bones turn to water. That awful moaning." She drank some more tea as if to steady herself.

They talked for a little while about the war, and the circumstances that had brought Katherine to England. Miss Parbury was a very sympathetic listener. Katherine noticed she wore no rings on her fingers.

"I think it's dreadful," she said at the finish. "And so you just have to start all over again, in a foreign country—start a new life altogether!"

194

Katherine moved the spoon in her saucer. "Perhaps so."

"When you think of it, we've nothing to grumble at in England, at least, I suppose I should speak for myself." Miss Parbury smiled brightly. "A home and enough to eat. And I've lost no-one."

Katherine agreed subduedly.

"Of course, it's been terrible," said Miss Parbury. She cocked her head as if thoughtful. "But if it had happened differently . . . I mean, I expect you won't think so, but wouldn't it have been rather—well—fun—to come to England?"

"I had been before," said Katherine. Two hours and five minutes after midday.

"Oh, had you? I only thought that it would be nice to be suddenly on one's own—if there wasn't a war, of course."

"If there wasn't a war, I shouldn't be here."

"Everything would be different, of course." Miss Parbury sighed.

"But to be on one's own is very lonely," said Katherine. "Don't you agree?"

She said this as a kind of bait for whatever lay unrevealed in this depressing, bright room.

"I expect so," said Miss Parbury, adding primly: "I've always lived at home."

"Oh yes." Angling in the dark, she said: "It isn't like having a home of one's own."

Miss Parbury shook her head. She did not seem communicative on this. But later she said: "After Father died, I felt I had to look after Mother."

"Yes, of course." Katherine could still see no trace of any other person in the house. "Is she out now?"

Miss Parbury looked up, as if startled out of a train of thought. "Oh no, she's upstairs. She's ill."

"Oh, I'm sorry." Katherine prepared to abandon the subject. "I hope she'll soon get better."

"No, she's an invalid." Miss Parbury sounded a little impatient that Katherine did not understand.

"Oh, I see. I'm sorry."

"When Father died," said Miss Parbury flatly, after a pause, "she had a sort of stroke." In the silence the wireless sounded still, now relaying a tango orchestra and she moved her head. "I think she likes to listen to the wireless," she said with a return to cheerfulness. "I think it cheers her up."

Katherine nodded vaguely.

"But the neighbours complain sometimes," said Miss Parbury, with the faintest indignation. "Of course, she does have it on all day. Though as I say, it's different when someone's ill, isn't it? You have to make allowances."

"Yes, of course."

Miss Parbury brooded a little.

"It is hard when a person's ill," said Katherine. "Won't she ever get better?"

A shade had come over Miss Parbury's face, as if speaking of sad things made her sad, in a childish way. Midway between youth and middle age as she was, her appearance called up both: it was easy to imagine her in ten years' time, more withered, more wispy, the veins showing on the backs of her hands, perhaps wearing rimless spectacles; but all the same there were moments when she looked simply like an overgrown girl, in her flat-heeled slippers. From the gawkiness of youth she was passing to the grotesqueness of age, and at no point would she touch the handsomeness of maturity.

"No," she said. "I'm afraid she won't. Just after the war started she had another stroke. She can't move now, it paralysed her right side. The doctor says she may live for some years yet. But eventually one will be fatal."

She put her head on one side and stared at the grate.

"What does she do all the time?" said Katherine. "Can she read?"

"Oh dear no," said Miss Parbury. From her decided tone Katherine might have suggested something far more unusual. "No, she doesn't read now, though once she did. . . . She can't, her mind sometimes wanders. One just has to be patient with her."

"Wanders?" said Katherine, with misgiving.

"Oh, she's all right some of the time. But sometimes she doesn't know who I am." Miss Parbury looked at Katherine as if willing to let her find this comical. "And she has sort of delusions. She thinks I'm trying to harm her—poison her food, and that kind of thing. The doctor says I mustn't take any notice. But I don't know what to do if she won't eat what I give her."

Katherine said nothing. The fire was burning sluggishly, as if resentful of the cold.

"And then she'll say—oh, all sorts of funny things, like that Daddy comes at nights and talks to her. I often hear her talking in the night. Of course, she means no harm, but it's not nice when there's no-one in the house." Miss Parbury spoke in a reasonable, slightly complaining voice, as if explaining why she was behind with her rent. She had an apologetic air. "She says he warns her that I'm trying to harm her. It's just impossible to make her see reason, be-cause she doesn't know what she's saying or doing. Once I was ill for a week and we had a nurse in. We had to, you see. And she tried to give the nurse all sorts of things —anything—spoons, vases, one of the clocks. Of course the nurse told me about it and didn't take them. But after she'd gone I found she'd taken mother's fur, a lovely fur I'd wrapped up in tissue and mothballs, one she wouldn't ever have used again. Mother must have said she could have it. She wouldn't answer when I asked her if she had."

A coal spat suddenly. The room was dark enough to have the light on. Katherine said:

"But you mean you have to do everything by yourself?"

"She's quite helpless."

"Helpless," repeated Katherine. "But with the work for you—it would be better if she were in a hospital," she added, rebelling against this conspiracy to make Miss Parbury into a tragic personality, which she was not, being rather comic.

Miss Parbury said in a surprised voice:

"But there's nothing she needs that I can't——"

Katherine blinked. Miss Parbury had taken the point exactly the wrong way round. More gently she said:

"It would be easier for you."

Miss Parbury seemed to consider the suggestion, though she must have thought of it many times before. She moved her head on her long neck, like a timid animal.

"No," she said finally, "I couldn't do it. These places, you know, they haven't the consideration, and the nurses eat the things you send. She wouldn't be happy there."

"But it isn't right, that you should have to be the one who suffers." As Miss Parbury continued to look enquiringly at her, as if she had never heard this viewpoint, Katherine sought to be reasonable. "I think, if someone is entirely dependent on you, there's something wrong somewhere. It shouldn't be asked, or given." And if she had listened to what she was saying, she would have visualized life and happiness like ration tokens, that once spent are never recovered, and are allotted equally to everyone. "When you make kindness a duty, everybody resents it—it's such a mistake, I think."

"One has to do what one can," murmured Miss Parbury, "surely."

"For a definite time, perhaps—three or six months. But for always—I should insist on a definite arrangement. It is always a mistake to be kind, because people are cross if you leave off then for a moment, and you are tied for life."

"To do for the best," Miss Parbury was excusing herself bewilderedly. It grew darker and their exchange died away in a mutter of Katherine's protesting it was none of her business, having just thought that no doubt that there was not enough money to send the mother to a hospital: the dull light hid their faces. But Miss Parbury settled this as quickly as if she had heard it asked, saying in a voice disclaiming personal implication:

"There is the money, of course. Father was in the navy and so there's a pension, but it would cost too much to—I have been having to think that over, as I have a friend who suggested we become engaged, and that would make things very much more difficult. Then——"

"Then she would *have* to be taken care of."

"Or live with us. That's what I think the best, because you can't ask an old person to make such a change, can you? But that doesn't suit all parties. My friend is very strongly against that, and, really, I can see his point of view, because it's always such an unsuccessful arrangement, isn't it? But what I say is, it's inevitable, and we should just have to make the best of it, that is, if we——"

"Well, and you are right, I think."

"The only thing is," said Miss Parbury, who, having started to tell the story because it oppressed her and because it showed that someone besides her mother needed her, was now quite wound up in the problem again and free from whatever embarrassment hindered her volatile spirit, "my friend says he is willing to help with what it would cost, sending her away."

Katherine looked across the hearthrug to where she sat, oddly like an incarnation of some loved childish grotesquerie—Rhoda Rabbit or Lolly Flopears—and thought that she had heard nothing stranger than this, a man paying to have Miss Parbury with him always, and that man to be Anstey: and at this she happened to see both of them less as people than as the "other person" who is so necessary. Looking at her, still hearing the unexpected sentence, she glimpsed the undertow of peoples' relations, two-thirds of which is without face, with only begging and lonely hands.

"And so," she said interrogatively.

Miss Parbury laughed, self-reproachfully. "I'm silly," she said. "I always have been. I know I'm silly, but, do you know, I can't decide. I don't like the idea, even now. It would be convenient, and so easy, and no-one could say anything very well, but I should never feel quite happy in my mind about it. It's the real test, you know, isn't it, when you feel: 'I shouldn't like it to be done to me.' "

"But it is surely reasonable——"

"Oh, but I couldn't think of her among strangers. There'd be times when she'd wonder where I was, the same as she wonders where Daddy is now sometimes. She doesn't understand, you see. And I should hate to feel I hadn't done all I could, if anything . . . It can't be for very long."

"But it seems so unfair that *you* should have to do it."

"There *is* no-one else. My brother is in Darlington, and he's got a family of his own. No," said Miss Parbury, as if gently rebuking her, "I've thought it all over. There's no other way. I suppose it's just bad luck, though it's wrong of me to say so. One has to look after one's parents when they're old and need you."

And Miss Parbury's manner, lacking both reticence and self-praise, seemed to take on a new grace, as if Katherine's reproval had stirred something asleep in her nature that had now risen gently to its full height, and which it was no use attacking. Because she did not quite understand it, she was resentful, and so called it stupidity. She was simultaneously aware that almost any member of Anstey's staff would have given a week's pay to be in her present position. "And what of your friend, don't you feel you owe something to him?" she countered, trading recklessly on what she had noticed, that people would tell her things they would not tell a fellow-countryman. "And yourself, too, supposing he will not wait."

Miss Parbury's hesitation was only very slight, but it made Katherine afraid that she had remembered what letter had been in her bag. But her expression when she lifted her head was quite undirected, only myopic with what Katherine recognized with a shock as sorrow.

"That's as must be," she said. "I don't want to hurt anyone except myself, but if I do, it's not because I'm being selfish. I may not be right, but all one can do is go by one's own judgement, isn't it? I can't understand," said Miss Parbury, pulling a handkerchief from her sleeve, "what people mean by a duty to oneself. It sounds so silly. I don't think I could ever like a person who didn't see what I meant, not in that way."

And to both their embarrassments she dropped a few tears, her shoulders being plucked lightly by the never-distant emotion of grief.

Katherine sat wretchedly for the half-minute it took Miss Parbury to stifle her sobbing, finished her cold tea, and put the cup aside. At what seemed the correct moment she said she ought to be going, and Miss Parbury regained the last trace of self-control. "Well!" she said, rising and touching her sickly lemon necklace. "I've been talking, as usual, talking and making myself miserable. I'm sure you want to be getting off. Now, have you got your friend's bag? It wouldn't do to take the wrong one this time! I'm very obliged to you for bringing it back," she added, as she held the door open and followed Katherine into the hall.

"I've never been in this part of the town before."

"Are you sure you can find your way? I'm afraid it's getting quite misty."

"Oh yes, I think I can find my way to the bus-stop, at least."

"It's an easy part to get lost in," said Miss Parbury,

going to the front door. As she did so, there came a noise from upstairs that sounded unnaturally through the small house.

It was as if someone were trying to crush a beetle by banging the end of a walking-stick on the floor. The blows were irregular, and unevenly loud.

Miss Parbury said nothing, but opened the door with a smile, letting in the cold.

As Katherine moved to go past her, the noise faltered, and was replaced by a voice. If it had been an ordinary voice, they could have heard what it said, for it was shouting. But it was not: there was only a series of distorted vowels, as might be uttered by a person without a tongue. It croaked and blurted, unexpectedly deep. After two outbursts it stopped. Then there was another thump. The sound of the tango orchestra continued undisturbed.

"Good-bye," said Miss Parbury. "And thank you again for all your trouble."

"Good-bye," said Katherine.

She hurried away.

4

Miss Parbury had been right about the mist. It had deepened until round the centre of the city it was nearly a fog. But it was not coiling or humid; simply a gauze, that might have been the accumulated breath frozen from many mouths, or a very incarnation of the cold. The buses she caught nosed through it cautiously, like fogbound ships, their shaded lights helping them very little, and it was fourteen minutes past three when she got back to the Library again, scuttling up the steps on the heels of Saturday-afternoon borrowers.

Quickly putting on her red overall, she went to the counter and started receiving books at once, her fingers flying over the tightly-packed files of tickets as if to make up for lost time. Miss Brooks was working there too, her hands defiantly mittened, but with the same watery good-humour. "Been on the spree?" she said. "Well, you haven't missed anything here."

"I got delayed," said Katherine.

"What's it like out now? Getting worse?"

"It's no better."

"I can feel it isn't." Miss Brooks put some money away and reached down for a book that had been reserved.

Miss Feather, who had been doing Katherine's work instead of her own, now returned from the shelves. Katherine could feel her approaching, and tried to busy herself, but just at that moment the influx of borrowers was slack. So she turned to face her.

"Oh, there you are, dear. I was wondering what had become of you."

"The fog was rather bad," said Katherine.

"Yes, it is bad, isn't it? We've been rather busy. Never mind." Miss Feather glanced conspiratorially round her. "Mr. Anstey would like to see you: I think he's in now. So would you go along and see him, dear? I'll carry on for the moment."

"All right."

"Oh, and just one other thing"—Miss Feather played with the ornamental and probably worthless old ring she wore on her left-hand little finger. "Just one teeny word of advice . . . It doesn't do, you know, to tell that Green child anything."

Katherine was puzzled. "Tell her what?"

"Well, anything, dear. It isn't wise. She repeats everything she hears—simply everything. It's best not to tell her anything at all."

"But I haven't been telling her anything——"

Miss Feather wagged her head, as if distressed at this refusal to accept a word in season, murmured something else and turned to three borrowers congregated at the entrance wicket, bending on her ancient legs to answer a question. Katherine, who had not given Miss Green a thought for some time, hesitated a moment, then pushed through the opposite wicket and walked slowly along the dim passage to Mr. Anstey's door.

She could hear Mr. Anstey telephoning, so prepared to wait till he had finished, leaning against the wall. What a day this was being! Her good spirits, desperately resisting the weariness of her errand through the streets strewn with worn-out snow, and Miss Parbury, whom she wanted to forget, were now swerving downwards because she was back where she started. It was strange that even after all these months she could never enter this mausoleum of a building without a bitter feeling of voluntary degradation. And what was it now, what would Anstey be bothering about? She could hardly bear seeing him again. She felt tired and raw, and in need of rest.

And everything was becoming so confused. It was three and a half hours after midday: Robin might have come and gone, because of her foolishness in leaving him no message. And what in the world had Miss Feather meant by saying that about Miss Green? She hadn't been telling her anything and didn't intend to. Why couldn't they mind their own affairs and leave her alone?

She wished she could throw everything up and go back to her room.

Mr. Anstey's voice was scraping away inside the door, and she winced at the thought of its being turned on her. He was so loathsome. Yet she realized with annoyance that she could not hate him as simply as she had done, now that she had come across this part of him that had no bearing on her. For her conception of him as a hostile cartoon she had to substitute a person who had and could

204

evoke feelings, who would undertake the support of an old woman, and on whose account she had seen another crying. Why had she been allowed to come across it all? It was repellent to her as an insanitary tangle of snakes in a crevice. It spoilt her dislike of him: when next she saw his mean face looking up at her, she would—if she were honest—be forced to juggle with rights and wrongs, instead of plainly wishing him dead.

This irked her the more because it hinted at things Miss Parbury had shown her that she did not want to recognize. Having tried for so long to live for herself alone, having concluded that not even the maximum selfishness would secure the happiness she felt herself entitled to, it was disturbing to meet one who valued these things so lightly. It reminded her of a girl she had known who had given up a career to enter a convent. During the one conversation they had had on the subject, the girl had said that care for oneself seemed to her less wicked than stupid—like carrying an umbrella on a cloudless day. Katherine had never forgotten her own surprise at this. If she thought on such matters, it was that one should try to accept any misfortune with equanimity. But this other viewpoint, that flung away at the start all conception of fortune and misfortune, this she found herself reluctantly respecting, and she could recognize her present respect by her knowledge that she would probably tell no-one of what she had learned that day. Certainly she would have liked to feed her contempt with giggling, but she knew also that if she thought long enough about it, the affair would make her feel small. Therefore she would sooner forget it.

When she heard the receiver being replaced, she knocked on the door.

"Yes, who is it there, come in," he shouted.

She entered resentfully. He was writing at his desk, the cigarette in his mouth having burnt so near to his lips that he held his head awkwardly back, squinting through the very bottoms of his spectacles. But he soon laid his pen aside, looking at her in an ugly manner.

"Yes, Miss Lind, I was wanting a few words with you. I've one or two little things I want to make clear." He blotted his writing unnecessarily, and thrust his head forward on his scraggy neck. She looked at the parting of his hair, wondering if she could hear anything in the world about him that would make her like him. It was improbable. "You have been with us now some time, six months——"

"Nearly nine."

He disregarded this, settling back for a harangue.

"And of course it was not to be expected that you'd pick up the job and start pulling your weight in the very first week, for the simple reason that the profession we are engaged in here is not one that any Tom, Dick, and Harry can qualify himself for, can *fit* himself for, in a fortnight or three weeks. Furthermore"—he took the half-inch stub carefully from his mouth and replaced it by a fresh cigarette from a paper packet on his desk—"there were a number of other circumstances or factors in your particular case which, to put it bluntly, made it a bit of a gamble to appoint you." He sucked the new cigarette alight. "I refer of course to the undoubted fact that in addition to your whatyoumaycall, the fact that you were fresh to this kind of work, you had by the nature of your birth and upbringing, more to learn than the average applicant about the kind of—*literature*, if we may so call it for the purposes of argument—with which, leaving aside for a moment other departments in which your talents and education would be a decided asset—you would have to deal. However, when I was consulted as to your appointment, I supported it notwithstanding these points, because I was of the opinion that a person of your education would have what is sometimes called the ordinary horse-sense to pick things up as you went along."

Katherine could not remember how many times he had said this. The first time was at their first interview. The last, for all she could recall, was probably that same morning. There was nothing in it she need pay attention to. She thought of Miss Parbury.

"Now," Mr. Anstey recommenced, "although I may not have said all this in so many words to you until today, I assumed, as I was I think entitled to assume, that these circumstances were as well known to you as they were to me." As if noticing that she was watching him only vaguely, his voice grew harsher and more deliberate. "However, it is beginning to appear to me that whether they were or not, you are going about your work in a casual way, a way which I don't hesitate for a moment in informing you to be *a way I don't like.* To put the matter bluntly, as I am accustomed to do, if you think that on account of the education you have received you are entitled to work when it suits your book and expect us to be grateful for the honour, you have got hold of the wrong end of the stick, Miss Lind, and the sooner you let go of it the better for everyone."

Katherine glared at him. He had certainly caught her attention.

"What are you complaining about?"

"I am complaining about your clearing off this morning, Miss Lind, without so much as a by-your-leave to anyone, and leaving the already-overworked staff to do your job as well as their own until such time in the afternoon as you think fit to honour us with your presence again." He had raised his voice to say this. "That is one of the things I am complaining of, Miss Lind."

"But you gave me permission yourself, or Miss Feather did," Katherine retorted. She hated his mean jaws looking up at her.

He made a contemptuous gesture. "The facts were, if I am correct in saying so, that one of the juniors needed taking to a doctor or a dentist by some responsible person. I am not prepared to split hairs in arguing how long that particular job or errand would take anyone, but it is I think obvious to anyone possessed of any intelligence that *at the very most, at the very outside*, it should not take anyone more than one hour, and probably a sight less," he added spitefully, with a look of such intensity that ash fell from the cigarette he had so far not removed from his mouth. She was going to say something, but he continued with an unfunny theatrical leer: "Naturally I didn't come to you and say, Oh, Miss Lind, be sure and come straight back when you've finished, don't stop at any sweet-shops or get carried off by the gipsies; that I thought would be unnecessary and uncalled-for, as I was speaking to a person of intelligence."

"What happened was this. Miss Green wanted to go home, so we took the bus to Bank Street. Then she felt ill, and I persuaded her to go to a dentist nearby. She had a bad time there and I took her to my room to rest. When she left to go home it was after twelve and I didn't think it was worth while to come back, just until one o'clock."

"And I presume you didn't think it worth while to have your lunch and then return straightway to make up for the work you hadn't done? Why, hang it, to use a common expression, you didn't even consider it worth while to be back at *three* o'clock, the normal time stipulated for your duties to recommence. And in any case," he said, sniffing vindictively, "leaving aside the hours from twelve till three, what takes the lynch-pin out of your story, what blows down the whole pack of cards, is the fact that Miss Green, however badly you say she felt and all the rest of it, Miss Green at least had the decency and the sense of— the *guts*, to put it crudely, to come back here at *half-past two*, in order to do the job she is paid for, and it seems to me as clear as daylight that if such is the case, as it undoubtedly is, your side of the picture or whateveryoucall looks pretty thin; in fact, I may say, to me, Miss Lind, it looks downright shabby."

"I think she was very silly to come back," said Katherine. So that was it. She was beginning to get angry. "I advised her not to for her own good."

Mr. Anstey lifted his chin. "Your position here hardly entitles you to tell members of the staff what to do. And another matter," he went on harshly, over something she burst out with, "another thing I don't want happening in future is to have your boy-friends ringing up whenever they please and sending messages and telegrams at all hours." He said this coarsely. "It is not my policy——"

"What do you mean?"

"*It is not my policy*, Miss Lind, to take cognisance of what members of my staff do when they leave this building after their working hours. I don't consider it is anything to do with me and frankly I do not give a twopenny damn, provided their work is done properly and they keep their affairs clear of mine—but when they don't keep to their part of the bargain, I no longer feel it incumbent on me to keep mine, and I take this opportunity of telling you that I don't want it to happen again."

"Who has been ringing me up?"

Mr. Anstey shuffled among the papers on his desk, and drew out a half-sheet. "It was a telegram sent by telephone," he said, sniffing. "Otherwise I should have refused to take it." He stared contemptuously at the four words pencilled in his own finical hand, then flicked it across to her.

She read it: "Sorry cancel meeting. Robin".

"Thank you," she said, and put it in her pocket.

He took the thin cigarette from his mouth and crushed it out. "Well, I have work to do, and so have you. The plain bones of the matter is just this: if you're prepared to work at this job, we shall get on splendidly. But if you're not, then all I can say is we shall get along without you very well. So if you consider yourself too good for us, well, you know what to do." He wagged a pencil at her and laughed, with an almost inconceivable hint of jocularity.

She snatched the pencil from him and stood panting a moment, as if going to fling it at his head or break it in two. He looked at her blankly with his shoulders hunched and bad teeth showing. Then she threw it down on the desk. "I will go," she said breathlessly. "I will—I hate——" To control her anger she threw up her head, finding it hard to breathe. "I'll leave now. How soon can I leave?"

"Your appointment was subject to a month's notice," he said colourlessly, as if considering something they were not talking about. "Notice of resignation should be addressed in writing to the City Librarian."

"Give me some paper. I'll write it now."

It was odd, if she had thought about it, that her outrageous behaviour had rather taken him aback without making him angry. "You can do as you please," he said, scratching his ear sourly. "But if you want my opinion you'll think twice before doing anything like that."

"I don't want it at all!"

"You could be a sight worse off, let me tell you, a sight worse off." He thrust his head at her again, but absently. "You're not going to find any job where you can do as you please, especially as you're situated now. You'd better by far stick at what you're doing, and be thankful, even though it may be unfamiliar to you. My advice——"

She would have liked to squash him with a great stone where he sat. "Oh, shut up with your advice, shut up. I don't want it, you bore me stiff with such things." She drew a deep breath to stop herself panting. "Keep it. Keep it for your Miss Greens and Miss Feathers and your silly Veronica Parbury," drawling out the last three words with an exaggerated foreign accent she had learned annoyed people.

She hardly knew she had said it till she saw its effect on him. It had exploded like a depth-charge. He sat in his chair as stiffly as a corporal who has been told to remain seated by a field-marshal.

That's finished him, she thought.

He began to speak as she left the room.

5

By four o'clock, all the lights had been switched on, and shortly afterwards the long black curtains were clashed together, each with the noise of a scythe-stroke, to shut out the pallid end of the day. Under the hanging lights the building seemed suddenly empty, and indeed fewer borrowers were coming in to shuffle their suspicious way round the shelves. They were going home for tea, or if they had not left home a glance from the window at the fog discouraged them from doing so. Katherine and Miss Brooks could therefore shelve the overflowing "returned" racks without interruption. They slapped books together, put them in alphabetical or numerical order, and bore armfuls of them off, to be nosed and slammed back onto the shelves.

For Katherine had gone back to work, hardly knowing what she was doing. And once back, she shrank from leaving conspicuously. It was easy, too, to join in the pallid duties as usual, it composed her trembling hands, and it prevented her thoughts from settling into colourless stillness, like stirring a teaspoon in a glass of cold water. So she worked on, handling the sombre leather-bound books like so many blocks of soft wood, making herself listen to the borrowers who came hurrying in from the cold and, as far as possible, finding them what they wanted. Their voices, and the hushed noises as the staff worked, did not press on her; they were indeed barely audible, as if this was the first half-hour after a loud explosion that had partly affected her hearing.

When every few minutes she turned to face what was in her mind, and the thought that Robin was not coming met her, her grief would break in a little shivering wave, and then reform. She need not have worried and reproached herself; he had not even started. How silly she had been, pretending to be at last turned outward to the people round her, trying to express her rediscovered gratitude to that sickening girl. Even more of a fool, because there had been other, unexpressed fancies: the way she would be swept off to their home, like a long-lost cousin, dropping an airy resignation to the City Librarian, to make herself useful about that fascinating house until Mr. Fennel could find her a remunerative job which she could do while still continuing to live with them; and then of course the slow ripening of her friendship with Robin into love, a love firmer and reciprocal, yet still bearing the fervour of their first acquaintance—or, if this last was too much to swallow, then at least some male friend of the family who would eventually hold out to her love, security, happiness, and a British passport. But disregarding such emetics, the plain news that he was not coming was enough to obscure her mind. Finding herself shut out into her own life again, all her nature beat upon his refusal, begging to be readmitted to the easy happiness she had been remembering. She was forsaken among the broken spars of the day. And because there was a trace of superstition in her, it crossed her mind that it was her fault for leaving him no word. She should not have been so proud and hesitant. She should have expected him, and then he would have come.

But nothing could argue away the loss. He had been the power that had set this extraordinary day moving, that increased its speed until she and a few other chance things and people were drawn up in a kind of whirling tower of air, their faces meeting, their hands touching, seemingly the only things left in the world. And now, like the switching-off of a current, he said he was not coming, and they were all left there, spinning in the emptiness, till the impetus should be exhausted and they were tumbled back on the floor.

Already she was falling. She had seen them as extraordinary, this Anstey, this Miss Parbury, this Miss Green, as if their faces were phosphorescent with a significance she did not grasp, linked with whatever had sent her to them. This was fading. And she had an unpleasant sense that she was going to fall farther than she had risen. She was gradually getting her recollections of her scene with Anstey under control, like a heath-fire, and viewed in the wintry light her behaviour had been serious. She had said and done things for which she might be called to account. But he should not have made her angry! She threw up her head as the sentences blazed again, scorching her. How vile he was, how deliberately he had told her about Miss Green and the telegram from Robin, treading her down, how glad she was if she had hurt him! Glad because there was no denying she had behaved badly, like a housemaid being ticked off and replying with personal insults. But at present she was too distracted to say more than, If that is how I react, if that is what I instinctively say, then it's my nature and I must abide by it.

This recalled Miss Green to her, and Katherine remembered that she still had her handbag. It had better be returned before Miss Green left work at five, though she would as readily have thrown it in the canal, but once it was given back there would be no more contact. That would be a good thing, at any rate. So Miss Feather had warned her that it didn't do to tell that Green child anything? That meant she had come back, ill as she was, full

213

of tales about the silent Miss Lind, how she lived alone, and how after six years she was meeting a strange love of her childhood. Katherine felt as if she had suffered a slug to crawl across her. And beyond that, weariness, oceans-long.

"These old things, they'd lose their heads if they were loose," said Miss Brooks in an undertone, for an old woman was insisting she had lost her purse. The old woman held her mouth very tightly and suspiciously, hardly moving her head, accusing no one but detailing the facts of the loss over and over again.

Katherine went out to the cloakroom, took the hand-bag from her coat-pocket, and went round to the Junior Library. It would be as well to get it over. When she saw Miss Green serving the shabby, clumping urchins she was not very angry. Her anger had spent itself earlier. She only wondered at her own blindness. As soon as Miss Green saw Katherine, she seemed to stiffen up and become busier, so Katherine had to wait a minute or two. How sly she looked, thin and cross. And the room was poky; it had been a storeroom till it had been converted, and it smelt inimitably of poor children. Katherine looked at the stock—disordered, upside down, lying on their sides —all beaten by use into a uniform dirty brown. Here and there were prettily-designed cards noticing certain kinds of books: but somehow these had got thumbed or even ripped, though there was no reason why anyone should touch them.

When Miss Green was free she went up to her.

"Here's your bag. I got it back all right."

"Thank you——" Miss Green seemed almost too confused to speak. "—good of you." She held her head back as if rearing from something unpleasant.

Katherine laid it on the counter. She felt it was no use saying much.

"So you came back," she said.

"Yes—I . . . after I'd laid down, I didn't feel so bad . . . take my mind off it——" Miss Green tittered inaudibly. "Er . . . who'd taken it?"

"A silly woman. She apologized."

There was a pause.

"Mother is washing and ironing the hanky you lent me," said Miss Green suddenly, as if this was a sentence she had prepared. "And——"

She took a twist of paper from her pocket and spilled five half-crowns onto the wooden counter.

"Here is what I owe you, thank you very much, it was very kind of you, I'll give you the hanky on Monday."

"Thank you," said Katherine. She took up the money and after saying a few more words went back to work.

In winter the library closed at seven o'clock, and usually the last hour was busy. This night there was enough to keep the assistants occupied, but because of the weather hardly as many people came as on a middle-week night. Those that did were people who did not mind the weather and had nowhere else to go; young mechanics, with oil engrained in their palms, one or two sixth-form children, couples of young married women who had slipped over from a nearby housing estate, coming in pairs because they were afraid of the darkness.

Time usually went quickly between six and seven, but with the unusual slackness it seemed to drag, and the day's business was petering out instead of rising to a sharp climax. Katherine hardly noticed it. On this night, as on a hundred other nights, she went about her work, dressed neatly in her red overall, under the electric lights that shone pallidly on her dark hair and composed, sullen mouth: except that she was a little slow when spoken fo, it could not be guessed that her thoughts were astray. Like the work she was helping to do, they were slowing, sweeping round in long circles that fell a little each time, touching

215

this, touching that, but always dropping further away from the exaltation that had faded with the daylight. The memory of the shelter by the icy fountain, where she had wished to help Miss Green more than even herself, was distant and despicable, and she avoided, too, thinking of Miss Parbury, for that was all ugly (making her ashamed). Instead she preferred to recall the look on his face—as if he had broken a tooth—when she had left him. Yes, there had been revenge there, and if she hadn't been so tired she would have warmed her hands at it, shutting out for the moment the uncertain state of things, whether she had resigned, whether she would have to leave. This was no doubt very important: it would knock away her security, that she had won so hardly, and set her once more on the move. She would hate that.

But did she really care what she did in England? There would be other things for her to do, and whatever it was she would do it unwillingly, obstinately, as if she were working in a field; what she did would be emptied away like a painfully-filled basket, and her time would be spilled away with it. There would be sleep, simply to freshen her again for work; there would be other Miss Greens, Miss Parburys, Mr. Ansteys; all this was inescapable, and it did not matter if she accepted it or not. It accepted her.

Only, there would be no more Robins. And as her thoughts came down finally to rest on his name, she knew what he meant to her. He was in the forefront of a time when she had come to this same strange country, and had been welcomed by strangers and taken in among them. She had moved into a world that might have been a country dance, when, dressed in white, she had momentarily joined hands with the one in yellow, the one in green, the lavender and the sprigged-rose. She saw herself attached first to one, then another, with emotions that could be snipped off like flowers, only to make the next crop more luxuriant. And she thought in some way he might lead her back to it. What a pretty thought it was, and how untrue. She had known it was untrue. It had kept her from writing to them as soon as she arrived, and when she had at last written to Jane it had been desperately, almost drunkenly; she had seized the slightest chance of escaping the desolation that was pressing upon her. It had lain at the bottom of her hesitation even that afternoon, when she could not think why she did not take every precaution against missing him.

Now she had missed him, she saw this clearly. Better sooner than later. And, with what strength she had left after this day, she had to face what remained. She did not bother to formulate it clearly; she knew well enough what it was. Life would be happy insofar as she was happy, sad insofar as she was sad. The happiness would depend on her youth and health, and would help no-one. When she was ill, it would drop away, like the flame of a wick being turned down; when she grew old, it would be thin and infrequent. And in these times no other thing or person would be able to help her, though they might try sincerely, and she might try equally sincerely to be helped. But they would not be able to touch any more than people standing ten yards apart can take each others' hands. Truly she had done more than come to England; in these past eighteen months she had broken ground she never dreamed existed, so that at first it had seemed an unreality. Now it had shrunken slightly into the truth.

The time came at last when work for the evening was nearly over. Miss Feather switched off lights over individual cases, as a hint to the few borrowers that remained, then, returning to the entrance, put out the first row of lights that hung at the far end of the hall. Katherine leaned against the counter and watched her do it.

Shadows appeared on the floor as they were extinguished. The hand of the clock moved precisely onto the hour, and the second row of lights went off. To watch them go out was like seeing the death of something. A woman dressed in black hurried to the counter, had her book stamped, and went quickly out, the wicket swinging back with a thud. The far end of the room was now quite dark.

"Another day gone," said Miss Brooks, with thin cheerfulness, coming to stand by her.

"And another week."

"Going away?"

"Are you?"

"Oh, I expect I shall go to my married sister's on Sunday. Usually do. Working on a Saturday doesn't give you much time, though, does it? You've no chance."

"Certainly you haven't."

They were silent.

"Saw you trapesing along to see Anstey again this afternoon," said Miss Brooks. "Had enough of him today, haven't you?"

"Too much. We had a real exchange of personalities."

"Oh dear. Well, I'm not surprised."

"I've a good mind to resign."

"What would you do?"

"I don't know. If I did I wouldn't wait."

"Not getting married or anything?"

"Getting married? Of course not. Where did that idea come from?" Miss Brooks looked rather ashamed. "Has our Miss Green been spreading romantic stories about me?"

"Oh, I wouldn't listen to anything *she* said."

Another row of lights went off.

"No harm if you did," said Katherine. "I only want to know what everyone thinks." As Miss Brooks kept stiffly silent she laughed and said: "I am not offended. I only want to know."

"Well, it wasn't Miss Green that told me," said Miss

Brooks, as if hurt that such a denial was necessary. Only people seemed to think you were late back because you'd met someone you used to know. And when you said . . . I thought you might mean that."

So that was all they had made of it.

"It was nothing like that at all. I met nobody."

She screwed up the pencilled message in Anstey's writing and threw it unobtrusively away. Miss Feather switched off the last set of lights, leaving all but the counter in darkness, and went along to the cloakroom. At the same moment Miss Holloway came up and leant across the entrance wicket. She had brisk black hair and horn spectacles.

"I left a pencil here somewhere," she observed. "Green, with a much-bitten end."

"Oh, I was using that. I was going to keep it."

"Shame on you. I say, did anyone find that book on Uganda?"

"Yes, I left it on your desk," said Katherine. "Didn't you see it?"

"Well, I never did. None so blind as them what will not see. I shan't bother now. Never do on Saturday what you can leave till Monday."

"If I don't feel better than I do now I shan't be here on Monday."

"Mittens no use?"

"You need mittens all over this weather. The pipes are stone cold. Feel them!"

"No thanks."

The three of them strolled along to the cloakroom, where one or two other girls were running combs through their hair.

"What about these questions," said Miss Holloway, tying a scarf round her head. "I'm convinced he's mixed us up with someone else, you know. Half the questions are things we've never touched."

She and Miss Brooks were both preparing by correspondence for the same examination.

"Oh, he was probably out on the tiles and couldn't think straight."

"I could do with a night on the tiles," said Miss Holloway. "I'm getting so horribly middle-aged. Do you know, a soldier gave me a seat in a bus today. Well, I mean, is that a compliment or not?"

"I feel a hundred, I'm sure."

In the entrance-hall the caretaker was following his broom about. "Good night," said Miss Holloway as they passed him. "Can't you get any more heat out of that boiler of yours on Monday?"

The caretaker burst into slow, incoherent abuse of his pay and superiors: he did not find speech easy and was content if his words were partially formed. This tirade followed them to the door. They chatted on the steps for a few minutes and then Miss Brooks left them, for she lived in the other direction.

"Good night, then."

"See you Monday."

"Good night."

"Can you see anything?" said Miss Holloway. "I'm not accustomed." She took Katherine's arm uncertainly. "Why do you dress up like a dirt-track rider?"

"Like a what?"

"This absurd coat."

"It keeps me warm. I know it's not elegant." The darkness had fastened tightly down onto the earth. There were no stars to be seen and although they knew their way to the bus-stop perfectly well, they edged forward very slowly through the blackness. Katherine slipped with a jar from the kerb to the gutter into the crusty snow. "Here, I thought you could see," grumbled Miss Holloway. She pulled her own coat closer round her neck. "This is the weather to lay you under the ground."

They rounded the corner and found their way to the bus-stop. To judge from their footfalls the fog had almost completely dispersed, and the air smelt frosty. Round the discreetly-lit door of a fish-saloon children clustered, newspapers of chips congealing in their bare hands. From a public-house, which had the word "open" cut irregularly into its matchwood blackout, came the sound of singing, accompanied by a piano of such distorted tone that it sounded like a mandoline. When they reached the bus-stop, they stood in silence for a time, for neither had anything to say that was worth the trouble of saying.

"I should like to ask your advice," said Katherine suddenly at last. Because they could not see each other she found it easier to speak. "I had a row with Anstey this afternoon. I'm not sure whether to resign or not."

Yet she said it almost for something to say. At the moment the problem seemed distant, and its different solutions indistinguishable from each other. However, to speak of it with someone else made it more natural, and among her casual acquaintances Miss Holloway was the one she would choose for such discussion. She was well-informed and unemotional. She would give an opinion quite uninfluenced by the fact that she was speaking to a person concerned. And Katherine felt this was the time she could best hear what Miss Holloway thought, when her own interest in the practical circumstances of her life had ebbed nearly to extinction.

"Surely you can please yourself?"

"I'm not sure if I can. You see, I lost my temper and said some things that mean you either resign quietly or get the sack." She waited a little, then said: "I said I'd resign, as a matter of fact, but I wish I hadn't. I've nowhere else to go."

"Well, then, don't resign. I wouldn't move an inch without knowing of a place to go to."

"Then I might get sacked."

"I doubt it," said Miss Holloway judicially. "Not unless you were really incompetent. You do your work all right, don't you?"

"Fairly well, though Anstey doesn't seem to think so."

"Then I don't think as things go at the moment that they'd ask you to go. Anstey has no powers of dismissal. They're bound to conscript women sooner or later, too, and I doubt if we'll be reserved—and I suppose you'd be exempt, wouldn't you?"

"I'm not sure. I did make some enquiries once, but they weren't very clear. I might be put in a factory."

"You see, you might be valuable in six months' time, when there's no-one but kids and old women, and I'll tell you another thing. Anstey did try to get someone sacked just at the beginning of the war, but Pollingbourne wouldn't have it: he just transferred her to another branch. That was rather a slap in the eye, wasn't it?"

"Mm."

"But I shouldn't ask to be transferred, because they'd just sit on you. And I shouldn't resign in the hope they'll transfer you, because they might accept your resignation and then you would be in a hole. Let them make the first move. I think, if you don't say anything, the whole affair will blow over."

"You don't think Anstey will keep on at me until I do resign?"

"No," said Miss Holloway. "I don't think I do. Anstey isn't that bad, you know. He's really quite decent. You see, he's got where he wanted to get, now, because of the war, and he's deadly afraid that afterwards he'll be stood down again. That makes him suspicious of everything and everybody. And he longs to be efficient, but he just isn't a big enough man for the job. I suppose he thinks if he can——"

At this point two slightly-intoxicated soldiers bumped intentionally into them, and apologized lavishly.

"That wasn't very clever of you," said Miss Holloway

coldly, as the soldiers grabbed theatrically at them for support in the darkness.

"Och, you don't know me," said one delightedly, in uncouth Scotch. "I'm a real clever chap."

"I'm sure. Wouldn't you like to take yourself for a little walk?"

He did not seem to grasp this, and, after a passing hiccough, added: "Ay, clever Jock, that's my name."

The other, who sounded much younger, clung round Katherine dazedly, saying in a fresh, slurred voice: "Where have you been all my life?"

The elder turned on him in apparent fury:

"Aw, get your legs under you, where's the guts Almighty God gave you——"

The other staggered, and at a heave from Katherine fetched up against the bus-stop, beginning to sing in a voice whose purity ebbed and flowed like the focusing and unfocusing of a telescope.

"Well now, it seems we're going the same way as you two young ladies," began the first soldier elaborately, but his grace bore no fruit because at that moment the double-decked bus loomed panting by the halt, lit from within by shrouded blue lights, and the younger soldier slid bemusedly down until he was sitting on the pavement with his back against the metal pole. The noise had gone out of him as from a slashed concertina. As they got onto the bus the first soldier called "Two bags!" in a clear, laconic voice, as if bidding at an auction.

"There goes your night on the tiles," said Katherine.

Miss Holloway did not go more than half-way with her, and they parted after ten minutes. "I should sleep on it," she said as she got up to go. "It will all seem different in the morning."

Katherine wondered if it would. She had half-dreaded to be alone, but now Miss Holloway had left her she found she was really too tired to feel it. Miss Holloway had been comforting: whether what she had said was true or not, it would relieve her of the trouble of doing anything. She wanted to avoid the fuss, it would be so meaningless. The bus rattled on. It was nearly empty. In front there were some girls and youths, talking noisily, who started to reiterate a song, a peculiar phrase that might prevent sleep at three in the morning. The blue light fell on their faces, the young men's hair coiled in unhealthy slabs, taking the colour from the girls' cosmetics, throwing ghastliness on their laughing faces. The floor was littered with tickets.

She got out at Bank Street. There were a few people huddled in doorways, or walking from cinemas, but the wide central streets were deserted of traffic, and the buildings were great silent locked shells. Here and there soldiers were shouting. At this time all the town had drawn within itself. The doors and windows were shut and curtains had been arranged across them, to keep the light and the warmth indoors. Outside there was none. There was no moon to show how the frost encrusted everything: the dark soared up like a cathedral, a blindness; it covered the town and the frozen allotments when the houses began to scatter into fields, then the brittle grass, and the woods. Convoys of lorries could get along the main roads with chains on, but there was no other traffic. She thought of the darkness covering not only these miles of streets around her, but also of the shores, the beaches, and the acres of tossing sea that she had crossed, which divided her from her proper home. At least her birthplace and the street she walked in were sharing the same night, however many unfruitful miles were between them. And there too people would keep indoors, and not think of much beyond the fires that warmed them, for the same winter lay stiffly across the whole continent.

It was a short walk back to Merion Street, and she knew it blindfold, therefore did not use a torch: only now and again she stretched out her hand to touch a wall or a street-sign. One of her gloves had a hole in it. Above all she felt tired, as if that day she had made a journey. When she got in, there would be her fire to put on, and she could sit in front of it and smoke and perhaps read. She knew she had made some discovery about herself, but just at the moment she had forgotten what it was, and inclined to think she had been fancying it. It would be too much trouble to make a proper meal: she would eat bread and drink some coffee with no-one to bother her. Then pretty soon she would go to bed and forget whatever it was in sleep. Among the blowing wastes that shifted around her there was still that much that she could enjoy. Though the city was gripped by the cold, and the room she had was no more her own than a tree belongs to a bird that perches in it, she could still sleep when it grew too much to face. She wondered in passing where Mr. Anstey lived (there had been no address on his letter), and whether he lived alone. If he did, it was ironical to think of them both going back to their empty rooms.

She knew Merion Street well, so that even though it was as dark as if the night had collapsed and was heaped all above it, she knew by counting her steps how far she had to go. At the twenty-fifth there was a grating where the heel of her shoe had once caught, and she avoided it. At the twenty-ninth, she opened her handbag for her latch-key, liking to open the door directly without lingering on the step. How tired she was. By that time she was passing the dentist's door—what had his name been? Tullidge? Wilmidge?—and six paces further she was home.

She swung up the steps. As usual she slid the key straight into the teeth of the lock, but as she did so she heard a breath intaken very close and near the ground, as if an animal were there. Then a voice said loudly:

"I say, is that Katherine Lind?"

It was Robin. He sounded rather drunk.

225

6

"You'd better come upstairs," said Katherine. She turned to her keys that hung abandoned in the lock. "For God's sake come quietly."

"Lucky I found this place by daylight," Robin said without paying any attention. "Else it would have meant a taxi." He was laughing.

This was terrible. She led the way up the narrow stairs, hearing him clumping and breathing behind her. So far she had not seen his face, but she was all at sea. This was too much to be confronted with. He had hugged her boisterously, seeming dizzy with good-humour. If there had been any light, he would have kissed her straight off.

He stumbled on the stairs. "Steady," she said, turning at the top along to her door.

"Well, you do hide yourself away," he called out, chortling as if it were a great joke. "Here, can't we have some light?"

"In a moment!" She had to go in and draw the curtains first, and finding a box of matches in the dark lit the gas fire. Then she switched on the light. "All right," she said.

In he came, easing off his cap and unbuttoning his gloves. It shocked her, Heaven knows why, to see him in uniform. The broad shoulders of his coat were swaggering.

The cap he threw onto the table, and the gloves into it, then he was after her again, seizing her by the shoulders and swinging her round under the light. She could not help·laughing, it was all so farcical, and he was roaring out something like, "Well, let's have a look at you" and "Well, it's extraordinary, I should have known you anywhere" until finally he really did start kissing her, as if it were the only possible alternative to speech, and she had to back away and shake her head and shout: "All right, please, for Heaven's sake!"

He released her and grinned. He was not very drunk, she thought, not as much as he pretended.

She shut the door. It was all quite unreal. He was a stranger to her. "Well, explain yourself," she said. He was coming at her again, and she had to push him away, back towards the fire. "Explain yourself! You said you weren't coming."

"Oh, did I?" He took off his coat unasked, smoothing his hair. "Today's been the most complete shambles. No-one knew what stood and what didn't. But I didn't think you'd get my telegram."

"I got it all right, it's practically lost me my job," she interjected, beginning to laugh. She took off her own coat and hung it up.

"But I sent it here," he went on disregarding. "And the old girl downstairs said you wouldn't be back till after seven."

"Oh, then they must have—— Well, this is all very strange. Sit down, make yourself comfortable."

He threw himself into Miss Green's chair. "Well, at any rate, here we are!"

"I know. It's extraordinary. I can't believe it's you."

"I'm solid enough," he guffawed, aiming a slap at her, which she avoided. "I'm not a ghost. Whooo!" He wailed and waved his arms as if they were shrouded.

She felt too weak to do anything but laugh. "Why are you so absurd? so drunk?" she asked.

"Drunk be damned." He sprawled in his chair, grinning up at her. "I only had a few while I was waiting."

"Well, it's had a very adverse effect on your behaviour." She held out a packet of cigarettes. He took one. She had no idea of what she ought to say to him. At present all this acted with her exhaustion to produce a sense of enfeebled absurdity.

227

"All right, then," he said, exhaling the smoke with a great sigh. "We'll be sober and serious. You start."

"I can't." She was heaving with silent laughter. "Stop making me laugh."

He made a weird noise.

"Stop."

He made another weird noise. This suddenly did the trick, and she leant back on her stool, feeling perfectly serious and smoothing her hair into place.

"Right," she said. She looked at him and saw him as he was, young and haggard. He must be as old as she, but did not look it. His face was sharp-featured, his jaw harsh from shaving, his teeth very white; his dark hair was no longer soft but brushed savagely away from his temples. When he laughed, wrinkles appeared round his eyes and he lifted his brows like a professional story-teller. His nostrils had a stretched, hungry look. He was an inch shorter than she was. "Where have you come from, when did you arrive, what are you doing, and everything else?"

He shut his eyes. "Military secret, half-past five, absolutely nothing, and same applies. I'm on thirty-six hours' leave. Look here! You've been in England for years. Why didn't you write sooner?"

"I don't know. I didn't know you still lived there."

"Of course we do. How long have you been here?"

"I came the autumn before last. I lived in London at first. I've been here about nine months."

"Why did you come to this hole, after London?"

"I got a job here. I wanted a change." She was answering almost at random. Robin was sitting there in her attic under the electric light, and it made no impression at all on her. What she had felt about him had long since worked itself out, and left nothing but blankness, and a certain irresponsibility.

"Oh yes, your marvellous job. Very learned."

"I'm lucky to have it."

"Did you get to your university?"

"Yes, oh yes. And you to Oxford?"

"Cambridge. Oxford's a little too near home." He jumped up restlessly and began walking about the room. "Jolly place, this. Live here alone?"

"I do."

"Like it? Being here, and your job, I mean?"

She began remembering. "Well, it's all right, but I may not have a job. All because of your telegram."

"What on earth has that to do with it?" he said, picking up a newspaper that lay on the table, glancing at it, then rolling it up to whack against his hand.

"The people downstairs must have telephoned it on. I can't explain, but it got me into a row."

"Well, they can't sack you for that."

"I can't explain, it's too complicated."

"If they do, you're well rid of the place, I should think. So this is your hide-out." He was making a tour of inspection, as if thinking of buying it, glancing into the alcove where her bed was, reaching up needlessly to touch the sloping ceiling. "You know, I wondered what happened to you, often."

"Well, I'm so glad." The thought was slowly become soluble in her mind, the thought that Robin was with her. This, she told herself, was the Robin she had written to in peace and comfort when she was sixteen; despite his harsh uniform and starched khaki collar that seemed to hurt his neck, they had shared many hours between them, in a time now forgotten. This was the Robin that had taken her to Oxford, that had met her at Dover, that had come up to the terrace from the tennis court when they had finished playing. She ran through these and many more incidents like an incantation, and gradually he seemed more familiar. If her mind had not been tired so that it could be swept along unheeding, his sudden appearance might have moved her. As it was, it failed to connect.

There were, she knew, things she should feel, things she should say; but whether through his fault or hers she had no command of them. She could only see their meeting in plain and uncoloured terms: a young man she had known once had come to see her this winter night, and now they were in a high-lighted room where there was a fire and what belongings she had, and below there was the street, the cold hunting through the darkness.

He came back to the centre of the room and sat restlessly on the edge of the table, swinging his legs.

"What are you going to do now?" she asked.

"Now?" He seemed both careless and nervy. "I'm going home, I think. There's a train about midnight."

"You'll be tired."

"Oh, sleep!" He flipped his hand vaguely. "One can do without sleep."

"No," she said, wondering at his off-hand tone. "You shouldn't do that. You look tired already."

"I'm all right." He drew at his cigarette and his nostrils dilated slightly. "The healthy open-air life."

"How long have you been in the army?"

"Around fourteen months."

"Do you dislike it very much?"

"Dislike it!" He slipped off the table and wandered over to the side-table, looking at what books she had. "Don't care much. Get as much fun as possible, that's the only thing."

"What are you in?"

"Artillery."

She covered a yawn. They might have been talking in a waiting-room.

"But what's your story?" he asked, turning back to her. "I don't know anything about you."

Pulling herself together, she began to tell him of the events that had led up to her arrival in England for the second time. She chose to tell them in a way that freed them of much of their unpleasantness, and made them sound like a series of actions taken of her own will. As she related them they sounded unreal to her.

He listened sympathetically, his forehead furrowed desperately. From the left breast-pocket of his tunic he took a long cigarette-case, and began to smoke again; she refused. As she spoke she considered dispassionately how he fitted her memories of him. His face was recognizable. But it had not achieved any maturity. Oddly enough she began to remember how Jane looked, which had been quite beyond her till now. But where had this jauntiness come from? and this restlessness, this perpetual unease? He reminded her of nothing so much as a boy in the presence of women.

In the meanwhile he smoked his cigarette hungrily.

"Filthy business," he said when she had finished. "It's pretty grim, isn't it."

He clasped his hands awkwardly.

"Would you like some supper?" she said, feeling more friendly towards him as he had heard her out respectfully. "I usually eat something about this time."

"Oh, but shouldn't we go out?"

"It wouldn't be any trouble. I haven't much, but there's enough."

"Well, I don't want to rob you." He went to sit down, then remained standing as she got up. "I haven't had anything since lunch, as a matter of fact," he added with a laugh, jerking his shoulders as if to settle his clothes more comfortably.

"If you want a proper meal we'd better go out," she said. "I could give you sausages and coffee."

"That'd be first rate, if you're sure you can spare it."

"Make yourself comfortable. I shan't be very long."

But he followed her out. "No, I'm interested in this place of yours."

Along the dark landing and in the bare little room where she did her cooking the air was chilly. In the corner was a

231

boiler wrapped in felt. The electric light made the sink and stove look peculiarly bleak.

She filled the kettle and put it on the gas. As she crossed to a cupboard he caught hold of her again and drew her to him as he leant against the wall.

"I'm sorry for you," he said. "You've had a rotten time."

He smiled at her in a way that would have been charming but for the shadows round his eyes and nostrils.

"You're behaving very strangely," she said, with amusement.

She let him kiss her. He did it eagerly but without grace, like a boy learning to smoke. All this was so extraordinary that it hardly registered: or rather, there was nothing to register. His manner was so unlike her recollections that he was still nearly a chance acquaintance to her.

"If you really want any supper you'd better let me go," she said.

He looked nonplussed. Then he laughed unconfidently and released her.

"Can't I help you?" he said.

"I don't think there's very much you can do. You can lay the table if you like."

She told him where to find cutlery and a table-cloth, and in the meantime unwrapped a paper of sausages and pricked them before putting them in a frying pan. There was half an onion that had lain in a saucer for several weeks, and she added a few translucent rings; also there were two cold potatoes that could be sliced and fried as well. After a time he came back and hung about watching.

"Why don't you go by the fire?" she said, warming her hands round the gas ring. "It's so cold out here."

"I'd sooner talk to you," he said doggedly. His hair was coming out of place where he had passed his hand through it many times. "What sort of a time d'you have, apart from what you do? Do you know many decent people?"

"No, I haven't bothered."

"You've been here long enough to know someone."

"I know I have. Somehow I haven't had the time. I don't really want any friends till I go home again."

"But that may be a long time yet," he said, as if eager to seize on something he could speak about with authority. "I honestly don't think you'll leave England for another five years."

"Five, oh, surely——"

"I don't see how it can possibly be any sooner." He went into a long forecast of military strategy and events. "Which adds up to five years," he finished, crossing his arms with a slight shiver.

"Well, you are probably right."

They talked in this way for some time, remotely. Yet he looked at her in an intimate, hungry way, as if aware she only vaguely recognized him. And infected by his distrust, her mind kept running to her and saying: This is Robin! This is Robin you were expecting! He's come. And soon he'll go again, so you'd better make the most of it. But the words struck no spark. She could not intoxicate herself with his presence, so that all else was shut out: yes, he was there, so briskly brushed, and smart, and self-confident (but there were rings under his eyes), but the rest were there too, the town, the boiler wrapped in felt, Miss Green, Mr. Anstey, Miss Parbury, in their separate ugly worlds, and soon they would all be asleep. Further, he did not seem open and friendly to her. His gaiety was automatic, restless, pitiful, but his eyes played on her, as if he wanted to tell her some trouble.

When the meal was ready, she made coffee and they carried the two plates along with a loaf of bread into the sitting-room. "This is the kind of meal I really enjoy," he said, pulling up his chair, but he ate scrappily, not clearing up his plate, and pushing it away, before she had finished, to light a fresh cigarette. Katherine had thought he was hungry and had planned to offer him cheese, but he seemed satisfied as soon as the novelty of eating had worn off again. She poured him a second cup of coffee, hurt momentarily. She wondered if he thought it had not been worth his while to come.

"Tell me something more about your family," she said when they had both finished. "About Jane, for instance."

"She's at home," said Robin briefly, stretching his legs under the table.

"And Jack?"

"Still in India. They're fairly stuck now."

"She did go to India, then?"

It was Jane, after all, who had been the mainspring of this meeting.

"Oh yes. She went back there with Jack. They lived there till war broke out. She was going to have this child then, and they thought it better she should come home, all things considered." He threw these sentences out moodily, as if they reflected discredit on his family.

"But why? India would have been safer, surely."

"I dare say it would." He hitched in his seat to get one hand in his trouser-pocket. "But they didn't think so at the time. It was all very confusing. You see, for one thing, children shouldn't stay in India after a certain age, and there was no guarantee they'd be able to send her back to England once the war got well started. And some people said it was just the chance for a civil war, if England started getting the worst of it. And then Jack wanted his children to be brought up in England," he added without irony.

Katherine nodded, her chin on one hand. The washing-up could be left till tomorrow.

"He's still there, then?"

"Yes, he's trying to get back for a bit. It's rotten all round."

"Will they go back?"

"I suppose they'll have to. Jane doesn't seem very keen on the idea, though. I don't think she liked the life out there much."

"Well, she knew what she was in for, I suppose," said Katherine, rising. As she glanced in the mirror from force of habit she could see that Robin had made her hair untidy, and she began setting it to rights, using her brush from the bedroom. "All the same, I'm sorry."

"I'm surprised that you should have noticed it in the papers, about the kid." He got up, and came as if magnetized to stand behind her as she attended to her appearance, smiling at her reflection in his professional way, yet looking as if he needed sleep. "I should have thought you'd have forgotten Jack's name."

She went on brushing. "It was such a funny name."

He looked over her shoulder, smoking as if being photographed. "That looks a very valuable hairbrush."

"I shall pawn it when I've no money."

He started to put his arms round her again, and she no longer felt tolerant of his behaviour, only somewhat irritated. Had he come all this way simply to mess her about? "Don't be silly," she told him. "You're not drunk any more."

A dark, wounded look came into his face, like the look of a child that has been refused something it believes its due. She saw that she had hurt him deeply, and it amazed her. Was she supposed to be flattered, that he had considered it worth while making a special journey on the off-chance of sleeping with her? For he would ask that if she made no protest. Queer, she thought, that he should have turned out like this. Someone must have given him the idea that he fascinated women.

"And the child?" she asked. "What did it die of?"

He had gone to sit down again, moving uneasily as if his pockets were full of unyielding objects.

"Oh——" he tossed his head. "That was a miserable

235

business. It just wasn't strong enough. Born with a defective heart, the doctor said."

"How bad for her," she said with a sigh. "Is she very depressed?"

"She was pretty cut up. I couldn't get down for the funeral."

Katherine put her brush back into the alcove, and returned to sit on her stool. "What will she do now?"

As she said this, the gas-fire began to fail and grow blue, and she realized the meter needed another shilling. Robin looked up quickly as the heat on his legs lost its steadiness, and dug his hand painfully into his hip-pocket for money. "Don't bother," she said, rooting in her handbag. But she had no appropriate coins and had to accept the shilling he held out. When she came back from the dismal landing the subject of conversation had passed from their minds.

She looked at her watch and saw it was nine o'clock, stifling a yawn and realizing that her weariness was being reinforced by boredom. Had they ever been at ease with each other? Or had her memory played her false? For there was nothing sympathetic in him. It seemed absurd that she should be obliged to sit and entertain him because they had met by chance when she was young; if she were introduced to him now she would not want to see him again. And this lack of contact was due to more than her temporary insensitivity. If it was only that, he could have amused her and gradually brought her friendliness into play again. But every word he had spoken fell short, leaving her untouched.

"When did you say your train went?" she asked at length.

Unintentionally this irritated him. "You aren't going to throw me out yet, are you?" he retorted, spreading a laugh thinly over the edge of his voice, and uncrossing his legs. "It actually goes at a quarter to midnight. I'll go if you want me to."

"Of course not. Would you like some more coffee?"

"Oh, don't trouble."

"No trouble." She had not meant to offend him. "Only there may not be enough milk. All my visitors have come on the same day, you see."

She stood weighing the coffee-pot in her hand.

"Well, if you're going to make some, I don't mind if it's black," he said ungraciously, as if cross that things were going the wrong way.

She collected the cups and went out: this time he did not follow her, and she was alone in the tiny, brilliant kitchen. Perhaps black coffee would keep her awake, for it certainly seemed that even if she did not let him do as he pleased with her, he was intending to stick there until it was time for him to go to the station. She caught herself up on this last thought and, watching the kettle boil again, wondered if she were as callous as that sounded. He had every right to expect a friend to welcome him, particularly a friend that owed him hospitality and had not met him for so long. If she could see her conduct from the outside, it might well seem at fault by human standards. But that was just where human standards broke down. What happened if she felt no humanity?

She did not think she was at fault; it was not as if she disliked him. What abstract kindliness she could command was at his service, but it was no more than she might show to a fellow-traveller in a railway-carriage or on board a steamer. Indeed, that was the strongest bond she felt between them, that they were journeying together, with the snow, the discomfort, the food they shared, the beds that were not warm enough. In this situation she need know nothing more about him: there was a fire, that he paid to keep burning; she had hot coffee she could give him; there was so much laconic mutual help, while outside lay the plains, the absence of the moon, the complete enmity of darkness.

She switched the light off and carried in the tray. He had got up again and was standing in front of the fire, as if fearing it might go out again. One hand jingled money in his pockets.

"Who are all these visitors you're talking about?"

She could tell by his voice that his irritation was very thinly hidden.

"I was only joking. I did have one girl in at lunchtime, who works where I do. I don't even know her Christian name. But she drank some of the milk."

"Then I come along and drink the rest." He gave a laugh, not wholly amused. "You know," he went on, swinging his weight first on one foot, then on the other, "you've changed a bit."

"Why do you say that?"

"I don't know," he said, stirring the coffee she gave him. "I can see you in thirty years' time, with a cat and a parrot——"

He tried to sound bantering, but there was constraint in his voice that meant his words hurt himself as well as her.

"I suppose you just don't give a curse for anyone," he ended rather bitterly.

She found it odd, that this was Robin speaking to her. No doubt he had learned to talk in this way at Cambridge. She leant easily on the table.

"Is this because I don't want you to kiss me?"

"No, it isn't." His denial was violent, disturbed: she had let the remark out casually, without realizing such an ordinary truth might offend him. Why, he was years younger than she was: it must be his English upbringing. "It's because you're about as friendly as a blasted block of ice."

He stood there foolishly, looking at the floor.

She thought of telling him that he was mistaken if he expected her to be flattered by his estimate of her, a foreign girl who could be relied on for a bit of fun. But her resentment was not strong enough. He could say what he liked. No doubt he would end by apologizing.

He stood there in silence till he had finished his coffee. Then he put the cup on the mantelpiece and threw himself petulantly into his chair again, his mouth resting against his hands. Katherine went over and reseated herself on the stool, taking up her box of cigarettes and finding there were only two left. She put one in her mouth, and threw the other into his lap.

In a minute or two he picked it up.

"I'm sorry," he said, clearing his throat. "I don't know why I said that."

She struck a match. "That's all right. We do seem to have lost touch, rather."

They lit their cigarettes.

"I suppose," he said, "we aren't really such very great friends. I don't mean to be rude."

"I suppose not. We only knew each other by chance."

"That's true. Tell me, why did you join that scheme? I always thought it wasn't your kind of show at all."

She laughed. "I thought the same about you. I can't remember why. I thought it would be fun."

"Oh, I was deadly serious about the language side of it. I read languages at Cambridge. I thought at one time of going into the Diplomatic."

"Can't you still?"

He rubbed his eyes. "I don't know. Everything's so uncertain."

"Well, at any rate," she said, "I enjoyed the holiday I had with you. That was a success."

"Did you? I had the impression you were no end bored. I'm glad."

"I always meant to ask you back."

"Well, you did ask me. But I was ill, wasn't I?"

"I think you were."

"And by next year there were war-scares every minute."

"And we'd stopped writing."

"Yes, we had."

Smoke hung under the electric light.

"A pity you didn't come over," said Katherine. "I should have liked both you and Jane to have come."

"Yes, it would have been grand."

"Perhaps," she said, "there will be time, after the war."

"I'm superstitious," he said. "I'm making no plans. After the war doesn't exist for me. I just look forward about a week." But his eyes looked as if he could see years ahead.

"Look, will you write to me?" he said later on. "I'm sorry I was rude just now."

"Write to you?" she said. Her eyes rested on his worried face. Did he really think, at this outpost of the conversation, that there was anything she could give him? "I will if you like."

"It'd be silly to lose touch. You don't have to write pages of literary stuff. Just a couple of sides would do. It's being in the army makes one feel like that, I suppose—being so cut off. It makes a letter seem awfully important."

He wrote in a small notebook, bound in soft leather, tore off what he had written, and handed it to her. It was a guarded military address.

"I'll do my best," she said. "I don't write much these days."

"I'd be no end grateful. And you must come to stay again as soon as you can. I'll ask mother to write to you about it."

"Jane won't want any visitors."

"Jane won't want anything. She wouldn't eat if someone else didn't get the meals."

"Perhaps in the summer!" she said, with a flicker of irony.

"I'm pretty certain to have left England by then. But you must go in any case."

The irritability had left his voice, the distress remained. He ran his fingers several times through his hair, and sighed once or twice. Their conversation was as barren as a field by the sea's edge, the grass littered with pebbles until at last the margin is all pebbles, dropping down steeply to where the clear water rises and falls against the stones. She felt very keenly that they were alone at the top of this building, and at this thought her spirits began to revive strangely, meaninglessly, like a rag caught upon a nail that flaps in the wind. She had been pushed so far that day into exhaustion that she had reached the boundary of a completely new land, where a wind seemed to blow and make her flutter like the last leaf on a tree, where all things tossed and shook in a kind of lonely exultance, irrelevantly, simply because they were alive.

And what of him? He sat with a dark face, shoulders hunched, his feet turned inwards. Something oppressed him continually, making him come to her or any woman, disguised by a jaunty philandering. He had lost the self-possession he had moved with when a boy, and was given over to the restlessness of his body. That was driving him, and because he could not control it he pretended he enjoyed it, to the extent of telling himself he was having a jolly good time and even if necessary that he loved her, which would not be true. It had driven him to play the gay officer, and in due course would cause him to play the forsaken boy, but it would be unkind to tell him so, because he had to do it and would be happier without the knowledge. But she felt superior to him, for she wanted nothing of him, but when he left her he would do so bitterly.

The silence was too long, and he seemed to feel it, getting up and pressing out his cigarette. "I think perhaps I'd better go now," he said, casting a look round the room. "You're probably tired out."

His voice was drab, and he gave his tie a jerk, tightening

it as if to hearten himself. In the light the lines of his face were drawn.

She was moved to feel sorry for him. It seemed a poor end to their meeting.

"There's no hurry," she said. "You'll have a terribly long wait."

"I expect you want to go to sleep," he said. "And I shall be giving you a bad name if I stay much longer."

It struck her that he did not really mean to go, that he had only suggested going to test her reactions again; she saw it with a clairvoyance that had somehow broken from personal interest. It was unlike anything she had felt before.

"Please yourself," she said, for some sort of answer.

He made a step towards her, and quietly took her hands as if to say good-bye. Neither spoke. Then he said:

"Shall I stay with you?"

"I don't think you'd better."

He changed his grip and held her, waited till her automatic movement away from him had spent itself, then kissed her, returning to kiss her a second time more fully. She wondered if this was supposed to make her change her mind. Afterwards he pressed his eyes against her shoulder.

"Let me stay with you," he said. "I wish you would."

She wondered how he could bring himself to keep on asking.

"There'd be no point in it."

He held her more lightly. "Why not?"

"Well, do you see any?"

He did not answer.

"It wouldn't mean anything," she pointed out.

"Damn it!" he said desperately. "What does that matter? I don't see that anything means very much. I spend all my time doing things that don't matter twopence. So do you." He had drawn himself up to say this, and now slackened in a kind of disgust. "Oh, well. I don't want to argue about it."

"I'm not arguing," she said. Truly she did not care one way or the other, being neither insulted or flattered. She could easily refuse, yet refusal would be dulling, an assent to all the wilderness that surrounded them. If she did not refuse, he would go back to his camp and boast about it, to cover the humiliation he suffered in making her accept. She did not mind. Her spirits were rising higher. He could not touch her. It would be no more than doing him an unimportant kindness, that would be overtaken by oblivion in a few days.

"It would mean a great deal to me," he said automatically, looking at her humbly.

"Well, all right." She named a condition that he accepted. "Stay if you like."

He released her, as if his desire had suddenly died out. She could almost see him wondering whether to accept her lack of enthusiasm: it was galling to him, and seemed all wrong.

"If you're sure you don't mind," he said hesitantly; this sounded so absurd she could not help laughing, and at this he seemed satisfied and kissed her again.

"There's no need to wait, is there?" he said, his eyebrows arching momentarily.

"I suppose not. Oh, Robin, there's just one thing——"

"What?"

"I think you should *pretend* to go. I don't want any trouble about this."

"Seems a bit unnecessary," he said stiffly, almost as if suspecting a trap.

"I'd feel much happier if you would."

He seemed impatient but submissive. "What do you want me to do, then?"

"Just go downstairs, open the street door, and shut it again. Then come back quietly. I don't suppose they'll be listening, but they might be."

"I'm not sure I know the way."

"The door is right in front of you at the bottom of the stairs. Be careful, there may be a bicycle in the passageway. Oh—Robin!"

"Yes?" They were whispering already.

"The sixth stair from the bottom creaks. Be careful when you're coming back."

"Oh, my God." He went.

Perhaps she should not have been alone so soon, for there came a slight backwash of shame at what she had agreed to, at letting it all end so badly. But it spent itself before it reached her. She picked up the saucerful of cigarette-ends and emptied it into the waste-paper basket, then went to the table to put their plates together. The door banged below. There was nothing to fear. If this was what he wanted, he might as well have it. In the past she might have been wrong, might have guessed or wondered, but that time was over. Now she could go through with her decision, and be sure that nothing would come of it.

She was laying his coat and cap over the chair Miss Green had sat in when he appeared noiselessly in the doorway. "It's snowing outside," he said. "I knew it would."

"Is it?"

He closed the door quietly, smoothing his hair. A snowflake had clung to his shoulder but quickly melted. "A rotten night."

"You'd better put all your things in the same place," she said, indicating what she had done. "It'll be easier for you."

He nodded. "What's underneath here?"

"A workroom, I think. There'll be no-one there now."

"Will anyone hear us talking?"

"I don't think so. We had better not shout." She looked at her watch. "And what about your train? When ought you to go?"

"Well, I needn't catch the midnight one. There's another back to camp about five. I'm not far away, to tell you the truth."

"But I thought you were on leave?"

He gave a slight frown, as if annoyed at being detected. "As a matter of fact, I'm not. We had embarkation leave ten days ago."

"But surely you shouldn't be——"

"Oh, it's all right." He gestured impatiently. "There's a man will cover up for me. I don't have to put in an appearance till eleven on Sundays."

There was another silence. At last she began to undo the cuffs of her dress. "Please put the light out," she said. He did so, and then turned out the gas fire.

7

"I suppose it's not very late," he said.

"A quarter past ten."

"Are you wearing a watch?"

"Yes, I'd forgotten it. I'll put it under the pillow." He laughed. "That's rather funny."

"Well, I always wear it. Otherwise it keeps me awake."

"Well, keep it on, then."

"I'll put it on your side. It won't bother me."

"Do you know where you're going?" she asked.

"Eh?"

"I said, do you know where you're going? When you——"

"Oh, well, not officially. They tell us on board. We can guess pretty well."

"I don't suppose you like the idea."

"Can't say I do." He was flippant. "But everyone's in the same boat."

He seemed restless and unsatisfied, as she knew he would be, and later on he began to talk again. "You will write to me, won't you? I mean, I can rely on it?"

"Yes, of course, if you want me to."

"I'd be glad so if you would. I don't get many letters. From home, of course . . . But one grows out of one's parents."

"I know that."

"I don't mean it—you know—it's nothing to be proud of. But my last leave wasn't up to much, pretty ghastly really. They tried to be so good and yet we just hadn't anything to say to each other. I mean, we were quite friendly and all that, but . . . I can't explain it quite, only I don't feel I want to see them again. Probably shan't, anyway. I say, do you mind if I put your watch somewhere else? It does make a row."

"There's a side-table by the bed, if you can find it."

In the darkness they heard some of the city clocks strike after a while.

"By the way, you'd better forget what I said about embarkation leave, it's supposed to be secret."

"Oh, I will, don't worry."

"I suppose we ought to go to sleep. I'm tired enough to sleep for a week, but I just don't feel like it. This war, it's mucked everything up. All happened so naturally, but my God it's made a mess of things." He paused. "Broken the sequence, so to speak. I mean, I knew pretty well what I was going to do, my career and so forth. All gone to blazes. Of course, if I come through, I suppose I can go on—but the funny thing is, I don't much care now. Awfully difficult to explain to one's parents."

"I say, I'm sorry, but this watch of yours still worries me."

"What?"

"Can I put your watch somewhere else?"

"Do what you like. I'll put it on again."

"No, don't. I don't want to hear it. Put it right away somewhere."

"Give it me. Go to sleep."

"But if one doesn't! . . . I mean, there aren't two ways about it. One's got to have some sort of aim in life, or you might as well be dead. Listen who's talking. My chances aren't worth much. But take these blokes who are getting married, there was one only last week; I think it's silly of them, downright silly. What's the point of it? You leave the girl, and get yourself wiped out . . . I don't only mean it from a practical point of view——"

"Go to sleep."

"I mean who's got anything to offer anyone these days? Badly put. I say, I'm sorry to burble like this. But it's not worth while. Obviously it's the only worth-while thing, a career and getting a family, increasing and multiplying, whatever that means. But when you don't feel it—I mean, if I asked you, for instance, to marry me, you'd refuse, wouldn't you . . . wouldn't you?"

"I suppose so."

"Well, there you are, then."

"Bit of a lark it would be, though."

"Aren't you asleep yet?"

"I was only thinking it would be funny. Lose one Katherine, gain another."

"What d'you mean?"

"My niece. How pompous that sounds. Jane's daughter. She was called Katherine."

"She wasn't, she was called Lucy."

"Lucy was only her first name. Jack called her that after his mother, who died—oh, it must be fifteen years ago. Before you met him. Her second name was Katherine —Jane chose that."

"I didn't know."

"So you see you are almost one of the family. There'd be no——"

"Robin, I do want to go to sleep. Don't say any more. I'm too tired."

There was the snow, and her watch ticking. So many snowflakes, so many seconds. As time passed they seemed to mingle in their minds, heaping up into a vast shape that might be a burial mound, or the cliff of an iceberg whose summit is out of sight. Into its shadow dreams crowded, full of conceptions and stirrings of cold, as if icefloes were moving down a lightless channel of water. They were going in orderly slow procession, moving from darkness further into darkness, allowing no suggestion that their order should be broken, or that one day, however many years distant, the darkness would begin to give place to light.

Yet their passage was not saddening. Unsatisfied dreams rose and fell about them, crying out against their implacability, but in the end glad that such order, such destiny, existed. Against this knowledge, the heart, the will, and all that made for protest, could at last sleep.